Spirit of the Jaguar

Abducted by an Uncontacted Amazon Tribe

David M. Schultz

Spirit of the Jaguar

Freewater Press

For permission requests, contact the publisher at:

Freewater Press: freewaterpress@gmail.com

ISBN 979-8-218-64969-2

Printed in the United States

Disclaimer:

Characters in this novel are fictious and not intended to represent any actual person or persons. Exceptions are historical figures Cândido Rondon, the Villas Boas Brothers (Orlando, Cláudio and Leonardo) and Sydney Possuelo, major advocates for the human rights and protection of ancestral lands of Indigenous peoples of Brazil's Amazon Basin.

River names within this novel are mainly fictitious including the Rio Sié, Rio Turi and Rio Celina. São Gabriel da Nazaré is a fictitious town.

The great Rio Negro is an actual river, the largest tributary of the Amazon River and one of the ten largest rivers in the world. It joins the Amazon near the city of Manaus, Brazil.

The Alto Rio Negro Indigenous Territory is an actual 30,880-sq.-mile protected area managed by Brazil's National Indian Foundation (FUNAI). Located in northwestern Brazil and bordered by Colombia and Venezuela, the region is a major rainforest drainage of the Rio Negro.

Amazon Indigenous languages Nheengatu and Tupi-Guarani are real. People of the Secret Village, the Igarapé and Arabox tribes are fictitious based on isolated tribes of the Amazon rainforest.

The name of any specific product, brand, institution, university, musician or company used within this fictional story does not imply affiliation, sponsorship, or endorsement by that entity. All product names and trademarks are the property of their respective owners and used herein within the doctrine of nominative fair use.

"I fight for the human rights of those who do not know that human rights exist."

Sydney Possuelo-renowned advocate for the isolated and uncontacted Indigenous peoples of the Brazilian Amazon

CONTENTS

CONTENTS

HISTORICAL FACTS

In 1541-42 Spanish explorer Francisco de Orellana and his crew became the first Europeans to navigate the entire 2,400-mile length of the Amazon River, a brutal but enlightening journey. From the base of the snowcapped Andes Range east to the Atlantic Ocean they searched the great river for its fabled El Dorado. While Orellana did not find the City of Gold, a wealth of rainforest hardwoods, fish and wildlife surrounded him while the gold he sought hid in river sediments. As they drifted downriver through present day Ecuador, Peru and Brazil, large communities of Indigenous people appeared from the jungle and sometimes clashed with the mysterious intruders. Many of the fiercest warriors were women reminding Orellana of the mythical Greek Amazons. He honored the river with their name.

Exploration over the following centuries uncovered new resources until the entire world coveted the Amazon's riches. The rubber boom commencing in 1879 set off large-scale extraction of Brazil's lumber, gold, fish, petroleum and biopharmaceuticals. Bulldozers, gold dredges, drill rigs, commercial fishing nets, chainsaws and cattle devasted large swaths of the immense Amazon basin, home to its native people for thousands of years.

Illegal narcotics smuggling thrived in the hidden jungle wilderness. Indigenous people of the Amazon fled deeper into the rainforest to avoid forced labor or violent deaths. Up to 90% of native populations suffered and died from European diseases. With no natural immunity to measles, influenza and other illnesses rarely fatal to westerners, Indigenous Amazon cultures are severely affected by foreign diseases to this day.

In 1967 the government of Brazil established the National Indian Foundation (FUNAI) to protect native cultures and their rainforest homes. FUNAI's mission is to represent the rights of native peoples through legislation and establishment of Indigenous Protected Territories. Non-native outsiders are excluded from *Terra Indígena* without special permission. FUNAI's task is to monitor Indigenous territories for illegal activities and allow natives a high degree of self-determination. Some native communities engage in commerce beyond their designated Indigenous Territory borders while others guide visitors on ecotours of their rainforest villages with the oversight of FUNAI. Isolated Indigenous peoples that avoid contact are protected from outsiders. Within the Indigenous Protected Territories of Brazil today it is estimated that up to 100 isolated and uncontacted native tribes live deep in the Amazon.

Yet despite FUNAI's oversight, the quest for natural resources within the protected territories, both illegally and legally by acts of the Brazilian Government, has not stopped. Bribes, corruption and deceit thrive where jungle extends beyond the horizons and law enforcement is thin.

CHAPTER 1
Realm of the Green Cathedral

Hidden within the vast Amazon rainforest, Indigenous tribes exist today as they have for centuries....

Mike Weston's guide warned him not to step into the jungle. Some of the world's deadliest snakes lurked in the shadows. Weston hadn't explored beyond the riverbank and tomorrow marked his departure from the Amazon wilderness. Beginning at sunrise, a five-hour float plane ride to Manaus followed by an overnight business-class flight would return him home to Silicon Valley.

Ellie would be disappointed his adventure hadn't risen to the life-altering experience she'd hoped for. His demanding BetaCorp Technologies' customers anticipated his return to work, always at their service.

Their guide Jairo ran his skiff onto a secluded beach to barbecue the peacock bass Mike's buddy Bill landed minutes earlier. A flock of green parrots flushed from the bush startling the men as they stepped onto dry land. Mike and Bill sat in folding chairs on the white sand as Jairo prepared their lunch.

The mysterious rainforest ten steps away called to Mike as they ate, his last chance to explore if only for twenty minutes. Jairo discouraged the venture but Weston knew he might never return. "I just want to take a few photos in there."

"Be careful!" yelled Bill wiping his brow as Mike stood and turned towards the shadows.

Weston entered the realm of the green cathedral. A moment later the tangled vines and broad leaves obscured him from Jairo and Bill…

Mike regained consciousness on his back staring into the fierce eyes of four brown-skinned rainforest men. He didn't trust his wavering perception. The men spoke in agitated snarls like the jaguars Mike had heard the night before from the safety of his deluxe air-conditioned riverboat. His senses cleared in seconds and Weston jumped to his feet, fleeing before fully upright. The men reacted immediately and tackled Mike on his third step. The rainforest men tied Mike's wrists together with strips of hide and lifted him to his feet. Two carried longbows and two hoisted wooden clubs. Pain throbbed on the back of Weston's head and he suspected his thick blond hair and blue polyester hoodie were bloodied.

The largest man, his face painted in diagonal black stripes like a jungle warrior, raised his club. Mike inhaled deeply expecting it to be his final breath. Instead the knotted branch came down on his iPhone lying in the mud. Moments earlier it had captured images of chattering monkeys and a bizarre multi-legged palm tree. Now it lay shattered and useless. The agitated warrior pressed a sharpened bamboo arrow into Weston's throat and pushed him forward as blood trickled down his neck. Mike staggered away from the river, tropical mist blurring the path ahead.

The barefoot men wore fur and fiber loin cloths hanging from their waists–nothing else. Their jet-black hair hung straight at cheek level, rough cut bangs exposing deeply set eyes. Mike guessed the young men to be in their early twenties. Three of them were much shorter than six-foot-two Weston but all were lean and strong. Their dark skin and muscular arms shined in the equitorial heat. The tallest of the men, the painted-face warrior, shouted at Weston, "Hatak! Hatak!"

The men forced Mike along a narrow bush trail that blocked any cooling breeze. He hadn't experienced such stifling humidity since his sauna in Aspen during the Artificial Intelligence Conference the previous winter. But this heat could not be escaped and Mike wobbled forward nearly passing out. Weston caught a glimpse of the river through the trees to his left. The guides would be searching for him soon.

When the trail met a placid lagoon the men pushed along its shore deeper into the rainforest and away from the main river channel. Long liana vines crawled into the jungle ceiling high above. A family of scarlet macaws squawked from the treetops.

Weston heard outboard motors racing in the distance. The search was on! Mike yelled for help but was immediately punched in the gut and fell to the ground. The angry warrior, his dark eyes glaring through darker painted stripes, kicked Weston repeatedly in the ribs. Again he pressed an arrow against Mike's throat and lifted him to his feet. The five men pushed on through the rainforest to a destination and fate unknown to the lone white man.

The forced march proceeded along the lagoon's shoreline for several more hours, the thin brushy trail undoubtedly used more by wild peccaries and tapirs than humans. A troop of curious monkeys followed them briefly, swinging from the treetops above. Weston staggered forward stunned with fear. "Where are we going?" he cried out. The rainforest men did not answer.

Eventually they arrived at a group of decaying thatched huts. Mike counted at least ten but most had molded and collapsed as the jungle reclaimed them. As dusk fell upon the Amazon, the rainforest men removed dry palm fronds from a damaged hut and laid them in a circle on the dirt floor of the most intact shelter. A hardened mud fire ring filled the center.

One of the men carried a small board and hard stick in slits on his waist belt. He picked up cottony pieces of fluff under a giant umbrella-like tree Jairo called *kapok* a few days earlier. The man set the board on the ground and placed a piece of kapok in a black indentation on the wood. He held the stick vertically between his palms and spun it quickly. After many minutes the kapok began to smoke and soon a tiny ember glowed. The man swept the ember onto a small pile of dry leaves and sticks in the fire ring. It smoldered lightly. He knelt and blew on the ashes and the glow brightened. The rainforest man blew again and the pile ignited.

As the sky darkened the jungle came alive with buzzing and chirping insects, mosquitoes dense among them. The hut was dreadful but the smokey fire kept some of the mosquitoes away and warmed Weston's tired body. The angry warrior tied Mike's ankles together with leather cord. With hands and feet tightly bound, all he could do was roll side to side on the fronds fearing for his life.

Mike wore his light blue polyester fishing shirt, a long-sleeved loose-fitting hoodie. The latest in technical wear kept a tropical traveler cool while repelling sun and some of the insects. The shirt reached well below Mike's waist over the pockets of his tan nylon pants. He wore nylon running shoes that might give him an advantage over the barefoot men. They seemed fearful of Mike's brightly colored clothing and avoided touching it as if their fingers would burn. All five men slept in fits that night. At least one rainforest man remained awake at all times to watch their captive. Weston slept for short stretches but woke continually due to his hard palm frond bed, stinging insects and state of bewildered fear.

At first light the brown men untied Mike's feet and resumed their march leaving the lagoon for the deep rainforest. The unbroken canopy a hundred feet above enveloped the five men in shadowy dusk. They trudged over decaying leaf litter and across creeks stopping to drink with cupped hands. They had not eaten in a day. The tropical air warmed uncomfortably but the rainforest men pushed forward with purpose, two in front and two behind Weston. The angry warrior usually led. Mike's clothing dripped with perspiration yet the native men barely broke a sweat. Giant honey bees added to Weston's torment buzzing and crawling over his face, perhaps mistaking his blue shirt for a jungle flower. Several stung him, the sharp pain throbbing for hours.

Animal whistles, chirps and howls echoed through the trees as the rainforest men continued their incomprehensible chatter. An unnatural drone caught Weston's attention. It grew louder until the distinct noise of an engine hummed overhead. Mike knew the plane was searching for him but felt immediately gripped in despair. Seven days earlier he flew into the remote Amazon tributary with Bill and eight other adventure-seeking fishermen. The five-hour float plane flight from Manaus, Brazil was a wonder. From two thousand feet above, the vast green rainforest extended out beyond the horizon in all directions broken only by low-lying clouds, scattered clumps of yellow flowers in the treetops and the occasional serpentine river. Other than some riverbank sandbars the ground was never visible through the thick vegetation. A search plane could fly directly over the men without a clue they were below.

Hours of low-level flight over the dense rainforest canopy reminded Mike of a *National Geographic* article he'd read years earlier while waiting in his dentist's office. The dramatic photos showed small clearings in the rainforest with thatched palm huts and men painted in red dye pointing spears towards the airborne photographer–Neolithic tribes of the Amazon isolated from the modern world. Mike's group of ten adventurers discussed it during cocktail hour their first night aboard the deluxe houseboat *Wild Amazon* anchored on a remote tributary in northwestern Brazil. Native villages could remain invisible to the outside world here in the endless jungle.

Weston's forced trek continued through the deep shadows. His legs burned but his mental anguish was worse. The barefoot men's splayed toes gripped firmly while Mike's shoes slid in the slick clay and decaying leaves. Overhead vegetation was so thick that ground dwelling plants could not grow in the dimmest sectors of the forest floor. Such areas could be easier to traverse but their gloom concealed hidden dangers. As Jairo had warned, venomous snakes including bushmasters, coral snakes, the swift fer-de-lance and myriad others hid among the tree roots, fallen limbs and leaf litter.

The angry warrior suddenly ran forward waving his club. A tree boa as long as the man hung low undulating in the branches. The powerful man swung hard as the snake lunged for him. His club connected and the boa fell hissing to the ground. It slithered forward but a sharp blow to the head silenced the serpent. The angry warrior slung the dead snake over his neck with the head and tail hanging down to his knees. His mottled brown jungle necklace twitched and writhed for half an hour.

Evening fell and the men set up their simple camp laying palm fronds in a circle with a fire in the center. Using a ground stone knife they skinned the snake and wrapped pieces around green sticks. It cooked quickly and Weston was offered his first food in two days. The youngest man that Mike guessed to be in his late teens handed him a fist-sized piece. Mike ate ravenously barely taking time to pick out the bones. The rainforest people secured Weston's ankles and wrists for the night. The men jabbered into the evening while lightning flashed on the horizon. Hours later the men quieted. Only the chirping of insects broke the silence.

When Weston was sure the native men were asleep he brushed his tied hands against his pants pocket. His Swiss Army knife was still there. Perhaps he could cut himself free and escape. Mike lifted the bottom of his shirt and used his fingers to quietly urge the knife out while squirming and straining. Just as the knife reached his pocket opening the guard snapped awake. In near darkness Mike Weston pushed the knife back into his pocket and covered it with his shirttail. The Swiss Army knife might save him, but not tonight.

The forced march continued the next morning. Mike was exceedingly weary but the brown men, especially the angry warrior with his perpetual scowl, threatened him with loud grunts and heaving of their weapons. At mid-morning they found a grape palm and gorged on ripe fruit. Rainwater pooled on game trails and soaked Mike's shoes. By that afternoon his feet itched incessantly. Sharp-thorned palms tore at his clothing and body as the brutal walk continued.

The rainforest men did not tie his feet on night three, apparently figuring he would not dare flee into the wild rainforest. Mike considered an escape but knew he would be hopelessly lost in minutes. If the jungle people had not killed him by now they might have other plans. Rain fell sporadically that night and doused the fire. Between showers mosquitoes swarmed mercilessly and covered every exposed part of Mike's body in burning red welts. He shivered and vomited until sunrise, rubbing his bound hands against any inflamed skin he could reach.

Again the men walked. Mike's fear morphed into a stumbling stupor. Emotional weariness and survival occupied his conscious thoughts overshadowing the pain of fungus thriving on his moist feet and festering insect bites on his face and hands. His physical strength was nearly exhausted. Three years of international flights and a full schedule of business meetings had kept him away from the gym and frequent runs that maintained his good physical condition through college and his early years as a computer programmer.

At midday the five men came to a smaller river; winding, dark and flowing easily. They searched along its edge and the two rainforest men with bows and arrows shot three fish in the shallows. One was an orange and gold peacock bass. Mike knew the species well–the target fish of his Amazon safari. He recognized others from the Manaus fish market he'd visited with Bill almost two weeks earlier but did not know their names.

Upstream a grove of slender palms arched gracefully over the water. Like much of the Amazon, distant beauty disguised intimate danger. As Weston walked through the palm trunks, sharp thorns tore at his legs and he recoiled in pain.

Late in the afternoon the men approached a long canoe tied to an exposed tree root. Swinging gently in the current, Weston could see it had been shaped from a single massive log. Hand-carved wood paddles lay stacked inside next to a woven basket. Near the canoe was a sandy beach where the men set up camp.

Although the river was smaller, the sugary white sand resembled the beach where Mike's ordeal began. Guide Jairo liked to run his outboard skiff onto the sand and set up comfortable folding chairs under umbrellas while preparing lunch for his anglers. Exposed during periods of low river flows, the beaches were comfortable and reasonably safe, unlike the rainforest a few steps away. Mike and Bill's fishing guides, many of Indigenous Amazon heritage, knew the jungle that appeared serene from the padded seat of a fast outboard skiff was full of hidden dangers. They discouraged exploration but could not always stop their fishermen who paid large sums to experience the deepest reaches of the Amazon.

Once the rainforest men set up their sparse beach camp, the youngest removed the leather bindings from Mike's ankles and wrists. All four native men and Mike Weston waded and bathed in the tea-stained water. Mike removed his shoes and the water soothed his itching feet. The brown men were completely naked as they bathed but Weston wore his clothing. The men seemed fascinated by his blue shirt but avoided touching the material as if it was cursed. They cooked their fish over the fire and the youngest shared with Weston.

As the forth night of Mike's nightmare began, the angry warrior once again bound his hands and feet. Perhaps he thought Weston would try to escape on the canoe and head downriver. Mike considered it. The warm sand made a better bed than palm fronds on hard dirt but did nothing to ease his throbbing headache.

During the night Mike thought about Ellie back in Santa Clara, his parents in Oregon, co-workers and customers at BetaCorp and Bill. By now they might have given up hope suspecting he'd drowned or been killed by a venomous snake or eaten by a jaguar. They couldn't have imagined his true fate. The search area on the Rio Celina must not have expanded as quickly as the rainforest men forced him through the jungle. Weston sobbed quietly in the flickering light of the fire. He glanced over to the sight of the prone young man staring into his eyes.

As they slept fitfully on the sand, Mike awoke and waited patiently while the buzz of forest cicadas gave him cover. He reached gradually with bound hands for his shirttail-covered pocket. The Swiss Army knife was still there but Mike's patience went unrewarded. The designated guard never slept. The glow of the fire reflected off his dark eyes.

Mike woke the next morning to a near-human scream. The young rainforest man emerged from the trees carrying his longbow in one hand and a furry carcass in the other–a freshly killed monkey. The limp body was loaded into the dugout canoe and the men prepared to board. The angry warrior untied Weston's feet and led him staggering down the beach. The men lifted him into the center of the canoe and sat him between the dead monkey and the woven basket filled with Brazil nuts.

The brown men grabbed their paddles and kneeled at even spacing from front to back. The woven fiber line was untied from the tree root and the canoe headed down the gentle current as the men paddled in rhythm. The dugout moved swiftly on the smooth flow. Travel by canoe was far more efficient than hiking the wet and tangled rainforest floor and gave Mike's aching legs time for rest. Yet his fear and confusion only grew as the dead monkey's human eyes stared into his.

The rainforest men paddled all day in the jungle heat with only three quick stops for water and Brazil nuts. As the sun settled low over the deep green canopy, the equatorial air cooled and a golden glow lit the river. Brilliant white snowy egrets roosting in a shoreline tree flew as the canoe approached. The men pulled into a small creek mouth. A palm-thatched hut stood on the bank several strides from the water, perhaps a hunting or fish camp.

After starting their nightly fire, the rainforest men cut the monkey into manageable pieces with stone knives.

They roasted hairy hunks skewered on sticks over the fire. The odor of singed hair and sight of the monkey's severed head lying in the dirt nauseated Mike who was famished moments earlier. He ate four Brazil nuts.

The following morning two of the men walked and waded the shoreline, bows and arrows ready. They returned an hour later with at least ten assorted fish hanging from their leather cord. The men loaded the canoe and paddled downriver. Mike sat in the middle, his wrists still bound. Several hours later he sensed a trace of smoke in the breeze. Within minutes a yellow haze appeared over the river. The angry warrior yelled out. A rainforest person appeared far ahead on the river bank, then another and another. They called back to the canoe.

Soon at least thirty native people–women, men and children–stood on the clay riverbank welcoming the young men back to their village. All had jet black hair hanging straight and cut raggedly in various lengths. The men stood lean and sinewy, the women slightly fuller. Some were painted in red and black facial dye, the men in bold stripes and the women in delicate patterns like the bird flocks flying overhead. The children were naked while the adults wore scant leather hides and straps with woven palm frond or leather waist coverings.

The canoe slid onto the shoreline as men and boys rushed down to pull it further up the flat riverbank. Commotion ensued as the four men disembarked. The villagers embraced and sang out. In a daze Weston was led by the angry warrior out of the canoe and into the curious gathering. Some of the children came up to touch him while startled adults called out to them. From their shocked reactions, Mike knew most had never seen a Pale Person.

CHAPTER 2
Secret Village

Pounding thunder woke Mike Weston back into his nightmare. Lightning flashes illuminated his desperate circumstance as haunting roars of howler monkeys echoed through the forest. Raindrops landed in thuds on the thatched roof overhead but he remained dry. A small fire flickered just inside the hut's entrance. Securely tied leather straps on his hands and feet prevented him from rolling over on the elevated palm frond mat. Mike strained to reach his Swiss Army knife but immediately realized it wouldn't matter. He could not survive the endless jungle alone. A week had passed since he last stepped off the luxurious houseboat *Wild Amazon* with Bill and his fishing guides.

Hours later the storm cleared and slivers of daylight crept into the rainforest and through the woven palm frond walls and door opening. Bird songs of every genre rose with the light. Weston laid on the mat aching, itching, terrified and confused still wearing his torn mud-stained pants, blue shirt and nylon shoes. Activity buzzed outside as incoherent voices broke through the chorus of birds. Unseen men argued, "Mba'ére pendejopy ko ava?"

Straining to hear, Mike understood nothing. Suddenly a fearsome man appeared at the hut's entrance with boar tusks protruding through his nostrils and face painted in diagonal red and black. Weston's only sensation was primal fear. Mike froze, his body trembling. He curled to a fetal position and closed his eyes for a moment praying the apparition would disappear. But it did not. The foreboding rainforest man's dark eyes bored into Mike's for a moment before he departed. Mike lay stunned, his chest heaving to catch his breath.

Soon an older woman entered the hut, dark brown and weathered with a wise face and long black hair with a trace of grey. She wore almost nothing, just a waistband with front and back coverings of woven fiber. Her bare breasts startled Mike until her caring eyes caught his. The woman carried an interlaced palm tray with bits of fruit, cooked fish and a stack of hand-sized leaves. She set it on Weston's bamboo-framed bed and walked out, returning shortly with a pottery bowl of acrid liquid.

The village woman untied the leather straps and removed Mike's moldy shoes exposing the peeling dead skin on his feet. Weston winced in pain. The rainforest lady dipped the leaves in the warm liquid and placed them on the most damaged areas. She coated her hands and gently washed the wounds on Mike's head and neck as she spoke softly. The words made no sense but her tone expressed concern. With two fingers she tapped herself below the neck. "Ticata…Ticata."

Weston took it to be her name and tapped his own sternum. "Michael...Michael."

Ticata handed bits of fish and fruit to Weston and he ate ravenously. The lady left the hut and returned with a bamboo container of rain water. Mike drank and fell back to sleep.

Weston slept for most of the day, his body wracked by the long forced march, skin infections and strange foods. He woke later in the afternoon as a wave of nausea swept over him. His moans alerted curious villagers mingling near the hut. They went to find Ticata and she returned to check on his condition. Weston rubbed his stomach and groaned. Ticata nodded and walked from the hut. She came back with a gourd cup of warm brew, some type of tea. Mike had little choice but to trust Ticata and sipped the elixir. When the cup was empty Weston fell back to sleep.

Weston woke to a dark man in his hut, the same young man who fed him during his forced march. The short but powerful jungle man tapped below his neck, "Jatabo...Jatabo."

Westin responded, "Michael…Michael."

Jatabo carried a bundle of sticks and laid them on the hut's packed earth floor near the smoldering fire. He pointed outside and Weston understood they would walk.

The young brown man offered a hand and lifted Weston to his blighted feet. The soaked leaves fell to the floor. Weston gestured for Jatabo to wait with his open palm before loosely slipping on his nylon running shoes. Jatabo grunted curiously.

The young village man guided Weston outside the hut to relieve himself in the forest followed by a brief tour of the village. At least twenty dome-shaped huts were visible, each made of bamboo poles covered in tall palm fronds. Lush banana trees sprouted randomly between the structures. Scattered rainforest people looked on as Mike walked, dripping from the heat. Many appeared curious and some seemed frightened. A few brave children ran up and touched Weston on the thighs, laughing as they scurried back to their group of friends.

Weston returned to his hut and laid down, his foot fungus, thorn cuts and leg muscles itching and aching. He felt his pocket for the Swiss Army knife. It was still there. Mike's immediate survival instincts receded enough that he once again thought of his family, Ellie, Bill and business associates at BetaCorp Technologies. By now the top management must have replaced him. They had too many valuable international clients to ignore for even a few days.

As daylight waned, the hum of insects intensified signaling the end of another Amazon day. Mike Weston fell to sleep.

Mike awoke in terror as the red-and-black-faced boar tusk man entered his hut the next morning. A necklace of long claws rattled as he approached. Weston gasped for breath and recoiled. The man moved deliberately and Mike saw he was older than his captors, perhaps a village elder. With a wave of his hand, the painted-face man signaled Weston to follow and he rose from his mat shaking.

The elder led him outside and walked with Weston to a large open-sided hut. Smoke rose to an opening in the thatched roof from a central fire ring inside. Five log benches surrounded the fire. Three other men were already seated. Mike recognized one immediately–the angry warrior who tormented him on their six-day forced journey. The other two appeared older and wiser, possibly more village elders. All four jungle men were naked except for their waist coverings.

The painted-face elder sat Mike on one end of the log with the three rainforest men on the other. He stood facing them and began to speak focusing on the angry warrior. The elder pointed to Weston and then turned back towards the angry warrior. He spoke forcefully, clearly aggravated. The other two older men spoke up seeming to chastise the younger warrior. Weston understood nothing but recognized their tone and facial expressions, not unlike some international business meetings he'd attended for BetaCorp. The painted-face elder and two older rainforest men talked with authority–obvious decision makers. As their conversation continued, villagers gathered and looked on while yellow parakeets chattered from the tangled jungle several steps beyond.

Weston knew the moment was right for a show of respect, yet had no way to communicate with the painted-face elder. The white tusks protruding from his nostrils gave him a frightening appearance, yet Weston sensed the demeanor of a benevolent leader. An idea came to Mike and he reached for the Swiss Army knife in his pocket as the dark men looked on curiously. Laying it in his own palm, Weston held the knife out slowly towards the painted-face man. The elder looked carefully at the red knife and then back at Weston. Slowly, Mike opened the shiny blade and cut a sliver of bark from the log bench. Then he opened the scissors and clipped a lock of his own blond hair presenting it to the painted-face elder. Mike closed the knife and presented it with both open hands. The elder accepted it and sat while opening and closing the many blades and tools, seemingly quite pleased. The painted-face man nodded his approval.

Weston tapped his chest and said, "Michael …Michael."

The painted-face elder tapped his. "Xapuri …Xapuri."

Xapuri rose from the log and signaled the four men, including Weston and the angry warrior, to follow. Xapuri led Mike Weston through the village as the other men followed. He called out and more naked village people appeared from their huts and the surrounding rainforest. They gathered around a central outdoor fire pit. Many foods unfamiliar to Weston soon arrived in baskets and woven trays and village women began to prepare them.

Fish and insect grubs the size of Mike's little finger baked on stones. The old woman Ticata was there and offered palm frond mats to Weston and Xapuri. Both sat on the ground near the fire. The kind old lady and a beautiful young woman with long black hair and amber eyes served the men on palm frond trays. The giant insect grubs made Weston queasy but he did not want to disrespect Ticata or Xapuri. In pursuit of international business deals he had dined on head cheese (sheep brain) in Glasgow, Balut (fetal duck) in Ho Chi Minh City and Hákarl (fermented shark) in Reykjavik. Mike popped the grub in his mouth and swallowed before he gagged. The fish followed and cleansed his palate. Ticata led Weston back to his hut to rest.

As evening fell and the chorus of rainforest insects awakened, Weston heard commotion from the village center. Voices rose as the entire village gathered. Yelps and laughter interrupted the conversations. Ticata summoned Mike Weston who followed her outside.

Villagers excited eyes followed him as Mike moved through the crowd. The elder Xapuri stood waiting at the central fire, his entire body now covered in red dye. He wore a neckless adorned with long sharp claws, perhaps those of a jaguar. Between the claws hung a red medallion, the Swiss Army knife.

Illuminated by the glow of fire, more villagers approached wearing ornamental necklaces of caiman skulls and teeth, claws, snake skin belts, and body markings of black and red dye. A masked man singing a staccato mantra pounded his feathered spear on the ground. The shaman?

Rainforest people began to chant and dance around Mike Weston–softly at first, but gradually morphing into a wild dervish. Some beat on stretched animal hide drums and others banged sticks to the rhythm. Villagers hopped and gyrated feverishly and Weston thought his end had come. Xapuri held a spear high over his head and called out repeatedly. The rainforest people responded echoing the mysterious incantation.

They chanted back and forth for several minutes until, suddenly, the village fell silent. The ceremony was over and Mike Weston had been spared. Ticata led him back to his hut. Again she wrapped leaves dipped in the acrid liquid around his bare feet. Mike looked into Ticata's yellowing brown eyes. They reflected a life of both sorrow and happiness, an accumulation of wisdom.

The next morning Weston saw his fungus-covered feet were healing, but three of the thorn cuts on his legs were infected. His first visitor was the young man Jatabo who brought a frond tray of nuts and cooked meat. The nuts were fine but the meat suspicious, probably monkey like he'd rejected a few nights earlier. But Mike was hungry so he tasted the roast monkey. He ate more.

Once again Weston walked among the village huts with Jatabo. His presence drew less attention than the day before. A vegetated area less tangled than the wild rainforest was cultivated on the edge of the village, a crude garden with three crops. Weston recognized the bananas. Several village women worked tending the plants and one waved. It was Ticata. She held a woven basket filled with tuberous roots. Mike waved to the kind old woman as he contemplated a way home to California.

Ticata visited Weston in his hut later that afternoon. Her first task was to swat a hand-sized tarantula off the wall and kick it out the entrance with her bare foot. Ticata treated Mike's feet and he showed her the infected thorn wounds beneath the torn fabric of his pants. Ticata held up a finger and walked out. Soon another village woman came to visit, the beautiful young lady who helped serve food to Xapuri and Weston around the central village fire. She carried a small clay pot. "Ipixuna," she said.

Mike gave her a questioning glance. "Ipixuna," she repeated.

Weston nodded and repeated, "Ipixuna."

The young woman smiled and Weston tapped below his neck, "Michael…Michael."

Ipixuna smiled, "Michael."

Tall and slender with streaming black hair, high cheekbones and smooth brown skin, Ipixuna's piercing amber eyes showed no fear of the blonde stranger. Like the other villagers, Ipixuna wore scant body covering–a woven fiber waist band and long feather necklace that, with her long hair, partially covered her breasts. Weston wondered how he might describe her if he made it home and recalled the Polynesian hula dancers he watched during a business trip in Hawaii. He guessed she was in her early twenties but couldn't tell for sure.

Ipixuna approached Michael and touched his legs searching for the wounds within the tatters of his pants. She dipped her fingers in the pot and removed them to reveal a red liquid the consistency of thick blood. Ipixuna applied the red nectar on Weston's wounds staining his worn pants. The sensation was soothing and Mike Weston felt some psychic comfort for the first time since his capture. Ipixuna rubbed the nectar on his legs until the pot was empty. She departed with the delicate grace of the smoke ribbons rising from the fire ring inside the hut's entrance.

That night another thunder storm passed over the village. At its peak Mike arose from his palm frond bed and walked out into the driving rain. He washed his dusty body and dirty clothing alone in the tropical rain and thunder, chaotic thoughts racing with the lightening. Weston felt a welcome chill as he re-entered the dry hut. He laid a small bundle of sticks supplied by the kind young man Jatabo on his smoldering fire. Fire was most important for keeping bugs away but on this night helped warm his wet body. As the thunder retreated into the distance Mike wondered, "Is that the direction of home?"

Again he considered escaping. He could easily walk from the village in the dark of night. But then what? His hut and the village felt like a lifeboat in the middle of an immense ocean. How could he reach shore?

Starting the next day Weston began to leave the hut for short walks without invitation. He listened carefully to the people's conversations but comprehended nothing. They reminded him of rainforest animal calls with added clicks and stops. Mike did, however, believe he could read the tone and facial expressions of the people. He was not threatened by the villagers but received scowls when he crossed paths with the angry warrior.

During the day the rainforest men left the village to hunt and fish. The women tended their crops, cooked and cared for the children. Late in the afternoon when most of the men had returned, the entire village walked the short distance to the river to bathe. Mike saw that about 80 rainforest people lived in the village. It no longer startled him to be it a world of naked people but he continued to wear his tattered clothing. Weston walked the village and edges of the jungle daily wondering how he could get home. His feet began to heal and his shoes that might be critical for an escape showed signs of wear. He decided to go barefoot.

With no practical way to shave Weston's blond beard grew, an obvious curiosity to the villagers who had little facial hair. Village children sometimes approached him and reached high. Mike leaned towards an outstretched hand and a fascinated child touched his honey-colored beard smiling and giggling.

As he walked the village perimeter the next day, Weston was surprised to see Xapuri. Perhaps, as an elder, he did not fish or hunt every day. Weston approached him and bowed lightly. Xapuri nodded. Mike did his best to demonstrate his desire to return home. He pointed to a hut and then at himself. Mike pointed far off and then held his hand over his heart. Again Xapuri nodded. Weston did not know if he understood.

Beautiful Ipixuna came to Weston's hut each day to check his leg wounds, always with exotic fragrances in her hair and a necklace of feathers and jungle flowers. The red nectar medicine she applied seemed to be the same dragon's blood tree sap the fish market salesman tried to sell Bill and Mike during their first day in Brazil. Always gentle and deliberate, slender Ipixuna spoke kinds words to Weston he could not understand. Mike began the routine of standing and squeezing Ipixuna's delicate hands before she departed his hut. She lowered her head and gazed at the floor with a shy smile.

On the third day Ipixuna brought a fistful of short green sticks the size of pencils to Weston. She handed one to Mike and placed the end of another in her mouth. Pointing to Westons's stick she directed it to his mouth. Mike imitated Ipixuna chewing his stick's end. The sweet wood soon foamed and masticated into tough fibers and Ipixuna used the fibers to brush her teeth. Mike followed her actions with his own rainforest toothbrush. Weston grinned and nodded as he realized how Ipixuna maintained her alluring smile.

Ticata continued to visit Weston several times each day, sometimes alone and sometimes with Ipixuna. Weston often saw them together in the village talking and laughing. The fungus on Mike's feet was nearly healed so Ticata no longer applied the leaves. Her main task was to make sure Weston had food and drinking water. By now she knew his favorite foods–fish, Brazil nuts, bananas and the grape-like palm fruit. But like all the villagers, Mike ate what the hunters brought home including monkey meat.

The village women cooked a type of porridge Weston enjoyed made from the roots grown in their fields. Digging the roots from the soil required a strong sharpened stick and great effort in the swelteringly heat. Four or five roots were placed in large baskets with head straps attached and lugged down to the creek to wash. Clean roots were cut into pieces to soak in clay pots, then boiled for hours. The final product was a starchy mash eaten almost daily by the villagers. Ticata placed it on smooth rocks around the fire and baked flat bread. Sometimes the hunters brought home honey from jungle bees and drizzled it on the baked bread.

Weston began logging his captive days on his hut wall with a black finger dipped in cold fire ash. He wrote the phone numbers of his parents and Ellie hoping it would aid his memory if he ever had a chance to use them. Ticata and Ipixuna stared curiously at the odd symbols.

On his tenth day in the village, the rainforest men led by the angry warrior brought nine pig-like animals back from their hunting excursion. Mike remembered the peccary Jairo had pointed out along the river. The successful hunting party emerged from the jungle chanting while holding their bows overhead in triumph. The women and children rushed to meet the hunters at the edge of the village clearing. Some yelled out "Hatak Hatak" and Weston recalled his first words from the angry warrior over two weeks earlier.

Was it a cry of conquest or the angry warrior's name? Maybe both. Mike sought out Ticata and tapped on her shoulder. She turned and Weston pointed to the angry warrior. "Hatak?"

Ticata nodded.

The villagers followed the hunters with their prized kills down to the river. With stone knives the men began the tedious task of processing the meat and hide. Xapuri came forward in toe-deep water wielding his Swiss Army knife. He opened the largest blade and joined his men. Their speed tripled as the sharp steel blade magically parted meat from bone and hide. Mike Weston knew he had bestowed a great gift to the people of the village. As the meat processing continued, blood flowed with the current and vicious piranhas swarmed in the deeper water downstream.

Soon the central fire was stoked and large chunks of meat roasted and smoked as the excited villagers milled about. As the meat cooked, Xapuri passed a wooden bowl of liquid through the crowd. Villagers held it to their lips and sipped as the feast began. Eating lustily with their fingers, the people that sometimes went days without a substantial meal gorged until they were stuffed. They chatted and milled about until they could force more of the delicious meal into their bellies. Mike Weston enjoyed the meat as well, a delicious jungle pork roast.

During the feast Mike watched his beautiful nurse Ipixuna stepping lightly through the throng, her long brown legs and shining black hair glowing in the firelight. She stopped next to the angry warrior Hatak. They were playful, touching and laughing. Weston's emotional response shocked him.

The festivities ended with the first sign of dawn as howler monkeys, as loud as African lions, welcomed the new day. The village fell silent and did not wake until late afternoon when the entire tribe bathed in the river. With no blood in the water, the piranhas had vanished.

Mike Weston gained strength as his injuries healed. He began to believe he could survive until he found a way home. Weston's basic needs were met yet he did not know the reason for his capture. As his body healed, Mike left his hut and walked at least twice each day. While he toured the village and its ragged jungle border, Weston made an effort to acknowledge the villagers without approaching too closely. Some smiled while others avoided him.

Weston came to recognize the bird-like songs of Ipixuna as she walked through the village and he heard her approach his hut the following morning. The men had just left to hunt as she entered. Ipixuna continued to attend to Mike's leg wounds even though they were nearly healed. She smiled and spoke softly during the ritual of rubbing the red nectar over his three scars. As she leaned over to begin the treatment, Mike noticed something different. Instead of her usual neckless of flowers and feathers, Ipixuna wore a new necklace with all the colors of the macaw–blue, scarlet, green and yellow. But the bright beads were not from nature. They were perfectly round plastic. Weston's mind raced. The modern objects did not come from the rainforest. They might be a thin thread connecting this secret village to the outside world.

CHAPTER 3
Ataqi's Journey

Eight years earlier.....

In his sixteenth flood cycle, Ataqi's people required completion of a great solo quest to achieve manhood. His time to set out approached.

The breathing organism of the deep rainforest, Ataqi's universe, held everything necessary for life. The jungle had nurtured his people as far back as their fireside legends recalled. Food, shelter, water and even medicinal plants were in abundance. Yet mysterious shadows beneath the towering canopy concealed a shroud of death.

Ataqi's ability to survive unaccompanied would prove his worth. If he could endure the rainforest for many days and bring a prize home to his people, a great celebration would ensue with chanting and dancing. Ataqi's body would be painted in red urucum seed dye and he would be proclaimed a man by the village shaman, worthy of joining the hunting parties that sustained his village.

The rainforest boy seeking manhood knew little of a distant world beyond the tall trees and liquid trails of winding *igarapés*, "canoe paths" in the Old Tupi Indigenous language. But his people sometimes told tales of an alternate realm. Ataqi wondered if he might encounter it on his quest.

The outside world knew of Ataqi's people from occasional aerial sightings. In small jungle clearings, their tightly-spaced huts might be spotted in an ocean of green. The nomadic tribe's villages appeared along small creeks so those on the outside called them the Igarapé People. Nothing else was known of them. Even the people of the Secret Village who lived in the same remote northwestern Amazon territory of Brazil knew little of the Igarapé People though their paths sometimes crossed during long hunting excursions.

The villagers distinguished themselves because the Igarapé People were generally taller and often used blowguns along with bows to hunt while the people of the Secret Village used only bows and arrows. The two peoples avoided confrontation when their hunting parties neared. Broken twigs hanging at eye level signaled caution, a caiman skull suspended over a game trail their final warning. Within their vast rainforest hunting grounds, the tribes preferred to use their weapons on peccaries, monkeys and tapirs.

Ataqi's father Iti prepared him well–how to shoot his darts and arrows straight, to recognize edible plants, to build friction fire and avoid the jungle's perils. While training his son, Iti allowed Ataqi to use a new innovation of the Igarapé People.

On a distant venture two flood cycles earlier, Iti and his hunting party came upon a group of Pale People. The aliens owned magic fire sticks to kill monkeys, boar and tapirs with ease. The Pale People, spirits perhaps, carried strange shiny objects that glistened like sunlight reflected off the river's surface. The Igarapé People knew of other shiny objects but they soared high above growling and out of reach–the great spirit birds of their ancestors.

Iti's five-man hunting party stayed hidden in the tangled foliage a safe distance from the Pale People. Under cover of darkness and complete silence, they entered the Pale People's camp and removed four of the silver objects.

The Igarapé People had no names for the two magic pots and two steel knives brought back to their village. Their pots had always been fragile clay, gourd or wood and their knives ground stone. They soon discovered the new metal tools were more valuable than the meat and hides that also returned with the hunters. Within days the ingenious Igarapé People were cooking meat in one of their new steel pots and replaced ten stone knives with two wondrous metal blades.

But the second pot was most valuable. They smashed it with stones until it lay on the ground in dozens of small shards. With much shaping and stone grinding, these pieces became the Igarapés' first metal arrowheads.

The great hunters who survived for hundreds of years with sharpened bamboo arrowheads now had a more lethal weapon. The village celebrated around the fire after the first steel arrowheads were fastened and tested. The shaman with a crown of vertical red, green and blue macaw feathers, and bamboo shoot jaguar whiskers piercing his cheeks, spoke to his people. The spirits had blessed them.

As Ataqi prepared to depart on his jungle quest he tied a brown-furred monkey pelt around his waist holding a stone knife and fire-making tools. He chose his father's hunting bow over the blowgun. Four sharpened bamboo arrows filled his fiber quiver along with two precious steel-tipped arrows.

Ataqi's bare feet slipped quietly over layers of decaying leaves as he departed. In dim light beneath the canopy with all his senses alert, he watched and listened for any hint of his next meal or a deadly fer-de-lance. The snake's venom could drop a man in two steps. A faint odor of mold and decomposition filled the rainforest but was so familiar Ataqi didn't notice. A capuchin monkey cried out in the distance perhaps warning of a stalking jaguar.

Tall for his age, Ataqi's muscles had filled out during the recent flood cycle. They glistened brown in the humid tropical air. Smooth jet-black hair hung to his shoulders and several whiskers began to sprout from his chin. He carried the bow in his left hand always ready to draw. His dark eyes scanned the forest shadows.

Ataqi's solo quest for manhood required that he bring home a prize, preferably the skin of a tapir, caiman or anaconda. The giant constrictor snake hid in shallow water preparing to strike its next victim and squeeze it to death in powerful coils of scaled muscle. The largest anacondas could swallow a large animal whole, even a human or alligator-like caiman.

Ataqi walked and searched for days through the trees, long liana vines and thickets. He crossed swampy creeks and moved quietly through the shadowy mist of the rainforest breaking twigs to mark his path back home. Brilliant green, red and yellow parrots sped in flocks through the clearings. Loud squawks gave away their location when they flew out of sight over the canopy. Parrots did not need to move silently to avoid death.

When he could find one, Ataqi's favorite nighttime shelter was the walking palm with teepee-like roots that held the trunk above ground. In a short time he could clean out the void between the roots and cover it with giant leaves creating a compact rain and insect-resistant shelter. As he tucked in for the night, sparkling fireflies lit the jungle for night-stalking creatures.

The next morning Ataqi climbed a tree to a buzzing bees' nest and thrust his hand into the waxy comb. Despite many stings, the sweet honey lifted his energy and spirit.

The following day Ataqi struck a small wolffish with his arrow and cooked it over a friction-built fire.

On the eighth day of his solo quest Ataqi came upon a wide slow-moving river. He stalked the bank looking for his village's prize or at least a meal of fresh fish. The only fish he spotted were enormous arapaima gulping air on the surface far out of reach. Frustrated, he continued on determined to capture a trophy worthy of his tribe.

On the ninth day of his journey Ataqi encountered a bounty greater than he could imagine. First he saw strange footprints on the riverbank similar to human prints but without toes. The feet that left these tracks in the mud had strange repetitive patterns not common in Ataqi's world except for the scales of snakes and caiman. Ataqi moved cautiously down the river's edge and saw men walking high on a distant bluff–Pale People.

Nothing Ataqi experienced on his quest surprised him until now. A village unlike any Ataqi had seen loomed high on the riverbank. He hid in the forest and observed for many hours. White huts like symmetrical pointed clouds lined the river bluff. A larger hut built of impossibly straight sections of tree trunks rose behind. Giant covered canoes swayed in the river near the Pale People's village.

Ataqi felt the urge to leave his cover and approach the village, but held back remembering warnings by his people. Stories of violent conflicts with Pale People were passed down for generations. These men had come into the

Igarapé People's jungle home many flood cycles ago seeking its natural riches. First they removed milky sap from "trees that bleed". Then the largest trees were cut down and fish hauled from the rivers until few remained. Pale People scarred the forests and polluted the rivers. Some rainforest people went to work for the Pale People voluntarily trading labor for food and goods. Many were forced to work as slaves.

Mystic Pale People carried black magic that could sicken an entire village and leave many dead. They killed villagers with their fire sticks when confrontations flared. The tragic lessons were passed down through many flood cycles of Igarapé People–acted out during tribal rituals as the central fire illuminated anguished faces. Many rainforest people fled deeper into the most inaccessibly dark reaches of the jungle to escape.

Yet Pale People had shiny knives and pots to prepare meat and make arrowheads. They had silver axes to shape dugout canoes, a great improvement over the stone adzes and fire used by the Igarapé People. If Ataqi could bring Pale People tools home he would be celebrated in his village, perhaps on a path to becoming chief many flood cycles in the future.

Aware of the risks, Ataqi set up a hidden camp, a small sleeping area in the bush where he could observe the new village. He planned to enter at night as his father had done. But first he must eat. It had been two days.

Ataqi walked the riverbank away from the Pale People's village where he would not be seen in the afternoon light. Skilled at shooting fish in the shallows with his bow and arrow, Ataqi stalked the water's edge. In a short time he spotted a redtail catfish resting motionless in shallow water no deeper than his knees. He stepped softly into the river and moved with stealth towards the fish so it would not spook into the depths. The firm sand and warm water soothed his tired feet. As he approached the oblivious catfish, Ataqi placed an arrow on his bow and drew. He aimed and steadied. The catfish finned casually, unaware of its impending fate.

But before Ataqi released his arrow a loud splash startled him. The fish hunter was also hunted. A caiman larger than Ataqi sprang from the water and grabbed his leg in its fierce jaws lined with razor teeth.

Ataqi dropped his bow and grabbed the thrashing alligator-like head attempting to pry it loose. He jammed his thumbs into the primitive beast's eyes. In the commotion the caiman dropped Ataqi's leg but immediately grabbed his hand and pulled him to deeper water. Ataqi felt the sharp teeth clamp into his waist.

In the frenzy Ataqi reached for his knife but it was pinned tightly by the caiman's powerful jaws. Out of the corner of his eye he saw an arrow floating next to him and grabbed it. Holding it short like a spear Ataqi thrust the arrow deep into the caiman's soft belly. He withdrew it and thrust the arrow again and again. The beast's life force faded and Ataqi moved away. Slashed and bleeding severely he waded to shore and pulled himself onto the muddy bank. Stunned but still alive, Ataqi called out to the spirits of his ancestors, "Save me."

They called back, "Go to the Pale People."

Ataqi's other choice was to die on the riverbank. He crawled naked towards the new village leaving a trail of blood. Ataqi recalled the blurry image of men running towards him before he lost consciousness.

CHAPTER 4
Village of the Pale People

Ataqi awoke in a curious environment. There were no trees, leaves or palm fronds. This hut had no thatched roof, no fire pit, no dirt floor. He wondered if he was a spirit. He felt afraid and didn't think spirits knew fear. Stinging pain radiated through his body.

Lying on a soft bed like none he had ever experienced, white wrappings stained in blood covered much of his mid-section, legs and hand. A clear vine of liquid protruded from his arm. Pale People in green and white moved with purpose around the hut. They spoke in a language that meant nothing to Ataqi but there was no anger on their faces. Shiny Pale People objects filled the room. A strange black entity flashed with miniature lightning and chirped like a parakeet.

Dizzy and bewildered, Ataqi realized not all in the maloca were Pale People. Dark rainforest people like Ataqi also moved in and out. Some approached him and spoke. The first two brown people spoke in sounds no more comprehensible than the Pale People's. Then a short dark-skinned woman approached with black hair cropped at her shoulders. Ataqi looked into her caring brown eyes. She reminded him of the young women of his village though she covered her body in soft green. His people wore scant body covering except during special celebrations. She spoke softly, "Ikanna."

Ataqi responded instinctively, "Ataqi."

"Ereko porã?" asked Ikanna. (Are you alright?)

"Aiko porã," replied Ataqi, pride overriding pain. (I am good.)

It was the simplest of verbal exchanges but lifted Ataqi's spirits.

Ikanna asked Ataqi what animal had attacked him in the Tupi-Guarani language spoken by many Indigenous peoples of the Alto Rio Negro region of Brazil near neighboring Colombia.

"Mba'é ryguata oinupã nde?"

"Jakaré," responded Ataqi. (Caiman.)

Ikanna nodded.

Knowing the native language had many local variations, Ikanna spoke slowly explaining that not all Pale People were evil. These white people had come to aid and protect the people of the rainforest with their shining tools and strong healing powers. Her message was difficult for Ataqi to comprehend but he was comforted by Ikanna's soft voice and thoughtful eyes. He did not understand why Pale People would build a village to help people like him.

Ikanna attended meticulously to her new patient Ataqi, visiting his bed many times each day. Their communication improved and Ataqi's understanding grew.

Ikanna served as one of four healthcare workers at a remote River Sié government control post. With few native Amazonians on staff, she usually made first contact with Indigenous locals coming for medical treatment by canoe or river boat. Two tents and four hospital beds comprised the entire medical clinic at the FUNAI outpost and checkpoint on the border of the Alto Rio Negro Indigenous Territory. Large signs on both sides of the Rio Sié warned boat traffic that they were entering a protected zone. In Brazilian Portuguese translated to English they read:

Federal Government of Brazil
Ministry of Justice
National Indian Foundation (FUNAI)
Protected Land
Indigenous Land Alto Rio Negro
Access Prohibited to Strange Persons
Article No. 231 of Federal Constitution
Article 161 of Criminal Code

Travel further upriver was forbidden except for Indigenous peoples and outsiders with special permission.

Everyone along the river knew of FUNAI though much of their knowledge was gossiped and erroneous. Ikanna learned about FUNAI in school before she applied for her medic's position.

Her textbook *History of the Amazon's Indigenous Peoples* translated to English read:

FUNAI (Fundacão Nacional dos Provos Indíginous) is Brazil's Government agency supporting Indigenous peoples. Their mission is to represent the rights of native people through legislation and establishment of protected Indigenous territories.

For hundreds of years, native people of the Amazon have been exploited, enslaved, forced to flee and even murdered as their extensive resources of rubber, hardwoods, fish, gold and petroleum were extracted by foreigners. Cattle ranchers and farmers leveled large portions of the rainforest that sustained native villagers for centuries.

Indigenous peoples of the Amazon suffered from European diseases for which they have no natural immunity and many died as they continue to die today. Measles, influenza, small pox, malaria, tuberculosis and pneumonia, by some estimates, decimated 90% of the Amazon's Indigenous population soon after the first Spanish and Portuguese conquests. Even pioneering Catholic missionaries inadvertently spread Old World disease into the South American continent.

In 1967 FUNAI was established to protect native Amazon cultures and their rainforest homes. The government designated large Indigenous protected territories, *Terra Indígena*. Non-native intruders are excluded without special permission. FUNAI's task is to monitor the Indigenous territories for illegal activities and allow the natives a high degree of self-determination. Isolated Indigenous peoples are protected from contact while other villages choose to engage in commerce with outsiders. Some Indigenous communities have established sustainable ecotourism where outsiders pay to visit the rainforest and learn about native cultures.

Many native peoples have retained their ancestral way of life while others have decided, often with tragic results, to integrate with the outside world. Some have fled the advances of technology, illegal resource extraction and disease into the darkest recesses of the rainforest to live in voluntary isolation. They are the uncontacted. FUNAI established a special division in 1987 to protect them.

Within the country of Brazil, attitudes towards FUNAI remain controversial. Brazil's citizens generally acknowledge the human rights of their first inhabitants, especially when considering the abuse, relocation and extermination of the North American Indians in the nineteenth century. Yet political controversy swirls. Extensive natural resources in the protected Indigenous territories are inaccessible to the majority of Brazilians, many who live in poverty. Should 400,000 natives in a population of 215 million control such a large portion of the country's land and resources?

Ikanna belonged to the Baré People who made contact with the outside world years earlier through desperation and force. Some of her people assisted FUNAI in their mission to protect Indigenous rainforest people and their habitat against incursions. Most of Ikanna's Baré People learned some Brazilian Portuguese. Other languages heard around the FUNAI control post were Spanish, Arawakan, Tupi-Guarani, English and Nheengatu. Also known as Modern Tupi, Nheengatu has become a universal language allowing many native cultures throughout the Alto Rio Negro region to communicate.

As Ataqi's communication with Ikanna improved, he learned his Igarapé People lived within the protected Alta Rio Negro Indigenous Territory and are considered by FUNAI to be among the uncontacted peoples of the rainforest.

"Yanderekan makura aymã munhã reta," said Ikanna as she stood by Ataqi's bed (Your wounds will take many days to heal.) The bite in his right thigh cut to the bone. Dr. Alberto Sanchez, director of the clinic, stitched the muscle and closed the gaping wound as best he could in the minimalist field hospital. Dr. Sanchez departed by riverboat the next day for his seven-day hospital shift far downriver in São Gabriel da Nazaré on the Rio Negro.

Ataqi asked if his attack would have killed other Igarapé People who did not receive the Pale People's magic.

Somberly, Ikanna replied "Hê."

Ataqi spoke about jaguar and caiman maulings near his village. Some of his people died immediately and others suffered for days before passing. Their mangled corpses were buried with provisions and gifts for the afterlife and the Igarapé People mourned for days until they spotted the shining spirit bird flying high above.

CHAPTER 5
Worlds Apart

Fate is not destined by the laws of probability....

While Ikanna comforted Ataqi in the FUNAI field hospital, 5,000 miles away Michael Weston followed the iPhone navigator to his new dormitory parking lot on the University of Oregon campus in Eugene. "Turn right in 300 feet." Mike pulled his rusted blue Ford pickup into the lot.

Mike knew no one on campus until he met Sarah on the foot bridge to Autzen Stadium a week after classes began. Well into his workout run, Mike stopped to take a break. "What are you looking at down there?"

"Salmon. Check 'em out."

"Oh that's cool. I guess they spawn further up the Willamette."

"Where you from?"

"I grew up in Vancouver, British Columbia ....Canada. I've seen a lot of salmon and even caught a few. My dad has a nice boat. I guess you could call it a yacht."

"I know British Columbia is in Canada," laughed Mike. "I fish quite a bit with my dad and brothers around Klamath Falls but usually for trout. It's fun but in my family it seems like we fish mainly to put food on the table."

Sarah was also a runner and they were soon jogging together, often stopping on the bridge to talk while staring down through the current.

"How are you paying for college?" asked Sarah.

"I have a scholarship but it doesn't pay for everything. I'm working part time."

"An academic scholarship?"

"Right. I've always studied hard for my grades. I'm determined to make it as a software engineer. Then I'll never have to worry about money again. I'll drive a Ferrari or at least a Tesla."

Mike grew up a three-hour drive from Eugene in Klamath Falls, Oregon. His parents both worked at Kelly Construction, Sue as an accountant and Dan a road construction foreman. Along with his younger sister and two older brothers, Michael spent much of his childhood playing in the woods and fishing the Williamson River and Klamath Lake near his home. Deer hunting each fall was a family tradition he never missed.

Mike's oldest brother Frank dreamed of becoming a master bow hunter and dragged him along to practice whenever he could. "Hey Michael, let's go shoot some arrows."

"OK I'll grab dad's bow and meet you in five minutes."

Frank owned a modern compound bow he bought at the local pawn shop and Michael used his dad's old fiberglass recurve bow. Their tattered paper deer target stood in an open field across the street from the Weston home.

"Nice shot kid!" said Frank as sixteen-year-old Michael's arrows struck near the heart. "Bow season starts in two months. You wanna hunt with me?"

That fall the brothers camped in the forest for three nights near a meadow northeast of home. Mike came along as an unarmed spotter to support his brother's passion. They woke in the dark each morning and ascended a ridgeline as first light illuminated the pine-rimmed valley. Mike scanned the meadow and surrounding trees with Frank's binoculars for hours. On the last morning Mike spotted a six-point mule deer below and upwind.

The brothers stalked quietly for twenty minutes through the trees and brush. The buck did not flee. At thirty yards Frank decided to shoot. He drew carefully and took a deep breath. His arrow flew true but the deer heard the woosh of the release and jumped to avoid its demise. "Wow, great shot Frank. You'll get 'em next time."

Sue painted beautifully with watercolors in her limited spare time and Michael inherited her talents. As a child he sketched forest scenes with colored pencils. In high school Mike won two awards at the Klamath County Fair for his landscapes of Crater Lake. Sue displayed the blue and red ribbons alongside Mike's winning artwork on her living room wall pointing them out to guests.

As a teenager Mike realized his family was barely getting by. Mike's parents shared a faded Highlander with 200,000 miles and there was usually no milk at the end of the month. Gamey venison and fish from their garage freezer filled Mike's dinner plate far too often.

During high school Michael worked weekends as a bagger at the local Ray's Market to buy the F-150 pickup from his uncle. For years the truck carried family on hunting, fishing and firewood cutting excursions. Winters are cold in Klamath Falls and the Weston's Franklin stove cut their utility bills in half when the woodpile was stacked high by Thanksgiving.

Mike ran for his Klamath Falls High School track team. Long training runs gave him time to contemplate his future and he decided during his junior year to become a software engineer. The best made great money.

In his senior year Mike applied for a financial scholarship to the University of Oregon and waited months for a response. When an envelope from the university finally arrived, he ripped it open in anticipation. Accepted! But then his stomach knotted–only half his tuition and housing were covered. He exhaled hard. "Looks like I'm still bagging groceries."

There was a Ray's Market in Eugene near campus and Weston was soon working three shifts each week as a cashier. The store manager allowed him to work around his class schedule but the combination of work, class and study time was exhausting, even for a nineteen year old. Mike's limited social life included study with classmates and conversations with Sarah while they ran the campus pathways.

Some nights Mike collapsed on his dorm bed wondering if he had the determination to keep up the pace.

CHAPTER 6
Field Surgery

Half a world away in the heart of the Amazon, Ataqi faced a different struggle–one of life or death. Writhing in pain in the Rio Sié medical tent, his caiman wounds festered and the bacterial infection in his right thigh spread. The remote medical outpost needed restocking and their supplies of antibiotics were low. Chronically underfunded, FUNAI did not have the resources to run medical clinics. They relied on outside donations from world-wide charitable organizations.

Supplies and pay for clinic workers were inconsistent. Yet the staff worked with dedication in the tropical heat considering their service an act of charity for the Indigenous peoples of the Alto Rio Negro. A primary mission of the clinic was to inoculate any Indigenous person who believed in the Pale People's healing magic against introduced diseases.

A shipment of medical supplies arrived in the frontier town of São Gabriel da Nazaré far downriver on the Rio Negro and Dr. Sanchez planned to bring replenishments back once he finished his rotation at the hospital there. But that was a week away and Ataqi needed more antibiotics immediately.

Ikanna spent hours comforting her patient, able to administer only half the recommended antibiotic dosage from the exhausted supplies. The clock ticked slowly. Patience was strength in the jungle but, this time, it did not help Ataqi. Ikanna contacted Dr. Sanchez on FUNAI's satellite phone to inform him of Ataqi's urgent condition. "Precisamos da medicação imediatamente!"

Ikanna knew the doctor did not always go through official channels to get the medications the clinic needed. Without official approval Dr. Sanchez appropriated additional amoxicillin and azithromycin from the hospital and hid the antibiotics among other supplies to be loaded on the dock the next day.

The Rio Sié control post relied on the creaky flat-bottomed riverboat *Tabatinga* to ferry passengers and supplies from downriver on the mighty Rio Negro. The 82-ft. shallow-draft wooden workhorse made the run up the Rio Sié every two weeks if she wasn't broken down or stuck on a sandbar. The FUNAI outpost was her last stop before turning downstream for the return trip to São Gabriel da Nazaré and beyond. Small by Amazon riverboat standards, bright yellow *Tabatinga* was better able to maneuver in the smaller Sié.

Dr. Sanchez departed the FUNAI clinic aboard *Tabatinga* each month for his one-week shift at the hospital.

He returned to the control post with supplies, but not just for the medical clinic. Building materials, food, tools, kitchen equipment and fuel for the outpost's generators rode in drums and pallets on the lower deck while passengers slept in hammocks on the open-sided upper deck.

The run upriver to the FUNAI control station normally took three days if the current wasn't running too fast like it often did during the rainy season. Six stops along the way served progressively smaller villages. River dwellers known as *ribeirinhos* assembled quickly on their village docks as they heard the throaty beat of *Tabatinga*'s twin diesel engines nearing, sometimes in the dark of the Amazon night.

The villages installed floating docks to accommodate extremes in river depth throughout the year. Depending on the season, *Tabatinga* might dock at elevations that varied by over forty vertical feet. River villages and outposts including FUNAI's Rio Sié were built on bluffs high above the river that might be near the churning water's surface during the peak of the rainy season.

Passengers of many descriptions boarded and disembarked along the river stops–ribeirinhos, traders, rainforest people and government employees. The arrival of *Tabatinga* was a joyous occasion, for many the only connection with the larger world on the great Rio Negro and Amazon Rivers downstream. The time between visits could seem like months, but patience was a necessity for anyone living along the liquid highway. Time moved progressively slower further upriver into the deep rainforest and wildlife thrived where humans lived at a slower pace. Ataqi's bacterial infection was no exception.

Ataqi faded in and out of consciousness as Dr. Sanchez hurried off *Tabatinga* onto FUNAI's narrow gangway. The doctor immediately began a drip of liquid antibiotics from the hospital. Dr. Sanchez decided he must open Ataqi's leg wound to clean out the infection but could not operate while his patient was so weak. Ikanna monitored the IV drip and comforted Ataqi. When his blood pressure slipped to 85/54 Ataqi lost consciousness again. Dr. Sanchez increased the antibiotic dosage.

Late the following day Ataqi woke and began to show improvement. Two days later he ate bananas and farinha bread, his first solid food in over a week. Dr. Sanchez planned surgery the next day. The medical tent that flapped in the wind made a poor operating room though the services performed there were considered miraculous by many who visited.

Dr. Sanchez did not have the tools to use general anesthesia so he injected a strong dose of benzocaine around Ataqi's infected thigh wound. He reopened the ten-inch gash down to Ataqi's femur bone and washed it thoroughly. Dr. Sanchez inserted a drainage tube and restitched the wound, remarkable field surgery in just over an hour.

The outcome was uncertain as Ataqi's fever continued for days. Ikanna monitored his antibiotics and cleaned the surgical wound while encouraging her patient to eat.

Ataqi was the only seriously ill patient in the two medical tents at the clinic. The second bed in Ataqi's tent sometimes served as a storage shelf and occasionally as a hotel bed. Indigenous people arriving for inoculations in their dugout canoes sometimes walked in unannounced at night and slept on the magic mattress. Some mornings when Ikanna arrived she would find three family members curled up together on a single clean white mattress. She gave them their shots or Malarone pills and sent them on their way.

Several dozen Indigenous peoples, some from Ikanna's Baré tribe, often lined up for immunization and malaria treatment outside the medical clinic. Some were adorned in bright macaw feathers, beads and body paint wearing varying degrees of clothing. Officially, all clinic patients were required to wear body coverings but not all complied. Clothing shipped from charitable organizations was available to the rainforest people but some refused to adopt the Pale People's ways.

When it was wasn't raining, FUNAI left old magazines out for the people to examine while they waited for treatment. They pointed and grinned at people and animals from around the world, *National Geographic* and *Smithsonian* magazines their favorites. Snow-covered mountain peaks and African wildlife, especially giraffes, drew sighs of wonder.

Setbacks racked Ataqi's body as he fought the insidious infection. At times his fever dropped but then returned a day or two later. Dr. Sanchez had to depart for São Gabriel da Nazaré and kept the tube in Ataqi's wound and instructing Ikanna to monitor the drainage while he was away.

Ten days after surgery Ataqi crawled out of bed and stood on the wooden floor. He couldn't put pressure on his right leg without throbbing pain. With a determined face, Ataqi spoke, "Ipitixu piru." (Bad pain.)

Ikanna worried, knowing the mental strength of the young man. Pain was never foreign to a stoic man of the rainforest. All had been stung by scorpions and swarmed by mosquitoes as they slept. Black palm thorns had pierced their calloused feet. Their stomachs often ached when they had not eaten for days. All had endured the brutal stings of bullet ants, the dreaded *tucandeira*.

Two weeks after he departed, Dr. Sanchez returned to the medical clinic. FUNAI official Orlando Rivas, director of the Rio Sié control post, greeted him at the dock.

Outpost staff members unloaded supplies from *Tabatinga* as Rivas tallied his new inventory.

Dr. Sanchez immediately tended to Ataqi and found he was able to take a few short steps. Drainage from the infection had stopped so he removed the sutures and tube from Ataqi's thigh. But Dr. Sanchez and Ikanna could see the tissue and bone were severely damaged. Ataqi might never move swiftly through the jungle again.

Ataqi's wounds healed over the following months and he was able to leave his hospital bed. Ikanna congratulated him on his resolve. She knew any man who laid for months in his rainforest village rarely rose to his feet again.

Soon Ataqi began assisting with chores around the clinic. He learned a few words in Portuguese and communicated with Ikanna in Nheengatu, similar to his people's tongue. Many languages were spoken around the outpost station. Other than Ikanna only one resident seemed to understand them all–the camp dog Carlos. Ataqi's new friend was a mutt of multiple breeds, perhaps German shepherd and hound but nobody knew for sure.

Ataqi spoke of his family often, of his desire to return to the distant village of his Igarapé People. But his damaged leg could not take him there.

Two months after Ataqi left his hospital bed Orlando Rivas invited Ikanna and Ataqi into the control post headquarters. Short and stocky with a permanent salt-and-pepper stubble, Rivas was a mixed blood *caboclo*–his father being of Portuguese ancestry and his mother an Amazon native of the Matis People. Rivas previously worked under legendary FUNAI sage Sydney Possuelo as they developed their philosophy for managing isolated Indigenous peoples of the Amazon, *Indios Bravos* as they were known. Under Possuelo's leadership Rivas became a full-fledged *sertanista*, a specialist in the undeveloped interior of Brazil.

FUNAI's Rio Sié control post near Brazil's border with Colombia monitored illegal narcotics smuggling, logging, commercial fishing and gold mining in the Alto Rio Negro Indigenous Territory. During their first meeting with Ikanna as interpreter, Orlando Rivas realized Ataqi's value to his mission. A complete lack of communication with a village under FUNAI's watch made it difficult to protect those people. What language did they speak? How far did they migrate during the annual flood season? Had there been confrontations with illegal trespassers? Ataqi seemed overwhelmed by the attention from a powerful man he didn't understand but, with Ikanna's help, he tried to answer Rivas's questions.

Inside the stark wooden headquarters building, the only permanent structure on the control post, Orlando

Rivas showed Ataqi his first map. Ataqi stared in confusion. Ikanna stood by his side and explained in Nheengatu that it was a miniature image of the rainforest as seen from high above–the view of the shining spirit birds. Ataqi's brown eyes widened.

Rivas pointed out the location of the control post where they stood and ran his hand northwestward, the assumed direction of Ataqi's village of Igarapé People. Ataqi appeared confused with the strange concept of a map and its snakelike blue lines. There were dozens, maybe hundreds, of creeks in that region of the Alto Rio Negro. Besides, the Igarapé People sometimes moved their village to search for better hunting or escape seasonal floods. Ataqi could not find his home on the map.

Orlando Rivas looked him in the eyes and shook Ataqi's hand. By his uncertain reaction, the young jungle man had never experienced such a gesture. "Você será convidado de volta," said Rivas.

Ikanna explained to Ataqi that they would be invited back.

As they left the headquarters building, an iridescent blue morpho butterfly the size of Ataqi's hand fluttered through the outpost grounds. The surrealistic creature bounced as it flew reminding him of his village where the spirit of each baby who died came back as a giant blue butterfly.

Ataqi longed to return to his Igarapé People but began to feel comfortable with his new life at the FUNAI control post, especially with his friend Ikanna who seemed like family. He helped preparing food and cleaning around FUNAI's kitchen always amazed by the Pale Peoples' shining knives, pots and magic gas stove.

Ataqi was not paid and did not understood the concept of currency. The only forms of exchange in the village of his Igarapé People were stone knives, animal pelts, leather cord, bows, arrows, clay pots and food. In his new FUNAI home he was compensated with meals, clothing and a comfortable place to sleep in a raised palm frond hut behind the control post. The edge of the rainforest was cut back to within two steps of Ataqi's hut and he sometimes had jungle visitors at night, usually snakes and tarantulas–nothing Ataqi hadn't experienced before.

On most evenings Ikanna dropped by to massage the deep scars in Ataqi's damaged thigh. It was painful but the wound had closed completely and there were no new signs of infection. Ataqi walked with a severe limp but knew he would not have survived the caiman attack without Dr. Sanchez, Ikanna and the Pale People's magic medicines.

Ataqi gradually grew stronger and helped out wherever he could around the FUNAI outpost. The kitchen crew began to rely on him and he helped with facility maintenance. The equatorial sun and driving thunderstorms tore at the structures as fast as they could be repaired. Ataqi liked the Pale People's tools and quickly learned their uses. He began speaking to Ikanna and the kitchen staff in broken Portuguese. With so much work to do the days passed quickly and Ataqi realized he had lived at the control post for two flood cycles. Ikanna called them "anos".

CHAPTER 7

Anthropologists

Four years after surgery saved his leg and his life, Ataqi helped erect a new tent structure at the Rio Sié control post. Even with his noticeable limp the 20-year-old rainforest man's determination made him a valuable member of the small maintenance crew.

A team of anthropologists moved in two months later bringing the number of personnel residing at the jungle checkpoint to an average of eighteen. FUNAI officials and assistants, medical workers, cooks, repairmen including Ataqi who received a small wage, and the new research team made up the mix.

As the anthropologists stepped off *Tabatinga* onto the aging wooden dock and into the tropical heat, amiable Ikanna was first to welcome them as the unofficial greeter of the remote Amazon outpost. "Olá e bem-vindos!" said the small native women in Brazilian Portuguese. The students reached out to shake her hand as perspiration dripped off their chins. They turned circles on the sun-bleached planks, eyes wide in awe of their temporary rainforest home.

Professor of anthropology Andrea Schmidt from the University of California, Berkeley along with her graduate students came to study Indigenous cultures of the upper Rio Negro. A former high school prom queen with caramel brown hair and hazel eyes, Dr. Schmidt hadn't bothered with makeup since her first days in the rainforest studying native cultures. Her epiphany occurred at the age of eighteen while watching a film in her high school history class, *Endangered Peoples of the Amazon*.

After twelve years of Amazon research, Professor Schmidt spoke Portuguese and required her graduate students to complete at least two courses in the language before spending a semester on the Rio Sié. The grad students, four at a time, studied the history of the Alto Rio Negro and its native peoples, conducted new research and assisted around the control post.

"This region's population is primarily Indigenous, many with some level of assimilation into modern society and its technology," said Professor Schmidt during their first orientation meeting in the outpost's big green dining tent. "While we're here we'll learn basic words and phrases in Nheengatu, the modern Tupi language common to northwestern Brazil."

Her sweltering students squirmed on wooden benches as a limping Indigenous man with deep scars on his arms and legs hoisted the canvas tent wall. A humid breeze blowing downriver crept into the tent.

"As part of your research you'll travel the Rio Sié aboard *Tabatinga* and speak with locals along the river's villages like we practiced on our way here. You will also have opportunities to interview river people waiting outside our outpost medical clinic. You can talk to fishermen and merchants arriving at our dock. Language will be an obstacle but most river dwellers speak some Portuguese and a few understand English."

Clouds darkened the sky and a haunting growl echoed through the rainforest. The students snapped their heads around towards the jungle and froze. No one spoke as a soft wind rustled through the trees a few steps outside. "Is that a jaguar?" questioned a student.

"Believe it or not it's a monkey–a howler monkey. You'll probably get used to their roaring though I have to admit they still startle me some mornings at first light," responded Professor Schmidt.

"Studying the isolated and uncontacted Indigenous peoples of the Alto Rio Negro presents a big challenge," continued Professor Schmidt. "Nomadic Amazon tribes leave little evidence of their existence after a village is abandoned. Organic jungle materials comprise their shelters, clothing, tools and weapons. They decay quickly into the moldy soil once abandoned, lost or damaged beyond use. A broken stone knife or clay pot fragment might be all that remains of a thriving village site deserted a few years earlier."

Andrea Schmidt took a sip from her water bottle. "Stone outcroppings are rare in much of the Amazon and, where they exist, petroglyphs are nearly unknown. Most of the remote Indigenous tribes have no written language. With so few remnants of their existence, isolated Amazon cultures can only be studied effectively through direct observation. But as you already know, we're not allowed by FUNAI to make contact or even trek into the rainforest home of the native cultures we are studying. History has taught us that an isolated Indigenous culture cannot be studied face to face without changing it forever.

OK let's break for the day. You're free to walk outside but don't go into any thick brush and keep a close eye out for wild animals. If you stay near our camp dog Carlos he'll bark to alert you of any dangers. We'll meet here for class again tomorrow after breakfast."

FUNAI was at odds with anthropologists who could be more interested in studying an Indigenous culture than preserving it. The Berkeley team signed a lengthy agreement with FUNAI and funded a portion of Dr. Sanchez's medical clinic as their entrance fee to the Rio Sié control post. The grad students were required to volunteer at least eight hours a week assisting the local population, usually traveling the river on welfare observation. Their interactions became part of the students' research and Orlando Rivas monitored their activities for FUNAI.

"I could eat this fresh papaya every day for breakfast," said a student as FUNAI staff departed the dining tent to begin their daily tasks.

Andrea Schmidt thumbed through her notes as the students arranged their seating.

"In the early 1900s Brazilian government expeditions making contact with isolated Indigenous communities officially began considering the well-being and rights of the natives. You'll often hear the name Cândido Rondon as you study the government's early interactions with Indigenous peoples.

As a Brazilian military officer, Rondon lead expeditions to build telegraph lines across the Western Amazon Basin in the late 1800s and early 1900s. These were true military campaigns and many of his men died of malnutrition and disease in the tropical jungles. Large teams he led conducted rainforest clearing, surveying, map making and scientific studies often putting him and his men in contact with isolated native villages. Some of those encounters were violent and Rondon himself was shot in the leg by a poisoned arrow. Yet he is famous for the motto he instilled in his men, 'Die if you must, but never kill.' His mixed African, European and Indigenous Amazon ancestry may have influenced his attitudes towards natives of Brazil as he lobbied the government for their protection.

Rondon was the first high-ranking government official to place the human rights of Indigenous peoples on par with all others. He became the first director of SPI, the Indian Protection Service, when it was established in 1910. In 1914 he co-lead an expedition with former U.S. President Theodore Roosevelt to explore the unchartered and treacherous River of Doubt now known as the Rio Roosevelt."

"I read about that. Some of the team members drowned in the rapids and Roosevelt nearly died of malaria," said a student.

"Correct. We will study Cândido Rondon and his work in more detail. We will also learn about the Villas Boas brothers, Orlando, Cláudio and Leonardo. The pioneering Brazilian activists and explorers dedicated their lives to protecting the Indigenous peoples of the Amazon. Starting in the 1940s, they led expeditions into the Brazilian interior and made early contact with many native communities, advocating for their rights and preservation of their cultures. The Villas Boas Brothers lived for years with Indigenous people in their native villages considering them equals. They brought previously hostile native communities together to resist the onslaught of outsiders seeking their valuable natural resources. The brothers were instrumental in the creation of the Xingu Indigenous Park in 1961, the first large-scale Indigenous reserve in Brazil. They continued to lobby the Brazilian government for native human rights and creation of large Indigenous protected territories. The Alto Rio Negro Indigenous Territory guarded from this control post is a result of their work."

Professor Schmidt fanned herself with her notes and pointed upriver towards the Indigenous zone she and her students could not enter.

"During the time of Cândido Rondon and the Villas Boas brothers up until the 1990s, the common belief was that most isolated native peoples would eventually integrate into modern Brazilian society as they learned of life downstream. Their goal as Indigenous rights advocates was to allow native peoples to assimilate at their own pace and discretion. Their well-meaning philosophy of willful integration was, sadly, a failure for many Indigenous peoples.

Even simple gifts of steel knives, machetes, pots, bright beads and mirrors left by outsiders wishing to make peaceful first contact often upended a stable age-old rainforest culture with inequitable wealth and greed. Imported diseases like influenza and measles that posed little fatal risk to outsiders decimated isolated Amazon tribes with no natural immunity. An entire village population might die excruciating deaths over a brief period as these illnesses ravaged the people. Imagine the horror."

"Damn. So to the native tribes, outsiders were a demonic death sentence."

"As terrible as that sounds it's pretty accurate," replied Andrea Schmidt.

The students took a break from their makeshift classroom as a flock of snowy egrets sped over the Rio Sié contrasted against the deep green of the jungle canopy. Ten minutes later, Professor Schmidt continued.

"Many isolated rainforest people were convinced to leave their villages for a better life in the world downriver, only to be exploited as uneducated lower-class laborers or worse. Some have been forced into slavery and sex trafficking. The result is that proud rainforest people are often reduced to poverty and depression when removed from their villages.

Today most isolated Indigenous peoples in the Amazon know something about the outside world. Many have fled deeper into the jungle to avoid its dark temptations. Their ancestors passed down stories of the brutal attacks and forced labor by invading rubber tappers, loggers, fishermen and miners of past generations."

Professor Schmidt described in detail some of the horrific conflicts between Indigenous Amazon villages and outsiders seeking the rainforest's wealth of natural resources.

"Philosophies for outside interactions with uncontacted and isolated people have evolved. Orlando Rivas's mentor is credited with this change in thinking. Mr. Rivas will explain the dedicated work of Sydney Possuelo next week. OK that wraps it up for today. Are there any questions?"

The following Tuesday morning as the mist cleared over the Rio Sié below, Professor Schmidt introduced Orlando Rivas as her guest speaker. "I believe you've all met Mr. Rivas, director of this station for FUNAI. Today he'll explain some of his early contacts as a young FUNAI agent, and how they shaped the bureau's current philosophy."

Orlando Rivas spoke over the distant hum of the outpost's diesel generator as the students opened their note pads and laptops.

"Bom dia and thank you for your interest in our native cultures. As a university student many years ago, I had your same enthusiasm. I still do today, but years of experiences have changed my attitude towards outside contact with our isolated villages here in the Amazon.

I joined FUNAI in 1985 right out of college. At the time our philosophy was to gradually introduce modern technology to the Indigenous people of the rainforest and allow them to decide when and how to incorporate it into their daily lives. We figured that many would assimilate into modern society and eventually be living like you and me. Some have and you know a few that work here for FUNAI. But we made a mistake thinking a parallel culture that has thrived for hundreds, perhaps thousands of years would drastically change in a few years. Let me give you an example.

In my third year at FUNAI I led a hospital boat up the Javari River to the edge of the greatest concentration of uncontacted people anywhere in the world. We had reports that an isolated village was suffering from tuberculosis. The disease probably came from an illegal mahogany logging operation encroaching on the village. Our plan was to diagnose and vaccinate as many villagers as we could convince to come to the hospital boat. Villagers with TB could stay on the boat and receive antibiotic treatment.

We were able to get the hospital boat within six kilometers of the village, a short walk through the jungle for the nomadic people. I led a small group in with gifts and two native speakers. We planned to lead the people back to the boat in groups of twelve for vaccinations and treatment. After two days we convinced the first group of villagers to follow us.

The chief sent a strong young boy along to mark the forest trail so his people could return back to their village after vaccination. This was a great honor for the boy who must have shown leadership skills the chief wanted to encourage. The important task of breaking tree limbs at eye level to mark the path was normally reserved for older hunters.

We set off for the hospital boat and my goal was to keep the group moving as fast as they could comfortably walk. But we had a challenge I hadn't expected. The boy stopped often to carefully mark the trail showing great respect for the trust of his chief. The entire group had to wait for him many times until I worried about making the boat by dark.

I pulled out my colored map and compass to show the boy, not exactly high tech navigation tools by modern standards but a wonder to the boy. My native speaker told the boy he could not stop to mark the trail any longer. His people could use my map to find their way back.

The young boy's eyes withdrew in sadness and his proud posture slumped. I knew immediately that his world had been shattered. Who was I to interrupt a thousand years of culture and tradition? This seemingly minor incident struck me to the core. Do we have the right to impose our ways on a civilization that has survived successfully in a challenging environment for millennia? Are they any less fulfilled than us? Less human than us?"

Orlando Rivas paused to let the students comprehend the weight of his words. Andrea Schmidt nodded as he continued.

"In 1987 my mentor Sydney Possuelo founded the General Coordination Unit of Uncontacted Indians within FUNAI. Our goal ever since has been to protect isolated and uncontacted people of the Brazilian Amazon from outside influences. In most cases that means no contact at all. Today we protect the human rights of people in our Indigenous territories that don't know they're being protected.

It's not that simple of course. The wealth of natural resources in the rainforest means that outsiders are always intruding, most illegally but some with the authorization of our government. As you can image, this causes great conflict in our capital Brasília. Our country has much poverty and some politicians believe we must maximize natural resource extraction in the Amazon. Others know this can't be sustained and could mean the end for our Indigenous people. Politicians wanting more outside access to the Amazon's natural resources, and there are many, terminated Sydney Possuelo's term as FUNAI's president in 1993."

The students passed a can of insect repellant as the air thickened with humidity and mosquitos.

"I consider myself an anthropologist just as you do. But I don't always agree with Dr. Schmidt. Over many years I've come to realize that it's better to know nothing about an uncontacted tribe than it is to study them up close and change them forever.

One more thing. FUNAI has law enforcement authority but we don't have the resources or personnel to fight large scale intrusions into our Indigenous protected territories. We consider ourselves to be the eyes of Brazil's police and military forces. That's why we're located here on a major gateway into the Alto Rio Negro. All of you can help. If you see any suspicious river traffic headed upstream, especially at night, make sure to tell me immediately. I can usually have an IBAMA plane, that's our environmental police force, check it out within a few days."

A thunderclap boomed nearby and the skies darkened. "OK we need to wrap this up. Thank you for your attention."

The students applauded.

FUNAI restricted the Berkeley team to second and third-hand accounts of life in the isolated villages. A ribeirinho who lived along the Rio Sié knew someone whose father had come upon an uncontacted village during a hunting trip twenty years earlier. The native people coming to the control post for inoculations were interviewed and some could relate stories of their ancestors' villages. "Você conhece alguma aldeia isolada na selva?" asked the grad students (Do you know of any isolated jungle villages?).

When their question elicited a confused grin, Ikanna translated the Portuguese to Nheengatu, "Inde r-eté marãka isaçu pepé awaúka?"

When she wasn't working in the medical tents, Ikanna spent progressively more time with the friendly research team. The Berkeley students often spoke of California and promised Ikanna they would take her there one day. The students brought music with them, small wireless speakers that worked off their computers. For the first time Drake and Rihanna were heard around the outpost.

Ikanna taught the graduate students and Professor Schmidt basic Nheengatu words and phrases as she learned English. Pieces of all three languages, English, Nheengatu and Portuguese filled the air any time their group met to dine, study or socialize. "Ikanna, I'm impressed with how quickly you're learning English," said Dr. Schmidt.

Two months later Ikanna joined them in the dining tent with notes she had written in English. "I must tell you about my good friend Ataqi. He is tall young native man, very shy, you see around camp. Maybe you noticed the scar on his leg. He attacked by big caiman and almost died. Dr. Sanchez operate and saved his leg. Ataqi comes from far-away village. His people hide in the jungle and they don't come out. Ataqi misses them and wants to go back to them."

The anthropology students and Professor Schmidt listened closely as Ikanna related Ataqi's story. They had never interviewed an Indigenous rainforest person who had lived with his people in isolation from the outside world.

The students asked Ikanna to introduce her friend. As they became better acquainted, the anthropologists often invited Ataqi and Ikanna to the dinning tent. Fresh fish sold by local fishermen that showed up randomly at the FUNAI dock was a favorite meal, especially when served with baked plantains.

Ataqi did not show up when Ikanna was busy in the medical tents. The anthropologists never pushed the issue with the quiet rainforest man. Though he had lived at the control post for over four years and wore cotton pants and shirts, Ataqi was still adapting to the strange new culture and technology.

Of all the Pale People Ataqi encountered, the anthropologists were friendliest but still peculiar like all Pale People. They had flashing boxes that captured miniature images of his world and other worlds he had never seen. Orlando Rivas had something similar on his desk but Ataqi had never observed it closely. Some of the scenes on the boxes moved, proof they were alive. Ikanna attempted to explain the basic concept of a computer but it did little to dispel the mystery Ataqi witnessed.

The anthropologists controlled the magic with their fingers but could not always master the enchanted boxes. At times the living scenes would not change when commanded by the students. Sometimes the scenes disappeared completely into a background as black as Ataqi's jungle at night. Their obvious frustration was a comfort to Ataqi who realized Pale People could struggle as he did.

The magic boxes had maps of the entire earth, a difficult concept for Ataqi. Ikanna pointed out the location of the students' university in California to her own astounded student, so far from his rainforest village. His jungle home seemed endless yet Ataqi could see it was a tiny leaf on the planet and a small part of the Amazon.

Although they lived in the wilderness, technology kept the Rio Sié control post close to modern civilization–computers, satellite internet and telephone, GPS, solar panels, medical equipment, diesel generators and power tools. Some students carried smart phones that Ataqi learned were miniature computers. "Oremi'ãma tapereira pirira, ikatu iñemoĩ asy tapema ñande kaxa," said Ikanna in Nheengatu (When they are closer to the cities downriver they can talk to people far away on those boxes.)

Over time, the shock of magic technology grew commonplace to Ataqi even though its workings were impossible to comprehend.

As Ataqi's confidence and understanding of his new home grew, his scarred thigh gained strength. His walks along the river increased and his limp subsided. Golden sunsets over the water reminded him of his family and his people. Ataqi longed to reunite. In his mind he saw their faces clearly though imagines of his village began to fade. Ataqi continued to grow and reached a height of six feet, tallest at the outpost.

Over the following few years Ataqi's scarred leg strengthened and he walked far into the jungle. His power and stamina increased as he explored deeper, once again part of his rainforest home. Chattering monkeys and bright toucans welcomed him back to his old world.

The anthropology students conducted their research at the Rio Sié control post for four months at a time and were then replaced by four other students. Some of them returned but many vowed never to come back to the realm of snakes, caiman, biting insects and suffocating tropical heat.

The students each selected a specialty of study— integration of Indigenous peoples into modern society, education, health and wellness of native people, religion and spiritualism, diet, language, tools and others. Some of the doctoral students returned to the Rio Sié control post three or four times to complete their research.

Professor Schmidt came to the remote outpost three times each year for the first month of each semester. New students learned of Ataqi and Ikanna before they arrived and met them as they stepped off *Tabatinga*. They looked forward to stories from the rainforest man.

With his daily interactions over the years, Ataqi's language skills improved until he spoke both English and Portuguese as well as Nheengatu. The students sometimes brought Ataqi or Ikanna along on *Tabatinga* to interview Indigenous peoples they met on the route to São Gabriel da Nazaré. Ataqi seemed to grow more comfortable with modern technology, no longer shocked by computers, smart phones, televisions or planes.

* * *

As Ataqi became familiar with his new life at the FUNAI control post, Mike Weston entered his final year of studies at the University of Oregon as a computer science major. His test scores remained strong. Between class time, studying and work at Ray's Market, Mike had little time for recreation other than his jogs around campus. Occasionally he took Sarah to a local restaurant or an Oregon Ducks' football game at rowdy Autzen Stadium but their relationships never grew beyond friendship.

During school breaks and holidays when he could take time off from work, Mike visited his family in Klamath

Falls. Several times each year his dad pulled their fly rods out of the garage and they fished the Wood or Williamson Rivers. Their drives together in the old blue pickup brought back good memories of family time together but also reminded Mike how much he wanted to break away from lower middle-class living. "It won't be long now dad and I'll be driving that Ferrari. I'll leave the truck with you to haul firewood."

As they neared their favorite fishing runs the snow-capped volcanic cone of Mt. McLoughlin rose high above the forest. Tall Ponderosa pines and clear spring rivers carried Mike back to his childhood.

CHAPTER 8
Affluence

"Let's stop on the bridge and look for salmon," said Sarah as they ran in misty Oregon rain.

"I don't see any but I need a break," replied Mike. "I haven't told you yet. I interviewed with another tech company yesterday. That's four so far. This one's my favorite, BetaCorp Technologies. They're making a big push into artificial intelligence. It's the wave of the future. We talked for over an hour and I think they're interested."

"That's great. You deserve it Mike. You've worked so hard. You're graduating near the top of your class and I'm going to need another year to get out of here."

"You'll make it Sarah. Besides, this campus is not a bad place to spend another year."

Recruiters from the computer industry visited the University of Oregon Campus beginning in the middle of the students' last semester. Weston met with four computer company reps and was most impressed with BetaCorp Technologies. The company flew him to Santa Clara, California for two additional interviews and made him an offer. One week after graduation Mike drove ten hours south from Klamath Falls to Santa Clara. The rusty pickup that blended well in rural Oregon felt out of place in Silicon Valley where Teslas, Mercedes and BMWs occupied most of the crowded freeway lanes.

Mike rented an overpriced one-bedroom apartment in neighboring San Jose his first year. His work schedule immediately ate into his free time. Artificial Intelligence fascinated him so much he found it difficult to shut his mind down, even at 2 AM when he should have been sleeping.

"Hi dad. Thanks for calling. How are you and mom doing? That's good. My new job is going well but I'm not sleeping like I should be."

"Are you getting enough exercise?"

"No. I'm thinking about joining a gym. There's a Summit Fitness down the street. I'll check it out."

Mike joined the gym where he knew no one. He was there to stay in shape and not to socialize so it barely crossed his mind...until he saw the cute strawberry blond for the third time. "Did she just look my way?" Two weeks later he mustered the courage to approach her as she finished a yoga class.

"I'm thinking about joining this class but I'm afraid I'll look like a clumsy fool."

"Come back for Thursday's class at seven and I'll help you get started. Don't worry. You won't be judged. We all started as beginners. I'm Ellie."

"Thanks Ellie. My name's Mike. I'll see you on Thursday."

Mike learned that Ellie taught fourth grade and lived in a tiny studio apartment in the same area. Nearly a foot shorter than Weston, she grew up in rural Eureka, California. After two years in San Jose, she was still adjusting to the fast pace of Silicon Valley. "My brother in Northern California has an old pickup like yours Mike. They stand out like a sore thumb in the parking lot here, but I don't mind. I know you're on your way."

Ellie and Mike met at the gym at least three evenings each week. Their similar rural upbringings made it easy to relate. Though Ellie didn't seem to care, Mike purchased his first new car a month later, an entry level Tesla. "Check out the parking lot. What's missing?"

"I don't see your truck."

"See the red Tesla? That's mine. I bought it yesterday. I'll never drive a beater again. Let's go for a drive."

Once a week they walked to the Starlight Cafe after workouts to share dinner and wine. A year into their relationship Mike suggested that Ellie move in with him.

"That's sweet of you Mike but I'm not sure we're ready. Maybe we can make more of our relationship with a little more commitment. Let's see where it takes us."

Mike's team at BetaCorp specialized in "theory of mind" machines in the first stages of self-awareness. The potential uses were limitless, nearly anything that related to human emotions in healthcare, sales, workforce motivation, government and military.

In his second year at BetaCorp, Weston attended the AI World conference in Seattle. He worked a booth to demonstrate his company's new robot "Professor Green" that gave lectures and answered students' questions on nearly any subject. BetaCorp's latest version PG2.c could scan a photo or piece of art and describe its emotions.

Mike excelled in AI programming but had even better skills selling BetaCorp's products. His managers saw Mike's potential and moved him into sales and marketing. With both salary and sales commissions Weston's earnings soared, but so did his time commitment to BetaCorp– international sales, long red-eye flights and foreign cities with challenging language barriers. Within eighteen months Mike traveled to Tokyo, Oslo, London (three times), Dubai, Paris, Reykjavik, Ho Chi Minh City, Singapore, Melbourne and Copenhagen. His amiable personality, knowledge of BetaCorp's products and youthful energy made him a top salesperson. A year later Mike was promoted to Vice President of Sales and his income continued to grow.

Mike bought a mid-priced multimillion-dollar home in Santa Clara and planned to purchase his Ferrari when he could find time to test drive all the models. His business life thrived but Mike's time with Ellie suffered. He traveled more than he was home and the long work days left little time for a relationship. Weston's fitness routine fell to almost nothing and he gained fifteen pounds, not too noticeable on his 6-foot 2-inch frame except to Ellie.

"Hey Mike there's a Billie Eilish concert here next month. Let's go!"

"Oh I'm sorry Ellie, I'll be in Glasgow for a sales conference."

Ellie invited Mike to her apartment for a special dinner to celebrate their third year together and discuss their future. He postponed twice but finally made the date.

"Is that veal parmesan? It smells amazing. Your mom taught you well."

"Thanks for the roses. Yes the Giovanni's know their Italian food," said Ellie with a strained smile. "Maybe you can come to Eureka at Christmas time and she'll make some of her favorites. Here, have some wine."

"That would be fantastic. I love your family's traditions. Everyone is so close. Unfortunately many of my international customers don't celebrate Christmas. Don't be surprised if I'm in Japan or India next Christmas season."

Their light conversation ended abruptly.

"Michael this isn't working. You know how I feel. It seems like you care more about your work and buying expensive things than you care about me."

"You know how demanding my job is."

"I do but it seems there's more to it. The money seems so important to you."

"That's no secret. We've had discussions about my childhood."

"It doesn't seem like it was so bad. At least your parents were there to spend time with you. Will you have time for our children? I love you Michael but you have some serious thinking to do. You should go on that fishing trip to the Amazon with Bill. The change of environment will be good for you."

Mike knew Bill Greer of ISB, Inc. from sales meetings, business diners and fly fishing talk. ISB was a major chip supplier for Beta Corp and they met often. They fished together once on a guided trip at a luxury lodge in Jackson Hole, the cost covered by ISB.

"Go fishing with Bill," said Ellie. "Take some time to relax and contemplate your future, our future."

No regular fishing trip, Bill invited Mike on an ecotourism adventure deep into the Amazon rainforest. The plan was to fly five-hours into the jungle on a float plane from Manaus, Brazil. The plane would land on a wilderness river and they'd stay on the *Wild Amazon*, a luxury houseboat with private chefs and air-conditioning. Each day the ten anglers on board would spilt into five pairs on fast twenty-foot aluminum skiffs, each with one English-speaking and one Indigenous guide. The target species was twenty-pound peacock bass. No other fishermen or humans were known to be in that part of the Amazon. The native villages were further downstream. Weston delayed giving Bill a response, knowing it would be hard to take ten days off work.

"Hi Mike it's Bill. Have you made up your mind? The trip of a lifetime!"

"It does sound amazing Bill but I'm getting close to some huge orders."

"Well, we'll be in the middle of nowhere but our houseboat has satellite internet so you won't be out of contact. And the peacock bass are huge, world record size."

"Yep, and Ellie really wants me to go……OK count me in."

CHAPTER 9
The Plan

Mike Weston's all-consuming and lucrative career at BetaCorp Technologies reached its fourth year when, a world away, anthropology professor Andrea Schmidt plotted a creative research plan. There might be a way to work around FUNAI regulations and interact directly with an uncontacted Amazon village.

Ataqi had resided at the FUNAI Rio Sié control post for eight years when Dr. Schmidt called a meeting with him, her four anthropology graduate students and Ikanna. Ataqi lit a mosquito coil in the dinning tent as the students took their bench seats. As they swatted insects, Professor Schmidt divulged a loophole that could allow outsiders to research an uncontacted tribe face-to-face without breaching FUNAI regulations.

Andrea Schmid dressed in olive cargo pants with her blond hair resting on the shoulders of a loose blue jungle shirt explained. "We know that only native people are allowed in the Indigenous territory without special permission. Ataqi, of course, can enter legally any time without official approval. I've known you now for four years and watched you gain strength on long hikes into the forest and along the river," she said looking into his eyes.

"With Ataqi's language skills and jungle experience he could lead an expedition. But we have another hurdle. Orlando Rivas has made it clear he doesn't want isolated villages to be contacted from the outside. But Ataqi is not an outsider. He's one of the Igarapé People. Ataqi, will you go with me to talk to Mr. Rivas? Maybe we can convince him."

Professor Schmidt knew Ataqi would not be surprised by her request. She discussed it with him two days earlier during a morning walk in the rainforest. He responded to her, "I want to see my people. We can talk to Senhor Rivas, yes."

Orlando Rivas had not supported the idea of sending an Indigenous team to make first contact with the isolated Igarapé People. Based on his interpretation, it was against FUNAI protocol. But the professor's new idea might change his mind. Her planned expedition would not be a first contact. Ataqi had lived with his people for sixteen years before setting out alone on his fateful quest. Orlando Rivas nodded and asked to reconvene the next day.

They met again in the control post headquarters the following afternoon–Director Rivas, Ataqi, Andrea Schmidt and Ikanna. While the ceiling fan squeaked,

Orlando Rivas laid out details of a contact expedition that could satisfy FUNAI's mission.

A small expedition team of no more than eight members with Ataqi as leader could explore the protected region thought to be home of the nomadic Igarapé People. Each expedition member must be related to a tribe of the Alto Rio Negro. Once the Igarapé People's village was located, only Ataqi could enter. Other team members would remain outside to reduce possible spread of disease. They could build a temporary forest camp at least one kilometer from the village. Ataqi would visit his people from there. FUNAI could provide assistance but did not have the resources to fund the expedition. The meeting adjourned as a tropical downpour approached.

With her basic plan set, Professor Schmidt lobbied her anthropology department at the University of California, Berkeley for funding. The opportunity to study an uncontacted Amazon tribe was unprecedented in recent years. The University of California pledged USD$50,000, the equivalent of R$250,000 Brazilian reais.

Notice went out to villages along the Rio Sié. Professor Schmidt's students rode aboard *Tabatinga* with fliers in Portuguese and Nheengatu that they handed to passengers and nailed to dock pilings. While many river dwellers who might qualify as expedition members were illiterate, important news spread quickly person to person along the jungle's liquid highway. For a two-month commitment expedition members would receive the equivalent of a year's pay for many ribeirinhos.

Each team member must speak Nheengatu or Tupi-Guarani and have rainforest subsistence skills. They would be well provisioned but the weight of supplies for an expedition that could last over a month was more than they could carry on their backs. So the men needed hunting and fishing experience as well as shelter building skills.

Professor Schmidt needed a team member to document the expedition. Many of the otherwise qualified job applicants would have poor or no writing skills. Ataqi had learned to communicate in four languages including Nheengatu, Portuguese and English. His native tongue was classified by associates of Dr. Schmidt from a recording as a Tupi-Guarani language related to Nheengatu. Despite his language skills Ataqi had not learned to read or write other than numerals and a few words in Portuguese.

Andrea Schmidt and Ataqi met weekly with Orlando Rivas in the control post headquarters. Director Rivas was the only *sertanista* at the control post, an Amazon outsider who had trekked the Brazilian rainforests in search of isolated native villages. He had years of experience on expedition teams back when contact or close observation of an isolated culture were encouraged by FUNAI.

The Berkeley graduate students often joined the meetings to take notes. Those new to the outpost might be surprised by their working conditions. "Professor Schmidt it smells like moldy socks in that office. Is that OK to breathe?"

"Welcome to the tropics. You'll barely notice in a few weeks."

Each week more details emerged from the planning sessions–navigation, gear, food, shelter, communication, safety and documentation. Rivas located the most recent satellite photos of the anticipated search area in the upper Rio Sié drainage. The resolution was adequate to view brown clearings through the nearly continuous green rainforest canopy. "A clearing is usually a village or hardwood clearcut. Logging of Brazilian mahogany was banned in 2001 and sale of the lumber is illegal in the U.S. But a black market still thrives for the hardwood," said Rivas as he tapped his mahogany desktop.

Based on their satellite photo review, the likely location of the Igarapé People's village was on the Rio Juri near the Colombian border 98 kilometers up the Rio Sié to the unnavigable rapids and then 45 kilometers northwest through the rainforest.

"You must paddle canoes upriver to the starting point of your jungle trek. We do not allow powerboats into Indigenous territories except in emergencies," stated Rivas.

A call went out along the river for two large canoes in good condition. Signs were posted at the docks, "Procura-se, duas grandes canoas em bom estado na estação Rio Sié."

The plan developed between Orlando Rivas and Andrea Schmidt took shape. If the expedition could locate the Igarapé People and if Ataqi was welcomed, he would give a verbal account of his experiences to the documentarian each night in the nearby expedition camp. If the initial contact went well Ataqi could stay with his people for perhaps a week to reacquaint before the team began their journey back towards the Rio Sié control post. Depending on the unpredictable outcome, Ataqi might return to his people in the future.

As emphasis shifted towards selecting the expedition team, a boisterous Indigenous man stepped off *Tabatinga* onto the control post's dock. Personnel near the landing, including Andrea Schmidt, took notice. Native people were usually more reticent than this dark barefoot character. In animated Nheengatu he asked for Professor Schmidt. She witnessed the brief exchange and met him face to face seconds later.

The deep scar across his cheek proved the sinewy brown man in worn cotton shorts and faded t-shirt was accustomed to confrontation. He surprised Professor Schmidt when he spoke intelligible English–with an Australian accent. "Nice ta make yah acquaintance ma'm.

Ace jungleman Urubu Pakha from the Warekena tribe he-ah fo yah expedition."

Dr. Schmidt took Urubu aside. "Where did you learn to speak like that?"

"Me Aussie friend along the rivah fo nine years. Came to the Amazon to dodge the law. Wanted fo murder in Australia but he didn't do it. A fine bloke he is."

Wide-eyed Andrea Schmidt nodded and reached out to shake Urubu's hand. As they shook he tightened his grip and reached for her blond hair with his left hand. With a swat, Professor Schmidt broke away. She barely noticed the black snake slithering into the grass in front of her as she steamed back towards the dining tent with Urubu following behind. "I kin lead yah bloody team," he called out.

"Meet us back here in an hour," she responded.

A re-composed Professor Schmidt along with her grad students and Ataqi assembled in the dining tent fifty minutes later. Urubu strutted in shortly after. "Where kin a man get a bite ta eat around here?"

"Have a seat," responded Dr. Schmidt. "Tell us about yourself. How can you assist our expedition?"

"Assist? I kin lead yah team ma'm."

"How?"

"I grew up in the jungle before me parents moved our family to the rivah. We started a farm and I walked to school most days where I learnt to read and write. Then I worked the field fo a few years until I got bored. I got a job as a deckhand aboard *Tabatinga* and learned to use all the navigation and communication equipment. Good experience for a young bloke don't ya think? Now I work fo me friend Doug's business. He knows how to make good money but his work's a beet slow these days. Doug's the Aussie I told ya about."

Professor Schmidt responded, "Your experience is interesting Mr. Urubu. We will need a team member to operate the GPS and navigate in the jungle. Sounds like you could document daily activities too. I'll give you a trial run. We'll be setting up a training camp over there."

Professor Schmidt pointed towards a nearby jungle thicket through the open dining tent wall. "Some of our gear has arrived. Why don't you and Ataqi start setting up camp."

"Yees ma'm. Ya won't be disappointed."

"I hope not," replied Professor Schmidt. "And Mr. Urubu. Remember to behave yourself."

Supplies and gear arrived from São Gabriel da Nazaré aboard *Tabatinga*–backpacks, hammocks, boots, tropical clothing, first aid kits, machetes, axes, knives, two GoPro cameras, hunting rifles, fish hooks and line, bows and arrows, beans, rice, manioc farina flour, coffee, pans and pots. Crucial equipment included GPS messenger units that would allow the expedition team and Rio Sié control post to plot their locations and communicate with text messages–if the signal could penetrate the dense rainforest canopy to satellites overhead. Orlando Rivas offered a handheld satellite telephone owned by FUNAI but the team determined their GPS messenger systems were more reliable and less expensive to operate.

Extra items were ordered as gifts to the Igarapé People. Dr. Schmidt and Orlando Rivas debated the list and quantity of offerings. It was customary for a contacting party to leave gifts on trails outside an isolated village as a sign of goodwill before face-to-face contact. A sudden unannounced appearance by outsiders could be interpreted as an attack and cause villagers to fight or flee. Gifts usually softened the initial contact. But how many and what kind?

As Orlando Rivas explained, It was difficult to appease the people of a newly contacted village without changing them forever. FUNAI was not against change, but it had to be driven by the will of the Indigenous people as they learned about the world beyond their rainforest home. History had shown that slow change or no change at all had the highest likelihood of keeping the people of a jungle culture thriving. They decided that extra knives, machetes and steel pots would be packed as gifts. Other offerings could be ornamental and less functional. Colorful plastic beads for necklaces were added to the cache.

The plan was to begin the expedition during the middle of the Amazon's drier season typically running from June through November. Unfortunately, selecting the expedition team took weeks longer than expected. Gear shipments to the control post were often delayed. A shipment of manioc flour was raided by rats and dried beef spoiled by mold. Some of the first aid supplies intended for the expedition were urgently needed by Dr. Sanchez and Ikanna at their medical clinic and had to be re-ordered.

Timing was not optimal but it gave Professor Schmidt and Orlando Rivas more time to train Ataqi, Urubu and their motley team of recruits. Three GPS messenger units arrived along with paper maps. The graduate students loaded the GPS messenger app to their computers. It tracked the handheld devices on digital topographic maps as they moved and communicated in text messages from the field. Two handheld units would travel with the expedition team while one GPS messenger would remain at the control outpost.

Orlando Rivas, Andrea Schmidt, Ataqi and Urubu assembled the ragged expedition team on the control post lawn one month before their departure date. Besides Ataqi's Igarapé People, three other Alto Rio Negro tribes were represented, the Baré, Warekena and Baniwa.

As the team waited for more supplies, training had to begin. Like Ataqi, most of the men were in their twenties though two didn't know their age. Urubu was the oldest in his mid-thirties. Three of the new team members were just one generation from an uncontacted tribe of their own people. Most went barefoot with widely splayed toes. All wore baggy shorts belted with rope and ragged t-shirts of ambiguous origin. One shirt sported the faded logo of the Chicago Blackhawks hockey team and another had the imprint of a newer model Chevy Corvette.

The expedition men were lean and strong though half could be considered emaciated, their disheveled black hair raggedly trimmed in bangs above their brows. Some had facial tattoos and pierced ears with decorative clam shell or caiman tooth jewelry. Ataqi handed his men their expedition wear–military jungle fatigues and shirts, two of each. They tried on tough nylon hiking boots. Some would wear them and others would walk the rainforest floor barefoot as their people had always done.

Tools were distributed–knives, axes and machetes. Backpacks, canteens and hammocks came next. Each hammock had a suspended tent cover that would prevent nighttime rain showers from soaking the sleeping men. They might keep some mosquitos, spiders, scorpions and ants off their tired bodies as well.

Ataqi and Urubu led their new crew a short distance into the jungle towards the training camp site. The rainforest closed in quickly, no less wild than if they had trekked for days. Capuchin monkeys stared down from the canopy but fled through the treetops as the men approached.

Within four hours the team finished building the test campsite Urubu and Ataqi had started three weeks earlier. Hammocks hung from trunk to trunk. The men constructed a crude table of bamboo poles and palm fronds. Nearby they dug a fire pit and covered it with a nylon tarp for cooking out of the rain. The team stocked a woodpile. Butane lighters were packed in every bag to avoid the difficult task of starting friction fires.

The practice camp was just that. Fire ants crawled on some hammocks mistakenly tied to tree trucks loaded with the stinging insects. There were no chairs except for fallen logs. Much of the firewood was too green to burn. One side of the palm frond table collapsed when the kitchen pots got too heavy. Arguments broke out with Urubu usually in their midst. Ataqi seemed distant from the jungle that was once his home, perhaps not ready for the role of expedition co-leader.

The next morning the team walked to the medical tents for physical exams by Dr. Santiago and Ikanna. Most had arrived at the FUNAI outpost with ailments common to residents of remote Amazon communities. Half showed signs of malnutrition and three had symptoms of malaria. The men were given Malarone and doxycycline, the drugs most commonly dispensed by Dr. Santiago. Ikanna instructed them to report each morning to receive their medications and gathered a supply to send with Ataqi on the expedition.

During their training period, the men hunted and fished every day to sharpen their skills. Pig-like peccaries were their primary game along with an occasional monkey or boar. They planned to carry two Ruger 10/22 Takedown rifles into the jungle along with two bows and three dozen arrows in the event their ammunition was exhausted. The team prepared, cooked and ate the game but their meals were heavily subsidized from the control post kitchen. Dr. Santiago and Professor Schmidt wanted the men as strong as possible before they departed.

The graduate students taught Ataqi to use the GoPro digital cameras. Urubu soon had the GPS messenger units tracking their location on the students' laptops, the red dots superimposed over digital maps of the area. Urubu typed out a message, "This is Urubu. Can you read my message?"

Two minutes later Urubu received a text message response, "Urubu this is Andrea Schmidt. I received your message. This will work well."

The team studied paper maps that Ataqi and Urubu would carry to the jungle. They learned that the GPS messenger units required clear space above to communicate with orbiting satellites, a challenge under the dense rainforest canopy. An open village site could be used to send an unimpeded signal but Orlando Rivas nixed the idea. "Ataqi we must hide our technology from the villagers. I don't want them exposed to any equipment they might consider black magic. The only exception is your camera."

Ataqi would photograph his Igarapé People–their shelters, food, ceremonies, body adornment, canoes, medicines, pottery, tools, gardens and weapons. Rivas and Professor Schmidt instructed Ataqi to keep the small camera as discreet as possible. "Ataqi, try not to show your people any digital images. They might think the camera has captured their spirits."

As the team continued training, their jungle skills returned. Ataqi gained respect from the men as they learned of his near-fatal caiman attack and long struggle to re-gain use of his crippled leg. The men spoke in their native tongues and in Nheengatu, the only language they all understood. Urubu and Ataqi often communicated in English. Orlando Rivas and Professor Schmidt seemed pleased with their expedition team's progress.

Several leads came through offering canoes for sale but they were too small. Each canoe had to carry four men and a month's worth of supplies. Eight meters was the preferred length. Finally a radio call to Orlando Rivas offered two serviceable canoes at a reasonable price. They needed inspection.

Rivas and Professor Schmidt called a meeting. The canoes were two days downriver in the village of Maracuá. Urubu spoke up. "I kin inspect and retrieve those canoes. That's just one stop down rivah from me home. I kin travel down in a fisherman's boat and return with the canoes on *Tabatinga*. Oh, I kin bring a messenger unit and we kin practice tracking and texting. What do ya think?"

The next day Urubu hitchhiked a ride downstream on a fishing boat delivering arowana and peacock bass to the control post. Andrea Schmidt refused to send more than a small amount of cash with him. "If you like the canoes, tell them Dr. Sanchez will stop in and pay the balance next time he heads down to São Gabriel da Nazaré."

"I'll be back in a week with the canoes. Bloody oath ma'm," shouted Urubu cruising away from the dock.

As he headed downriver to Maracuá, Urubu pulled out one of the expedition team's new GPS messengers and typed out a note. "Doug its Urubu. Will be there in 2 days."

CHAPTER 10
The Aussie

Urubu disembarked in Tirinba, an hour upriver from Maracuá where the canoes were located. Doug, more often known as Nick, met him on the creaky old dock. As the only redhead for many river miles he was difficult to miss. "G'day dark man. Watch yah step. Let's see what ya got?"

Urubu handed the GPS messenger unit over. "Here ya go Nick. They think yah name is Doug at FUNAI."

"Let's keep it that way. Oh that's a nice one, the newest model. A cracker in a sweet little package," said Nick. "Better than me old model. Let's turn the tracking function off now. We don't want ta leave a trail."

They walked the short distance on a red earth path to Nick's house overlooking the Rio Sié. The freshly-painted blue two-story on the bluff was the nicest along that stretch of river. The rainforest closed in tight but Nick had a gardener who maintained a lawn and tropical flowers around the home.

"Have a seat, I'll be right out."

Urubu sat on the elevated front porch and watched the S-shaped wake of a ten-foot caiman cross the Sié. Nick returned shortly and cracked open two Brahma beers.

"Ya know the plan. When ya reach the big rapids hide the canoes in the bush. Ya don't want them disappearing while yah trek'n the bloody jungle. Send me the coordinates so I kin pass them on to me friends and I'll arrange the rendezvous. They'll reach the Rio Sié far upstream in Colombia on an old logging road hidden under the trees. Keep me informed of yah progress. Got it mate?" questioned Nick.

"Got it. Can I trust these guys?" asked Urubu.

"The blokes will need ya again."

"Let me see that messenger unit," said Nick. "Come on in. I'll show ya some tricks."

The men sat at the kitchen table with Urubu's device as Nick attempted to get the GPS coordinates. Nothing. "Good. The double roof is blocking yah satellite signal. This is what'll happen in most of yah jungle camps with trees overhead. It might as well be turned off. No GPS, no communication, no tracking."

"Here's how ya turn the tracking function on an off. Very important. You'll want to leave tracking off except when yah far away from a camp. If things heat up we don't want FUNAI knowing the coordinates of our hiding places."

"They won't be suspicious if ya turn tracking on during the middle of the day out on the rivah. Then your professor and her students can follow yah progress. They'll just figure the forest canopy is blocking yah signal at the camps. Make sense? asked Nick"

"Gotcha," responded Urubu. "What about our spare GPS messenger?"

"That's an easy one. See this? It's how ya access the SIM card. You pull it out and replace it with this. Looks the same but it's broken. Let's try it outside."

They stepped out and the correct GPS coordinates flashed on the small screen. Urubu pulled out the good SIM card and replaced it with Nick's.

"Good on ya mate. I'm getting noth'n, said Urubu."

"Looks perfect but it won't work. Put the good card back in and don't lose the bad one."

"Excellent. And don't forget–you don't know anyone named Nick."

"Got it Doug," laughed Urubu.

Nick ran Urubu downriver to the next town of Maracuá in his powerboat to check out the canoes. "Be in touch mate. Best of luck," called out Nick as Urubu walked up the wooden gangway.

Nick sped off upriver and disappeared around a forested bend.

The two aluminum canoes were large enough for the expedition but banged up from years of river rock collisions. The owner selling the boats spoke the local Nheengatu that Urubu often used along the Rio Sié. They questioned and bartered.

Urubu wasn't sure the canoes were in adequate condition for the expedition. The owner pulled out a repair kit with rivets and aluminum repair plates and laid it in one of the boats. With Ataqi and other ingenious repairmen at the Rio Sié control post, Urubu determined the canoes could be made river worthy. Besides, there weren't any other options. The wet season was a few weeks away and the search for Ataqi's Igarapé People had to get underway.

Urubu offered the man less than he was asking. They bartered and agreed on R$15,000 reis, the equivalent of $3,000 US dollars. Ten percent now and the rest when Dr. Sanchez came by on his next trip to São Gabriel da Nazaré.

"Katu?" asked Urubu.

"Katu."

The men shook hands and called two other villagers to help them carry the canoes down to the dock. *Tabatinga* was scheduled to stop on her way upriver the following morning. Urubu slept that night on the splintered wooden dock near the canoes. He didn't want them to disappear in the darkness. Mosquitoes swarmed any time the river's breeze died but it was nothing he hadn't experienced a hundred times before.

Tabatinga arrived two hours late the following day, punctual in river time. The crew helped Urubu slide the canoes onto the lower deck and they cast off upriver towards the FUNAI control post.

CHAPTER 11
Preparation

As the expedition team trained at the Rio Sié station, Mike Weston scrambled to organize his work load at BetaCorp in Santa Clara. Ten days' absence while fishing the upper Amazon could leave valuable clients hanging. Mike expected his deal to sell five Professor Green PG2.c AI robotic units to the Norwegian University of Science and Technology to close soon. "You know how it goes Bill. They always have more questions."

"They'll be able to reach you," assured Bill. "We'll be in the middle of nowhere but, as I've told you, our big houseboat has satellite Wi-Fi….and a gourmet chef."

Ellie grew more distant but they spoke on the phone most weeks and met at the gym when Mike could get an hour away from work. With their relationship frayed, Mike questioned his decisions. It wouldn't work with him traveling the world on business trips while Ellie stayed home with the children she desperately wanted. "I hope your time in the Amazon gives you the space to evaluate our relationship," she said before he left.

As the major chip supplier to BetaCorp, Bill's company ISB had money in their marketing budget to spend on valued clients. Bill routinely asked Weston to join him on fly fishing adventures but Mike usually declined the offers–too many deals in the works.

Bill invited Mike on a one-week trip to the South Snake River in Jackson, Wyoming a year earlier where the fly fishing and affluent western ambiance could reward ISB's best customer. For once Mike agreed.

As their guide spun his high-bowed drift boat around with an expert's touch on the oars, the three men bounced through a chute and slid into a pool of rising trout. Mike barely noticed, staring at his iPhone screen to see if the signal strength was adequate to call out. Weston sat in the back of the drift boat on an important call while Bill hooked one cutthroat trout after another from the bow. Each rise on his elk hair caddis dry fly evoked a whoop from Bill. "You're up Mike. Grab your rod."

Mike signaled to keep the noise down. "I need to make a call." Their guide frowned.

Nothing against Bill or fly fishing but Mike declined most of his offers. The Deschutes River, Belize bonefish, and the Alagnak in Alaska all sounded good but Mike couldn't take the time off work. He hadn't planned on taking up Bill's offer to fish the Amazon before Ellie's urging.

Bill scheduled their trip through Amazon Frontiers, an ecotourism company in São Paulo that guides anglers to remote Indigenous Protected Territories. The AmFron website described their mission.

> "Amazon Frontiers (AmFron) works with FUNAI and local Indigenous communities to guide adventure-seeking anglers into rarely visited regions of the Amazon Basin. Native people make up half our workforce needed to house, feed and guide our anglers aboard custom deluxe riverboats.
>
> AmFron's ecotourism adventures bring jobs to remote villages while sustaining their rainforest homes. Nearly all fish landed by our anglers are released after being measured and weighed. Fishing logs are maintained to monitor the health of the rivers we fish over the years. AmFron riverboats depart Indigenous territory waters and head downriver for maintenance each year as the rainy season begins."

Weston received a package from Bill two weeks before their departure. Mike was surprised to find a new top-of-the-line Orvis 10 weight fly rod, Nautilus fly reel and a dozen seven-inch-long streamer flies in flashy colors meant to tempt ambushing peacock bass. Also included was the latest in hi-tech tropical sportswear, a blue FreeFly long sleeve hoody and tan nylon pants.

Mike kept his trip gear to 30 pounds including polarized sunglasses, light hiking shoes, two fishing hats, light rain jacket and his laptop computer. His red Swiss

Army knife with two blades, scissors, cork screw, can opener, screw drivers and awl traveled with him as usual. His parents gave Mike the knife on his twelfth birthday.

Bill worked from ISB's headquarters in Chicago and Weston would fly out of SFO. They planned to meet in Panama City and fly Copa Airlines to Manaus, Brazil.

* * *

Back at the FUNAI control post Ataqi and Urubu worked with their expedition team, Ataqi leading by quiet example and Urubu by emphatic, often annoying chatter. The team broke down their training camp, trekked deeper into the jungle and set up a new camp to test their preparedness.

As the season of heavy rain approached, Professor Schmidt and Orlando Rivas decided to cut the one-month training session a week short. It was early November and the expedition party was ready to head out, as ready as they could be.

CHAPTER 12
To the Amazon

Bill waited in the terminal as Mike Weston deplaned in Panama City. "Glad you decided to come along. Ready for our big adventure?"

With a six-hour layover Mike and Bill decided on a two-hour taxi tour of the Panama Canal and old colonial town center. Afterwards, they relaxed on soft reclining chairs in the airline lounge while Mike returned client emails and business calls.

Their flight arrived in Manaus, Brazil at 2 AM. An AmFron representative greeted them there and shuttled the men to the Opera House Hotel. As AmFron recommended, Mike and Bill arrived a day before their long floatplane flight to the Rio Celina. A missed connection would mean a missed trip so some leeway between flights was recommended. Besides, a guided day tour of Manaus was a must-see according to the AmFron website.

They slept until after 9:00 the following morning but were up and ready for their 10 AM tour. As they sipped coffee and waited on the hotel's veranda under the warming equatorial sun, Bill read a description off the Internet.

"Manaus, Brazil is located in the heart of the Amazon just south of the equator on the shoreline of the Rio Negro. The bustling boom-and-bust city of over two-million people has a rich but gritty history. The waterfront, lined with weathered docks and swarming with activity, serves as a gateway to the vast wilderness beyond. The fish market, a hub of commerce and culture, teems with vendors selling fresh catches from the rivers, creating a sensory overload of sights, sounds, and smells.

Amidst the vibrant Latin hustle and bustle however, Manaus harbors a darker side. Poverty and gangs run rampant. Illegal activities are persistent with organized crime syndicates vying for control. Petty theft is common on the desperate, crowded streets. Despite efforts to improve security, the city's reputation as a haven for illicit activities persists, adding an air of danger to its exotic allure."

Mike missed much of the city's description as he checked his phone messages. Their tour guide Pedro picked Bill and Mike up at 10:15 AM. As they rode in the air-conditioned van, Pedro described his city.

"Manaus was originally a Portuguese fort built in 1669 at the junction of two of the world's largest rivers, the Rio Negro and the upper Amazon. Locals call the upper Amazon River the *Solemões* but most maps label it Amazon all the way to its headwaters where Peruvians call it the Marañon on the eastern slope of the Andes Mountains. The big Amazon, really big, starts where the two rivers meet just downstream of Manaus. The river here is so wide you often can't see from one bank to the other and it's still many days by riverboat to reach the Atlantic Ocean.

Manaus is the center of activity for nearly every enterprise in the Amazon. The city grew rapidly in the late 1800's when the rubber boom flourished. Sap from our rubber trees made the first tires, industrial belts and rubber shoe soles for the world. Hardwoods, especially teak and mahogany, were logged in hundreds of tributaries upriver and floated down to mills here. Many years of over-harvesting and clearcutting scarred much of our rainforest. Now it's illegal to log teak and mahogany in most of Brazil. But there's still a black market for those beautiful hardwoods. Other Amazon species from the rainforest and from tree farms support our lumber industry today.

If you've eaten Brazil nuts they probably passed through Manaus. Manioc farinha flour is big business here too. Commercial fishing in the rivers is a large industry. You will see when we tour the fish market."

They reached the busy waterfront where a multitude of flat-bottomed riverboats of every vintage, size and color rested briefly on their docks and moorings. *Itaberaba, Hilda V, Aqua Nera, Delfin II* and dozens of others prepared to depart for exotic ports and villages.

A few well-maintained riverboats gleamed with fresh paint but most were rust-stained and deteriorating. Trucks pulled up to the largest riverboats the size of ships as crates of supplies were offloaded. Passengers lined up bound for journeys to unknown destinations that could be over a thousand miles in either direction. Mike and Bill watched passengers stringing their colorful hammocks up on the covered decks.

"That's how you sleep on our riverboats. Everyone brings a hammock and picks their own sleeping spot," explained Pedro.

The river flowed like syrup far below the frontage road, the shoreline littered with worn tires, broken pier pilings and assorted trash. A massive old concrete retaining wall separated the elevated roadway from the water. The stained wall was marked every vertical meter to measure the river's elevation, the highest mark nearly 20 meters above that day's water surface.

Pedro parked the van and the men began a walking tour of the immense Manaus fish market. Amazon fish of every description cooled on ice trays–arowana, pacu, bizarre armored catfish still squirming, giant arapaima and brilliantly-colored peacock bass, the target species of Bill and Mike's fishing trip. Venders called out like auction dealers, some wearing the gold and green jerseys of their esteemed Brazilian national football team.

A booth on the far end offered native medicinal products from the rainforest. Like many venders at the market, the salesman spoke some English. "What's that one?" asked Bill pointing to a yellow-labeled plastic jar.

"It's the red healing sap from our Amazon dragon's blood tree. It's been used by native Brazilians to treat wounds for longer than anyone knows. It really works."

"How about that one?" asked Mike.

"Boiled anaconda fat…from the giant snake of the Amazon. It's one of our best medicines. Rub it on cuts and they heal fast. Drink a tablespoon twice a day and it reduces inflammation."

Bill and Mike tasted a few drops. Bitter! They each bought a small plastic bottle of the elixir to reward the energetic vender for his good sales pitch.

Pedro drove Mike and Bill back towards the waterfront. "You've probably been told this already. Be very careful at night on our streets. Stay in large groups and don't go far from your hotel. Tourists are easy targets for street gangs here. I blame the government for our poverty and crime. Brazil could be a rich country but we can't get to our natural resources," lectured Pedro.

"Tomorrow you'll fly into one of Brazil's protected Indian territories, one of our governments worst ideas. They've decided these lands are not owned by the Brazilian people–just a small group of *indios*. There are enough natural resources in the protected *indios* lands to make all Brazilians comfortable. Yet the *bugres* won't use them. It's time the *indios* are brought into the modern world."

An outboard motorboat sat waiting at the waterfront. Mike, Bill and Pedro sped off towards the junction of the mighty rivers, the breeze comforting in the stifling tropical heat. There was no question when they arrived. The dark waters of the Rio Negro contrasted distinctly with the tan water of the Solemões, each tributary many miles wide. "The Solemões runs strait off the glaciers and snow fields of the Andes Mountains and is filled with mud and silt. The Rio Negro water percolates through wetlands in its headwaters in Colombia. Dead leaves stain the water like tea, but it's quite clear," said Pedro. "Once the two rivers meet to form the mighty Amazon, the two colored ribbons of water do not fully mix for many kilometers downstream."

Their boat motored to a floating wooden platform moored on a calm section of river for a unique Amazon experience. Bill and Mike removed their shoes and were instructed to sit on a bench at the river's surface. Their legs dipped into the silty water. A man brought over a bucket of dead baitfish and began splashing the water. Within minutes two pink hulks rose from the murky depths. River dolphins! The *botos* as they are known on the Amazon were wild but had learned to stay near the platform for an easy meal. The man fed each dolphin as their long toothy jaws rose above the water. "They must weigh three or four hundred pounds!" exclaimed Mike, a bit nervous as he reached out to touch one.

"Our Amazon botos are grey when they're young. But they fight with each other, especially the males during mating season. Their teeth marks leave wounds that heal as pink scar tissue. So maybe the river dolphins with the pinkest skin are the biggest fighters," explained Pedro.

Their last stop along the river was another floating platform. This one was open to the water in the middle, actually a square floating walkway supporting a submerged net pen. Bill and Mike were each handed a stout bamboo pole with a short hookless line. Dead baitfish were tied on the ends.

"Try your luck," shouted the attendant.

Mike and Bill dipped their baits into the giant net pen. Within seconds the water erupted as two massive scaled creatures lunged at their baits. The men could barely hold the rods as huge arapaima fish pulled until their bait came free.

"Arapaima can reach 600 pounds but these are small ones, only two or three hundred pounds. Do you want to try again?"

Bill and Mike hooted and laughed as they cast their hookless lines and the prehistoric fish put on a feeding frenzy.

"Arapaima that we also call pirarucu are delicious. They have been fished out in many parts of our Amazon. These fish here are raised in lakes along the Rio Negro and removed with nets. We are trying to replace some cattle ranching with arapaima farming. Cattle need big clearcuts in our rainforests...not good," explained the attendant. "Arapaima farming is more better."

The motorboat returned the three men back to the Manus waterfront in time for Pedro to drop Bill and Mike off at the hotel for their AmFron orientation meeting. All ten anglers arrived and they introduced themselves.

"We will meet for breakfast here in the restaurant at 5 o'clock tomorrow morning. Bring all your gear downstairs with you. The van will take us to the airport at 6:00," instructed AmFron host Margarite.

"As you know, AmFron has obtained special permission to fish the Rio Celina in the Alto Rio Negro Indian Territory. Very few outsiders are able to trespass and fish this protected Indigenous zone. Please pay your $600 tribal entrance fee to me in U.S. cash after this meeting. All the money goes to protect the Indians and their territory. You are also required to sign these release forms to enter the special zone. I hope you all have a great adventure and catch some big peacock bass."

The two-page contract to enter the protected Indigenous Territory was labeled:

INDIVIDUAL RESPONSIBILITY TERM – FUNAI
– National Indian Foundation

The contract began:
I _____ am a guest of the Alto Rio
Negro Indigenous Territory, of the Rio Celina
Fishing Project for the permanent possession of the
people Baniwa, Warekena, Baré and other people of
the indigenous territory both known and unknown.
I will respect the customs, beliefs and indigenous
traditions and observe the other provisions of the
1988 Constitution (Articles 231 and 232) of Law No.
6,001 / 73 (Statute of the Indian) and the
Convention 169 of the ILO - International Labor
Organization work (incorporated into the Brazilian
legal system by Decree No. 5,051 / 2004).

The contract disallowed firearms, hunting,
commerce, extractive activities, research activities,
proselytizing, or giving alcoholic beverages or addictive
drugs to the native people. All guests were required to
remain with their applicant's representatives and not go
into areas other than those pre-established in the Visitation
Plan.

"The main thing is to respect the native people and
their land," explained Margarite. "Each of your fishing
skiffs will have two anglers with one native guide and one
English-speaking guide. In late afternoon the five fishing
skiffs will tie up to your houseboat and you'll encounter
other native staff members working to make your stay in

the Amazon as comfortable as possible. Communicating will be difficult but a smile is always appreciated. You are encouraged to tip the staff at the end of the week."

All ten anglers walked down the street that night for a group dinner before their departure to the Rio Celina the next morning. Pirarucu (arapaima) was listed on the menu. Both Mike and Bill ordered the fish and agreed the texture and flavor were excellent. "They put up a great fight too!" laughed Bill.

The van picked up the fishermen and their gear at 6:00 the next morning. After check-in at the airport they were bussed out to the tarmac. Two chartered Cessna 208 Caravan amphibious float planes waited. Each had eight passenger seats, two pilot's seats and ample storage in the flotation pontoons and belly compartments. Protruding fore and aft on each of the two pontoons were wheels allowing the planes to land on both water and paved runways.

Three AmFron staff members loaded boxes of food and assisted the ten anglers with their gear. All three boarded the planes for their one-month work shifts on the distant Rio Celina. Soon they lifted off and the city disappeared quickly as the two planes headed north. Scattered rural settlements along the twisting creeks and rivers dotted the jungle landscape below, evident by their agricultural clear cuts and tin roofs. Small boats worked the rivers. Signs of civilization faded until, twenty minutes later, all were gone.

Mike knew from his guided tour the previous day that large barren swaths scarred the Amazon where logging, gold mining and ranching had flattened much of the rainforest. But most of the deforestation was further south. Weston gazed out his window amazed at the extent of the tangled jungle a few thousand feet below. A vast canopy of treetops in every shade of green spread to the horizons, some capped in bright flowers. Tall palms poked their fronds upward through dense foliage. Mike saw no sign of human activity. If there had been it wouldn't have been obvious under the thick vegetation. They flew on for nearly five hours deeper into the Amazon. Scattered clouds floated below just above the tree tops.

The infinite rainforest was interrupted occasionally by serpentine creeks the Brazilians call "igarapés". Mike and Bill saw the name on maps of their fishing area the day before. Igarapés are headwater tributaries, they learned, large enough to navigate by canoe. But it became apparent to Mike as they flew on that many Amazon waterways labeled "Igarapé" would be considered full-fledged rivers just about anywhere else on earth. Riverbanks gave the passengers their only view of the rainforest's full height. While the trees reached high competing for sunlight, the darkest spaces beneath were more open. Large animals, no doubt, prowled the forest floor.

Humans also lived in the rainforest and Mike thought back to a *National Geographic* article he'd read years earlier. The lead photo, taken from a low-flying aircraft, showed a thatched hut in a small clearing. Standing just outside staring upwards at the plane were black-haired men, their naked bodies stained in red dye. Their painted faces expressed both surprise and anger. The men held spears and bows high threatening the skyward intruders. Mike looked for similar clearings but saw none.

The floatplanes finally reached the Rio Celina and turned upriver with no evidence of boats or any human activity below, just more winding river and rainforest. Finally, they spotted their sanctuary in the most spectacular but hostile wilderness cruising the river ahead, the *Wild Amazon*.

Mike and Bill's plane dove sharply towards the gently flowing surface and then leveled off. With a soft thud the pontoons made contact and white spray splashed to window height. A moment later the plane came to rest followed by the second floatplane to their right. The planes taxied to the wide stern of *Wild Amazon* and crewmen tied them up.

Ten anglers disembarked the float planes balancing along the pontoons in steaming jungle heat. Minutes later they relaxed in the air-conditioned lounge of the deluxe riverboat. Cold sodas and beer were opened while Mike pulled out his laptop to check the satellite Wi-Fi. The weak signal eventually downloaded 31 work emails and one from Ellie. Mike waited impatiently for hers to open. "Enjoy your trip Mike. Focus on the nature surrounding you and try not to be consumed with work. Love, Ellie."

Weston spent the next two hours returning client emails.

Each morning after a big breakfast the anglers walked to the stern of *Wild Amazon* at anchor and boarded their fast outboard fishing skiffs. English speaking guide Jairo and indigenous guide Aruaú waited ready for Bill and Mike to board. Each of the five skiffs were untied and raced out to different locations along the Rio Celina to begin their fishing day. Other than their own boats, they saw no sign of human activity–just dense rainforest rising far above the riverbanks, colorful birds and monkeys. Mike felt like a first explorer of the jungle wilderness. With no Wi-Fi or cell signal he focused on fishing with just a trace of anxiety.

Their target was the *Temensis* peacock bass, a giant version of the popular Jack Dempsey and Oscar aquarium fish that also come from the Amazon. The largest *Temensis* peacock bass reach fourteen kg or 30 pounds though a twenty-pounder is considered a trophy. The AmFron Rio Celina project is a fisheries research study so every *Temensis* caught was measured, weighed, photographed and released. Some of the smaller brightly-colored butterfly peacock bass were kept for meals.

Jairo pulled the skiff into an oxbow lake, a former bend in the sinuous main river channel that eroded outwards over many years until it joined another bend to create a new straighter channel. The old curved river channel remained as a swampy backwater lagoon, prime hunting ground for ambushing peacock bass.

Jairo selected two large streamer flies from Bill and Mike's fly boxes. The flashy seven-inch-long orange-and-green-hair streamer flies imitated favorite baitfish of the peacock bass. The huge flies, far from the tiny insect imitations Mike cast for Oregon trout, looked like juvenile peacock bass. "Yes they are cannibals," said Jairo.

The fly rods were also stouter versions of the light 4 and 5-weight trout rods Mike was familiar with. "Those trout rods would shatter like toothpicks when a big peacock strikes," answered Jairo. "Besides, you couldn't cast these heavy streamer flies with a trout rod. That's why we usually use 9 and 10-weight fly rods here on the Rio Celina."

Mike and Bill stood on the bow and stern decks of the 20-foot skiff casting their streamer flies towards the bank. The closer their flies landed to reeds, submerged trees and aquatic vegetation the better. Peacock bass use them as cover and wait patiently to ambush their prey. Jairo used a small electric motor to move quietly within 60 feet of the shoreline brush. In lower clearwater conditions they might see the largest fish underwater, but rain falling in the Colombian headwaters had flooded the Rio Celina. The Amazon's dry season was coming to an end.

Mike rolled out a long cast along a submerged stump and hooked the first fish. It didn't fight as hard as he expected and he soon saw why. "It's a black piranha Mike," said Jairo. "Watch those teeth. Hand your rod to me and I'll unhook it."

Jairo grabbed the plate-sized piranha and expertly removed Mike's fly from the razor sharp teeth. He held it briefly for a photo and flipped it back into the water. Mike's streamer fly looked as if it had met a garbage disposal. "We better change that mangled fly. Take it home for a souvenir."

Bill's first fish came an hour later. As he retrieved his fly to imitate a fleeing fish, the line suddenly tightened. Bill pulled back as hard as he could to keep the strong fish from retreating back into the tangled underwater branches. The brightly colored peacock bass responded by shooting into the air spraying thousands of water droplets like liquid diamonds. The heavy fish strained Bill's fly rod to the breaking point as it surged towards the submerged brush. The tug of war continued as Bill made progress only to lose his gains seconds later. With a powerful surge, the peacock bass battled into the branches of a partially submerged tree and wrapped the strong line.

Jairo pulled the skiff close as Bill reeled his line. "There it is Bill," said Jairo.

A bright peacock bass still attached to Bill's line rested hopelessly tangled in the branches. Jairo called to Aruaú who stood up and removed his white long-sleeve T-shirt. Aruaú dove in and swam for the tangled fish. It required three attempts but the determined native guide finally came up with the spectacular gold, orange and black fish in his hands. Aruaú spit water as he swam the short distance back to the skiff, depositing the fish in the net held out by Jairo. He weighted the heavy fish and Bill held it for a photo. "Why is its tail so ragged?" questioned Mike.

"It's a vicious world down there," replied Jairo. "Piranhas do that."

Bill reached over to shake Aruaú's hand, his black bowl-cut hair still dripping.

They motored back to the main river channel just as their mothership *Wild Amazon* passed by headed upriver. "If we go farther upriver we may be able to find lower water," explained Jairo. "The fishing should be better."

Over the next five days, *Wild Amazon* motored higher into the headwaters of the Rio Celina than she had ever explored. "When the rain stops up there, the upper river will clear first," explained Jairo.

Each day's routine was similar and, while the fishing was not great, the experience was. Jairo was a master at spotting wildlife along the shore and pointing it out to his fishermen. "Look over there by the dead tree. Those are peccaries, like little pigs. The natives hunt them and they're one of their favorite foods."

"You see that animal moving on the shoreline? It's a capybara, a giant rodent that thrives in South America."

Jairo's best observation was a tapir crashing through the shoreline brush. "It looks like a cross between a baby rhinoceros and an anteater," laughed Bill.

At lunchtime Jairo usually tied the skiff to a shoreline root. "We prefer the white sand beaches for lunch but most of them are underwater now. Maybe we'll find some further upriver in a few days."

Mike asked if he could step onto the bank and walk into the jungle as the others finished their lunches. "We don't recommend it," responded Jairo. "We have many venomous snakes; fer-de-lance, coral snakes, bushmasters, all kinds of snakes that can drop a man in seconds."

That night around the dinner table, one of the anglers passed his phone with a photo of a coiled fer-de-lance. "It was five feet from our boat."

The staff abord *Wild Amazon* worked hard to keep their anglers safe and comfortable in the harsh environment. They cleaned sheets and made up soft beds in the air-conditioned cabins while their guests fished. Picture windows in each room provided a thin barrier between regulated comfort and the uncaring Amazon wilderness. Top chefs prepared dinners of prime rib, swordfish and king crab. Attention to detail made luxurious *Wild Amazon* a secure fortress against ever-present danger, especially at night when jaguar snarls echoed through the jungle and the green glow of predatory caiman eyes shined on the river.

By the fifth night *Wild Amazon* had motored further up the Rio Celina than she had ever been. After dinner Jairo showed Bill and Mike their location on a map of the region laid out on the table. "Rio Celina is a tributary of the Rio Sié. This is their confluence. You flew over it on the way in. Eventually Rio Sié flows into the Rio Negro from the northwest, still 600 kilometers upstream from Manaus."

"It looks like we're close to the Colombian border now," said Bill. "Do you ever see other boats up here?"

"I've never been this far up the Celina," replied Jairo. "But in my six seasons guiding here I've only seen one other boat. It was coming downriver and looked suspicious–maybe a cocaine smuggler. The captain notified the police in São Gabriel but we never learned what happened. I've heard rumors of illegal gold dredging in the upper Celina but we haven't seen a rig pass by. They usually move at night so it's hard to say. Our environmental police force IBAMA tries to monitor this region from the air but it is basically endless and their budget is small."

With cold drinks in hand Mike and Bill made their way to *Wild Amazon's* upper observation deck. A golden sunset approached the treetops and lightening flashed among distant clouds. Howler monkeys roared to warn of impending darkness. The buzzing hum of millions of insects soon filled the night. Mike Weston went back to his room and returned client emails.

The anglers woke to a beautiful morning on their last day of fishing, determined to put in a full session on the water. Breakfast concluded earlier than usual and within minutes the anglers stepped onto the wide stern of *Wild Amazon* loading their skiffs with fishing gear and lunches. Bill and Mike's fishing boat was untied first and sped off upriver. Jairo wanted to explore ever further into the headwaters. The river level had dropped and several white sand beaches began to show, a favorite lunch stop of Jairo's.

Jairo continued until he found promising fishing water near a grassy island. Mike and Bill each landed and released heavy peacock bass. Jairo stowed a smaller butterfly peacock bass into his ice chest for lunch. Fishing was good until two pink river dolphins as large as the men came over to check out the commotion. Their show entertained the men but sent the bass into hiding. Jairo cranked up the outboard and they headed for a new spot.

At noon Jairo found a white sand beach and ran his skiff onto the soft bank, an idyllic spot to enjoy their final lunch of barbecued peacock bass and tropical fruit salad. The men hopped onto the sand as Aruaú set up folding chairs beneath an umbrella. Bill and Mike's steps were their first on dry land since the tarmac in Manaus and it was their last day in the deep Amazon. By noon tomorrow they'd be well into a five-hour float plane ride to Manaus followed by overnight business-class flights back home.

The mysterious rainforest ten steps away called to Weston as they ate, his last chance to explore if only for twenty minutes. Jairo discouraged the venture but Weston knew he might never return. "Let's check it out Bill."

"No, I'm staying on the beach. But don't let me hold you back."

"I just want to take a few photos in there."

Mike Weston entered the realm of the green cathedral. A moment later the tangled vines and broad leaves obscured him from Jairo and Bill…..

Manaus Waterfront

Weston's jungle walk

Capuchin monkeys

Lurking anaconda

Manaus Fish Market with arapaima

Manaus Fish Market with peacock bass (center)

Amazon Sunrise

CHAPTER 13
Jungle Expedition

The expedition team moved quickly to shore as *Tabatinga* rounded the bend churning upriver. Carlos the mutt, sensing their excitement, came running and barking alongside his buddy Ataqi. As the riverboat thumped against the dock, Urubu hopped off to welcome his men. "Eremiara sukurí iunara igara." (Help me unload the canoes.)

While *Tabatinga's* crew tied up, the expedition team boarded and hoisted the canoes off the deck, up the slope and onto the flat lawn to the side of the headquarters building. Subtle groans reflected the condition of the boats that could carry the men up the Rio Sié to the rapids. "No worries mates," said Urubu. "We'll have em fixed in a flash."

Grey clouds and afternoon showers cooled the men from the oppressive heat but also warned of the coming wet season. They planned to depart on their journey up the Sié in three days if the canoes could be patched in time. The expedition team organized their supplies under cover of the dining tent and packed them into nylon sacks, waterproof river bags and backpacks. They carried the packed food and gear downhill to the dock to open much needed floor space in the dining area.

Orlando Rivas notified the men that a final health screening was required before they could depart in search of Ataqi's people. Ikanna explained the necessity of the tests to the restless expedition crew. She had seen the tragic outcome of carrying normally benign diseases into a population isolated from the outside world.

Ataqi, Urubu and another outpost handyman reshaped the dented sections of the canoes with hundreds of hammer taps. Power saws removed the most damaged pieces. Fortunately there was no significant structural damage to the canoes' ribs. The men shaped replacement patches with sheet aluminum that came as part of the deal and attached them with the same silicone sealant that found myriad weather proofing uses around the control post.

Without the proper rivet gun, securing the aluminum patches to the canoes' hulls was the most challenging part of the repair. But living in the Amazon is a constant series of improvisations and the men soon had a solution. With two men, a sledgehammer as a backstop and accurate taps with their carpenter's hammer, the aluminum rivets were seated.

Two days after the canoe repairs commenced, Urubu pronounced them river worthy. New canoe paddles were part of the team's gear and the men carried them to the boats for a test run. The excited team walked the canoes to the dock, dropped them in the river and climbed in, four to a boat. Ataqi and Urubu each had their own small crew of native men looking fit in matching jungle fatigues and the Australian bush hats that Nick recommended to Urubu.

Anyone growing up along the rivers of the upper Amazon has canoe experience and the men of the expedition were fine paddlers. They practiced for an hour working up and down the Sié becoming two well-synchronized teams. Leaks at the repair patches were minor. Water accumulating in the canoes from rain showers would need more attention.

The big aluminum canoes weighed a fraction of the traditional Amazon dugouts and moved swiftly over the river's surface. Paddling upstream with a full load of supplies would not be easy but the men's chatter and body language showed confidence.

Ataqi and Urubu met with Andrea Schmidt and Orlando Rivas that afternoon and declared they were ready. "There's no time to lose. Can you depart tomorrow?" asked Professor Schmidt.

"Yees ma'am," replied Urubu.

The men loaded their expedition's supplies into the canoes before nightfall. The grad students, Ikanna and other staff organized a send-off celebration with singing and guitar playing around the fire pit. Ataqi made a short speech, first in Nheengatu to his team members and then in English.

"I want thank Professor Schmidt, Meester Rivas and friend Ikanna for help to find my people. I want bring back pictures and many stories for you. Aguyjevete!"

They hooted and clapped for the jungle boy who fought back from near death and a crippling injury. Ataqi stared at his feet embarrassed by the praise.

The expedition team gathered for breakfast before sunrise. At first light they boarded the canoes and prepared to cast their dock lines. Urubu activated his GPS messenger's tracking function and its location coordinates were transmitted to Professor Schmidt's. She looked at her hand-held unit, identical to Urubu's, and waved to him from across the dock. Two students preparing to follow the expedition on their computer app received the coordinates and gave a thumbs up from the grassy slope below the headquarters building. With dock lines freed, every control post resident stood by to wish the team good luck as they paddled up the Rio Sié into the unknown. It was November 10th.

The heavily laden canoes struggled against the current but were able to make several kilometers per hour according to Urubu's GPS. The river averaged one hundred meters wide and the canoes crossed from shore to shore searching for the easiest current. Not wanting to push too hard their first day, Ataqi directed the men towards shore for a thirty-minute lunch break. With their canoes in the shallows tied to shoreline roots the men waded to land, always wary of hidden dangers–caiman, anaconda, electric eels and freshwater stingrays among the deadly mix.

Lunches were quick meals that included beef jerky or dried fish, crackers and dried banana chips or acai berries. The team enjoyed breaks from the intense sun but Urubu rushed them back to the canoes. "E'waka'i kuyawë rë mura'tu." (It's time to get back on the river.)

An afternoon rain shower cooled the tired team as they paddled on. As the men bailed rainwater and leakage from their canoe with cooking pots, Urubu pulled the GPS messenger unit from his pack and shut the tracking function off. Professor Schmidt and Orlando Rivas had enough location coordinates for the day.

Before sundown the two canoes pulled into the mouth of a tree-shrouded creek, its left bank a potential campsite beneath the rainforest canopy. A sweep of the area found a venomous coral snake coiled under a fallen log. Valued team member Pelém of the Baniwa tribe dispatched the snake and carried the log to the kitchen area for seating.

The minimalist camp went up quickly with use of the team's axes and machetes. The men lashed hammocks to trees and attached their suspended tent covers. Kitchen tarps covered the fire pit and the team constructed a makeshift table of lashed bamboo and palm fronds. The men felled a small tree and cut it into sections for additional chairs. They collected dead branches for firewood.

"The mossies are a fright here," complained Urubu as he slapped his cheek. Some of the men applied bug repellent but most didn't bother. A few moist sticks tossed into the cooking fire created enough smoke to subdue the bugs.

They planned to eat canned ham for their first camp's dinner, but one of the men spotted a heavy redtail catfish in the creek upstream. Pelém returned with his bow minutes later and secured a favorite meal for the entire team with a single arrow strike behind the gills. Bare-chested and wearing a necklace of armadillo claws he rarely removed, Pelém lifted the catfish from the creek as a dozen red piranhas appeared, attracted by the splashing and blood scent. Three piranhas held the big catfish with their razor teeth and wriggled in the air for a moment before dropping back to the water.

Shortly after the catfish dinner, as the hum of evening insects grew, the tired expedition team crawled into their hammocks. Their first day had been a success. Team leaders Ataqi and Urubu inspected the dark camp with their headlamps and then sat by the dying fire to discuss the next day. "I'll grab the messenger unit," said

Urubu as he stood and walked the short distance to his backpack.

"The canopy's too thick here. I'm not geet'n a signal," said Urubu as he walked back towards Ataqi to show him the non-responsive signal. "No worries. I'll get coordinates tomorrow on the rivah."

The men crawled from their hammocks at first light to alarm clock howler monkeys. Coffee was soon on the fire followed by warm farina bread and plantain chips. The team packed their camp within an hour and boarded the canoes.

As soon as his canoe cleared the tree cover, Urubu had his men hold steady in the soft current and grabbed his GPS messenger unit. He double-checked that tracking mode was off. With clear sky above the GPS coordinates flashed.

Urubu typed a message to Doug who he knew as Nick, "Camp 1 Rio Sie 1° 13' 55"N 67° 08' 34"W Canoes hidden under canopy in creek mouth. Cant be seen from river or air. Good camp. Urubu out."

Then Urubu typed an alternate message to Professor Schmidt at the Rio Sié base. "Camp 1 Rio Sie 1° 14' 11"N 67° 10' 17"W. Problems with unit 1 GPS tracking function. Seems to work intermittently. Will switch to GPS messenger 2. Day 1 successful. Day 2 promising. Urubu out."

Twelve minutes later he received a response from Professor Schmidt. "Message and coordinates received.

You are 78 km from rapids takeout. Is tracking function on? Good luck. A. Schmidt out."

"Yes tracking on." typed Urubu. It wasn't.

On day two the eight expedition members made good progress paddling 21 kilometers up the Rio Sié. At midday Ataqi directed the canoes to an exposed sandbar for their lunch break. In good spirits the men joked and laughed as clouds shaded them from the equatorial sun.

That afternoon the team paddled into an oxbow lake to search for a suitable camp. Soon Ataqi located a clearing in the shoreline underbrush and beached his canoe followed quickly by Urubu's. With their machetes the men slashed out a suitable campsite. A bounty of fish filled the lagoon but swarms of bugs did as well. Dead branches provided an abundance of firewood and insect-repelling smoke once the campfire burned.

Nauta, one of Urubu's canoe men, sat slumped over a stump during camp preparation. His paddling on Urubu's canoe was weak that day forcing Ataqi's canoe to wait several times for Urubu's men to catch up. Urubu walked towards Nauta. "We need everyone's best effort mate. This team is too small ta have anyone not carrying hees weight."

Nauta did not seem to understand and stared blankly. Short tempered Urubu shot back, "Bloody hell I need ya to work!"

Ataqi approached and spoke to Nauta in calm Nheengatu. Nauta responded weakly. He had been stung by bullet ants while taking down camp that morning and was ill. Ataqi suggested he rest and drink more water than usual. Urubu stomped away.

Rain fell most of the night and the team woke to a campsite of mud. The men refilled containers with fresh rainwater accumulated in the canoe bottoms. They rinsed muddy backpacks, storage containers and boots in the lagoon before loading the canoes for the day's journey.

Urubu asked his paddlers to hold in the lake just meters from camp once clear of the canopy cover. The GPS coordinates flashed. Urubu typed a message to Doug, "Camp 2 Rio Sie 1° 24' 39"N 67° 09' 29"W Calm lake hidden from river. Good hiding place. Beached canoes not visible from aircraft. Urubu out."

Urubu sent a second message to the Rio Sié FUNAI base. "Camp 2 Rio Sie 1° 25' 41" N 67° 07' 56"W All is well. Urubu out."

A response came minutes later. "Thank you Urubu. Not tracking your GPS messenger. Your coordinates place you 55 km from rapids takeout. Be safe. A. Schmidt out."

To avoid the Rio Sié's stronger midriver currents the expedition team paddled near the shoreline, sometimes in the shade of the rainforest. As they moved upstream into the zone of the uncontacted, wildlife grew more abundant. Monkeys of different species moved with ease in the treetops and often came to the river's edge to inspect the intruders. Flocks of green parrots and blue parakeets zipped by. A huge harpy eagle, the monkeys' greatest enemy, soared above the canopy. The intricately patterned black, white and grey bird of prey with banded legs and long black feathers streaming behind its sinister head stared intently hunting for its next meal.

Later in the afternoon the men spotted a pack of wild boars drinking along the shoreline. Urubu signaled his paddlers to approach cautiously and pointed to Pelém's rifle lying against the canoe's stern end. The master hunter lifted the .22 and took aim. Four shots rang out in quick succession. Boars squealed and mud flew. A minute later the shoreline went silent. Urubu held two fingers in the air as he waved Ataqi's crew over. Each team loaded a boar the size of a farina flour sack into their canoe.

In a calm section of open water Urubu checked the GPS coordinates on his messenger unit and then activated its tracking function. He sent a message out to Professor Schmidt and her students following on the app. "Good progress. Team mostly strong. Check tracking coordinates on your map."

Andrea Schmidt responded. "Yes we see you at 1° 33' 17"N 66° 49' 16"W Glad all is well. A. Schmidt out."

Late in the day Urubu once again disabled the tracking function. The expedition team searched for their third camp. Nauta appeared to gain strength throughout the day and Ataqi thanked him for his effort.

The canoes moved another kilometer upriver before a suitable landing beach and campsite were located. As the men carried supplies to camp Urubu noticed another message from Professor Schmidt, sent an hour earlier. "Lost tracking again. Our last coordinates have you 39 km from rapids takeout. Storm coming from N. Will hit you soon. Be safe. A. Schmidt out."

By the time camp was set and the boars butchered, tree tops above began to swirl. The lighter breeze below the canopy kept the bugs away as the campfire grew. The brown men laughed and sang as they roasted fist-sized chunks of fresh boar on sticks. Warm grease ran down their chins as they devoured the delicious meat. They finished in light rain that quickly turned to showers and doused their fire. The team retreated to their covered hammocks for the night. Some immediately crawled in beneath the suspended micro-tent covers while others stood washing in the warm rain before retiring wet but clean.

The storm raged throughout the night and wind whipped the river's surface until bands of thick foam formed against the shoreline. In their cocoons the men stayed comfortable but their prospects of upstream progress looked dim as the grey light of morning illuminated the angry Rio Sié.

The morning of day four came grudgingly as dark clouds blocked the sunrise. Strong winds from the north blew down the Sié creating dismal prospects for upstream paddling. Rain dripped and flowed off the canopy of leaves over camp but the wind barely penetrated. One by one the men came out of their hammocks and walked barefoot to the tarp-covered fire with time for a long breakfast. Thick strips of boars' bacon sizzled in frying pans alongside manioc flour beijus pancakes. With dried acai berries sprinkled on top and strong coffee the team enjoyed a jungle feast.

Ataqi and Urubu walked out to the exposed shoreline, pelted by horizontal rain as soon as they emerged from the trees. "Looks like we not moving now," yelled Ataqi.

"No way mate."

Often stifled by bad weather, men of the jungle accepted it as normal and spent the day under their tarp patiently sitting and chatting. By late afternoon the storm began to abate and the energy of the refreshed team's conversations grew. Ataqi smiled at their laughter and back slaps.

Day five broke with barely a cloud in the sky and a light breeze blowing favorably from the southeast. The men packed quickly and began paddling before the sun rose above the treetops. At midday the two canoes beached on a sparsely vegetated island. As the men ate, Urubu logged the GPS coordinates and allowed the FUNAI control post to track his location.

"You haven't made much progress in two days. What's happening?" messaged Professor Schmidt.

"Could not move for entire day in storm," responded Urubu. "River is higher but weather good."

"OK take care. A. Schmidt out."

By day's end the canoes reached the mouth of the Rio Celina flowing in from the west. It appeared to account for half the Rio Sié's flow as they approached. Their location was just a single day's paddle from the rapids where their land trek towards the Igarapé People would commence. Ataqi determined it was too late to cross the Celina so the canoes landed on the south bank of the confluence. A sand bar there created a shallow backwater, an easy place to unload. The men walked their canoes in tannin-stained red water to the base of a tree. They tied off and passed their camp supplies man-to-man onto the bank. The team splashed and swam in various stages of undress as the sun sank towards the treetops. Lightening flashed in the distance but did not threaten as it drifted away.

Before he ducked under the tree cover, Urubu sent a message to Doug. "Mouth of Rio Celina 1° 49' 03"N 67° 15' 36W. Missed a travel day due to storm. Many hidden campsites here. One day to takeout at rapids. Urubu out."

The team enjoyed their easy camp that night but for the hordes of bugs that always materialize after heavy rainfall. They secured their hammocks' tent covers and mosquito nets securely and slept well.

The men woke excited for their last day of upstream paddling. The retreat down the Rio Sié at the expedition's conclusion would be twice as fast with half the effort. But one more day of hard paddling lay ahead.

The mouth of the Rio Celina flowed slower than the Sié so the men paddled their canoes from camp directly across to the northern bank of the Celina before continuing onto the Sié. Urubu estimated their paddling time to the rapids as five hours if the gradient and current speed did not increase.

Random large boulders appeared breaking the river's surface like half-submerged hippos. They might have been if the men were paddling the Congo or Nile. Environmental conditions are perfect but hippopotami have never lived in the Amazon–though there is a curious exception. Urubu told his men a tale in Nheengatu as their paddles dug deep and pulled the canoe forward.

Notorious drug lord Pablo Escobar smuggled four African hippos in a chartered aircraft to his private Colombian estate in the 1980s. The hippos thrived in his lake, roamed to nearby rivers and reproduced until, forty years later, 200 wild hippos were believed to roam the remote wetlands of Colombia. Over the years some might have found their way to Brazil. Urubu pointed to a rounded boulder the size of an automobile protruding above the river's surface. In Nheengatu he called out, "Peabiru u hippopotamus!"

The men howled with laughter.

The team paddled upstream from one large boulder to the next using current eddies to avoid the faster water. Two hours later the expedition team heard faint rumblings. With the rounding of each river bend the intensity increased until they sighted a roaring cascade ahead.

CHAPTER 14
Trek to the Unknown

As the fierce Rio Sié rapids came into view the team searched for a landing beach and base camp. The confluence of the Rio Juri, thought to be home to Ataqi's Igarapé People, flowed into the Sié from the west 27 kilometers further upriver. But the rapids blocked access by canoe so the expedition planned to trek through the rainforest.

After a 40-minute search the team found a landing gradual enough to beach their canoes. With great effort and loud grunts they dragged them into the bush high above the river for hiding. The men hadn't spotted another human in six days but could not risk the disappearance of their canoes before they returned. Their only other option for returning to the FUNAI control outpost was a brutal jungle trek down the banks of the Sié.

Wading knee-deep into the river clear of overhead trees, Urubu received the GPS coordinates 1° 57′ 32″N 67° 27′ 53″W. He typed a message to Doug. "Made it to rapids. Found good spot to hide canoes in the bush downstream. GPS coordinates to come later."

He send a message to Professor Schmidt. "Made it to Rio Sie rapids in good shape. Overland trek to Igarape People to begin tomorrow."

Minutes later he received a response from Andrea Schmidt. "Glad to hear youre at the rapids. Im in Orlandos office. He wants you to test the other messenger unit."

As soon as he grabbed the team's second GPS messenger Urubu blurted out, "Damn the batteries are bloody weak. I have spares in me bag just down the way. Be right back."

Urubu carried the unit to his backpack out of Ataqi's sight. As Doug had instructed, he removed the good SIM card and replaced it before returning to Ataqi.

"I'm not geet'n bloody reception but I probably need ta wade back out in the rivah. Come with me."

The two men waded out clear of the jungle canopy and tried the second unit again. "Damn no success with this one," said Urubu faking his disgust.

They walked back to shore and grabbed the working GPS messenger. Once he had a clear signal Urubu texted a message back to Professor Schmidt. "Tell Orlando we cant get reception with the second unit. Fortunately the other one is working. Urubu out."

The team set up camp and still had two hours to organize gear and food for the overland trek to begin in the morning. Ataqi had his men remove everything from the canoes and lay their supplies on the camp clearing.

Packaged food rations were holding out well. Hunting and fishing success while paddling the Rio Sié saved much of their food supply. Once they took inventory of their expedition gear the men repacked.

Jerky, dried fruits, coffee, beans, rice and farina flour filled their backpacks. The rifles were cleaned and four boxes of .22 cartridges loaded. Pots, knives, machetes and axes were set aside. The machetes might never see the inside of a backpack as the men slashed at vegetation and snakes impeding their progress. Each man packed his extra set of fatigue pants and shirt. The rain tarp and hammocks would be packed in the morning. Urubu changed batteries in the functioning GPS messenger unit and packed more batteries for the trek.

Pelém demonstrated many skills and could write in Portuguese. Ataqi and Urubu selected him as their second documentarian. Urubu would text messages to Professor Schmidt when he received a satellite signal while Pelém would log their activities in Portuguese each evening. Paper and pencils were sealed tightly in plastic bags to keep the tropical moisture and decomposing microorganisms away.

Ataqi filled his backpack with gifts for his people–knives, machetes, steel pots and colored beads. Just enough space remained to load his GoPro cameras. The men turned the canoes upside down to keep rainwater out and remaining supplies that could not be packed were stored beneath. The expedition team camouflaged the canoes under piles of palm fronds and sticks.

With extra food available the men stuffed themselves that evening but ate less in the morning, a light meal of beijus pancakes and more dried açaí berries. The physical effort required to walk the treacherous jungle floor packing heavy loads would be even more difficult on a full stomach.

The team set off early on day seven leaving the Rio Sié on their shortcut towards the village coordinates of Ataqi's Igarapé People. Five wore boots while three including Pelém went barefoot as their people had always done. Ataqi and Urubu considered trekking north along the Rio Sié 27 km above the rapids to the mouth of the Rio Juri before heading west. But they estimated the shorter route directly northwest could save three merciless hiking days.

Like their ancestors, the sinewy dark men moved smoothly over the forest floor even with their packs weighing 20 kg, over 40 pounds. Narrow shafts of light passing through gaps in the canopy illuminated the dim green cavern below. The lead man never walked directly over fallen logs but stepped on top first and inspected the backside from above. Not a day went by when at least one bushmaster or Amazon rattlesnake lay poised to strike.

GPS coordinates were poorly received through the rainforest canopy so Urubu relied on the simplest of tools for navigation, a compass. He directed the team from behind while the lead men swung their machetes clearing the path. The expedition crossed many streams often wading directly through or, for wider crossings, locating a natural log blowdown bridge. Other than the swarming mosquitoes, the creeks made good resting areas and the team often stopped for water breaks in the intense jungle heat. Some men drank directly from the natural flow while others treated the water with iodine pills in their plastic water bottles.

The larger streams sometimes opened the canopy enough for Urubu to receive a clear satellite signal. Late on the first trekking day he sat on a decaying log with blue sky above and activated the GPS messenger. A message popped up from Doug. "Send GPS coordinates for hidden canoes."

Urubu messaged a response. "In due time. I dont want them disappearing while Im away. How are our Colombian friends progressing?"

The GPS coordinates for the team's new position flashed on Urubu's messenger unit. He sent out identical messages to both Doug and Professor Schmidt. "Making progress with heavy loads. Current location 1° 57' 41"N 67° 29' 18"W. Dense jungle."

Doug responded back. "Our friends have almost reached the upper Rio Sie in Colombia. Its slow hauling a boat trailer on the muddy road."

The expedition team had hiked an estimated twelve kilometers when Ataqi called an end to their first day's progress. In thirty minutes the men hacked out a suitable clearing and hung their hammocks. With no fresh kills the team was happy to lighten their backpacks of canned beans simmered with dried tomatoes and beef jerky. The men wiped their plates clean with flatbread and retreated for the night.

Splats of raindrops on giant leaves woke the men early the next morning, the eighth day since they departed the FUNAI control post. With Ataqi leading, the men slogged through the day wet, muddy and largely silent, their senses elevated for the slightest hint of danger. Once again they saw no sign of other humans in the endless wilderness.

Just behind Ataqi, Pelém carried his .22 rifle on lookout for game. Late in the day as the rainfall lightened, Ataqi stopped and pointed to a swampy meadow. Pelém stalked forward as the team stopped to rest. Minutes later three shots rang out. The men watched as Pelém walked forward and lifted two hairy bundles off the ground. The team cheered the fresh peccaries for dinner.

On day nine the men hacked through especially dense thickets but were rewarded late in the day with a fine campsite requiring minimal clearing. Their bush camp went up quickly and the hammocks were soon lashed to sturdy tree trunks free of fire ants. Four men set out hunting. Less than an hour later normally composed Pelém ran into camp screaming, "Nauta fer-de-lance Nauta fer-de-lance!"

Urubu heard the frantic calls first and yelled out to Ataqi, "Get the antivenom. Let's go!"

Ataqi reached into the first aid kit assembled by Ikanna and pulled out the snake antivenom kit. He ran into the forest with Urubu following Pelém. The men moved fast dodging downed trees and dangling lianas vines. Moments later they came upon Nauta lying in a bed of decaying leaves and moaning. His pant's leg was pulled up to the calf exposing the two sinister puncture wounds of a pit viper.

Ataqi rushed to open the antivenom case and loaded the syringe with serum as Ikanna had shown him. He stabbed the needle into Nauta's leg near the bite marks and injected the first dose. Nauta barely responded, his breathing shallow and pulse weak. The men stood by and Ataqi injected a second dose ten minutes later. But it was too late. Softly groaning, Nauta succumbed to the venom.

Ataqi, Urubu and Pelém walked back to camp without saying a word. When they arrived, Ataqi delivered the sad news. The expedition team's somber responses might have surprised those who hadn't grown up in the rainforest. All had witnessed sudden death at the hands of nature.

The remaining seven team members carried Nauta's lifeless body back to camp as darkness enveloped the jungle. They laid him on a mat of palm fronds and flowers, chanting and singing far into the night to lift his spirit to the sky.

The following morning the men dug a grave to bury Nauta and protect his soul from jungle predators. They placed his knife along with acai berries and manioc flour next to his body to sustain him on his journey to the afterlife. The remaining seven laid palm fronds over his prone body before covering him in soil. The men broke camp and carried on towards the Igarapé People.

A few hours later the team came upon a path more heavily worn than the sparse game trails they sometimes followed. With his compass, Urubu confirmed that it led towards the northwest. The men continued on the pathway at a pace double their speed in the untrodden jungle.

They stopped at an open creek and Urubu pulled the GPS messenger from his backpack. The GPS flashed 1° 58' 15"N 67° 51' 07"W. "Õ mairỹ ĩhẽ." (Men we are close.)

Urubu sent the coordinates to Professor Schmidt. With no emotion his satellite text message ended with, "Nauta is dead from snake bite."

With Ataqi leading, the men continued along the trail. Pelém noticed a broken twig at eye level and whispered to Ataqi. A kilometer further along Ataqi stopped suddenly. The team came forward and recognized the sign. In the crook of a trailside tree rested the skull of a caiman–a warning sign to keep out. Further inspection revealed more twigs partially broken but still hanging from their branches across the path, universal Amazon trail markers warning outsiders to turn back. The expedition team proceeded cautiously. The pathway widened and smaller side trails split off into the rainforest.

An hour later Ataqi detected a vague odor of smoke in the air. After a brief discussion with Urubu he decided the team would progress no further. The Igarapé People were near. In a heavily shadowed area with sparse undergrowth, he directed the men to set up camp.

As the team cleared the campsite and hung their hammocks, Ataqi walked on alone in a state of high alert. Smoke became more pronounced and he recognized the odor of roasting meat. Ataqi could not tell if it was peccary or capybara but, moving closer, he soon knew. Delicious peccary baked on a fire.

He proceeded forward both excited and frightened until the wall of a thatched hut appeared through the jungle thicket. Ataqi decided to go no further. He removed his backpack and spread gifts along the trail. Knives, pots and a machete were laid out in an even parallel pattern. He hung ten strings of brightly colored plastic beads in the branches above. Ataqi turned and headed back to his men at the expedition camp.

CHAPTER 15
Contact

Mike Weston recognized the bird-like songs of beautiful Ipixuna as she walked through the village. The rainforest men had already set out to hunt that morning as he heard her approach his hut. Ipixuna continued to attend to Mike's leg wounds even though they were healed. She enjoyed the ritual of rubbing the red nectar over his three scars. As she leaned over to begin the treatment Mike noticed something different. Instead of her usual neckless of feathers and jungle flowers, Ipixuna wore a new necklace with all the colors of the macaw–blue, scarlet, green and yellow. But her bright beads were not from nature. They were perfectly round plastic. Weston's mind raced.

* * *

Ataqi, Urubu and the five other remaining expedition members improved the campsite they'd cleared the previous day. The seven men built a palm frond table with sturdy bamboo legs, cut log benches and gathered firewood. A creek flowed nearby and the men filled their water containers and pots.

Ataqi asked that the rifles remain silent except in emergencies. A shot from their fire sticks would startle the Igarapé People and they might flee or fight. The expedition team could hunt with their bows and arrows.

Ataqi was anxious to return to his people but waited until midday so they could find his gifts on the trail. From the expedition camp, the distance to the village was less than two kilometers. Alone once again, he walked barefoot to check on the offerings. He wore the black underwear briefs he'd become accustomed to during his years at the FUNAI control post. His bare arms and legs revealed deep scars so his people would know he was not a spirit. The souls of his people did not carry wounds of the living to their afterlife.

As he approached the village Ataqi saw nothing on the trail or in the branches. The gifts had been removed. He carried more–two pots, two knives and a machete. Ataqi proceeded slowly until huts were visible through the dense foliage. He moved forward and began to speak out in his native Tupi-Guarani. "A'ewa tekotehỹ." (I am a friend.) Over and over he said the words. He continued towards the village center with the new gifts. Four naked children played, their long black hair waving as they jumped and laughed. Ataqi walked slowly until they saw him. The children stared for a moment and then ran off towards the manioc fields.

A lone elderly woman appeared that Ataqi did not recognize. She did not seem afraid and walked forward to meet him. "Ore, oñe'ẽ nẽ mba'e'e ngara'y Ticata." (Hello, I am Ticata.)

Ataqi knew her words and responded, "A'ewa Ataqi, Iti ra'y." (I am Ataqi, son of Iti.)

Ticata nodded but seemed uncertain. Ataqi realized she did not know his father. Ticata motioned for him to wait and walked over to a larger hut. He turned to inspect the village. The large round maloca was not the communal longhouse of his people. The palm-thatched huts in the village were rounded while the huts in his village had pitched roofs like the FUNAI medical tents.

An elderly man emerged from the larger hut with Ticata. His red-dyed face with diagonal black stripes and boar tusks protruding through his septum indicated a man of prominence. As the elder walked towards him Ataqi noticed something unusual hanging from his neck. He recognized the versatile tool used at the FUNAI outpost. Orlando Rivas and several others owned them–a red Swiss Army knife. Ataqi knew he was not the first outsider to contact the village.

The elderly man approached Ataqi. "A'ewa Xapuri," he said in a deep voice.

"A'ewa Ataqi, Iti ra'y," replied Ataqi, holding the gifts in his outstretched arms. Xapuri took the machete and asked Ticata to carry the pots and knives to his hut.

Xapuri did not know Ataqi's father Iti and asked him to follow and sit with him. As they walked, village women looked up curiously from their tasks. Some crushed and soaked manioc roots. Others cooked over scattered fire pits. Several ducked in and out of their huts with children. Two of the younger women wore Atagi's bead gift necklaces.

They entered the communal open-sided maloca hut and sat on a log bench. Xapuri asked about the strange cloth Ataqi wore around his waist. Ataqi asked about the Swiss Army knife. The men knew both had come from Pale People.

Ataqi told his story. He came from a nearby village that spoke the language of Xapuri's people. During his solo quest to become a man, a caiman attacked him and he nearly died. Pale People and a native woman with remarkable healing powers saved him. He lived with the Pale People in their mysterious village for eight flood cycles they called "anos" or "years". He learned many of their ways.

In the Pale People's village he met other people from a faraway land called California. The California People helped him form a team to find his village. His expedition team, all men of the rainforest, was camped nearby. They canoed and walked for many days and found Xapuri's village. "Arovia aju che Igarapé ava reta ojejuhu," said Ataqi (I thought I found my Igarapé People.)

Xapuri asked, "Tupe karai oîhu Avá Karai nhande rekoa?" (Do you know the language of the Pale People?)

"Oîhu," replied Ataqi.

"Opotî ngara'y, peteî moîhỹa ĩhẽ oîhu." (Come back tomorrow and we will talk again.)

The men stood and Ataqi bowed in respect to his elder. He asked Xapuri the name of his people and he replied, "Amo'u mbya rekojera." (We are the Secret People.)

Their introduction was brief but Ataqi knew he had much to contemplate. He walked swiftly back to camp to share his news. Pelém took notes as Ataqi told of the new village. They were not his people, though similar. He planned to return in the morning with his camera.

"I need to tell the FUNAI station," said Urubu. "We haven't communicated in two days."

He walked for nearly an hour that afternoon until he found a clearing in the jungle canopy where the GPS messenger could communicate with overhead satellites. Urubu activated tracking mode and sent identical messages to Doug and Andrea Schmidt. "Expedition camp location approx. 1° 58' 20"N 67° 59' 14"W. Ataqi contacted a village today 2 km northwest of camp. Not his Igarape People. He will return to village tomorrow. Urubu out."

Urubu followed with another message to Doug. "How are my contacts progressing?"

Urubu waited until Doug responded. "Contacts approaching upper Rio Sie in Colombia towing boat on unmapped logging road hidden under trees. They asked about your canoe coordinates again."

"Tell them I will take them personally to the canoes."

"Dont play with fire mate."

"I want to be as valuable to them as possible. Urubu out."

CHAPTER 16
Salvation

Slabs of boar meat sizzled near the hottest embers of the expedition team's campfire as Ataqi recounted his first contact with Xapuri's Secret People. The expedition team had not found the Igarapé People though Xapuri might assist in their search. "Ixy oikuaa che reta rehe," said Ataqi. (He knows of my people.)

The men divided the remaining plastic beads and strung twenty necklaces for Ataqi to gift the next day. With less than 100 beads remaining, each necklace had only four or five. But every colorful bead would be considered a gem by the people of the Secret Village.

Ataqi returned to the village the following day carrying the necklaces and GoPro camera concealed in a black cotton bag. Along the trail he encountered fresh jaguar tracks and stepped around them to respect the jungle lord, symbolic of strength, stealth and wisdom. The great spotted cat could be the spirit of his grandfather Inapari, celebrated shaman of the Igarapé People who died from a mysterious fever when Ataqi was a young boy. Ataqi remembered many days of ceremony and grieving. Every flood cycle thereafter his people told the story of

Inapari's powers to talk with souls of the dead through dance and song.

At midmorning Ataqi entered the village's open-sided maloca and sat on the log bench. Once again the younger men were away and the women he could see were busy harvesting bananas from the broadleaf trees growing randomly around the huts. They noticed Ataqi but did not acknowledge him. Children turned to stare at the stranger who looked like their fathers, only taller with deep scars and wearing a strange waist covering.

As he waited Ataqi laid the bead necklaces on the log. One curious woman with yellow feather ear trinkets noticed and came over to inspect. Soon a disorganized group of women and children formed chatting happily. Their curious smiles and laughter rekindled memories of his people. Ataqi handed out the bead necklaces until the log was bare. Those left in line did not seem disappointed. Perhaps they expected him to bring more gifts the following day.

Ataqi sat patiently facing Xapuri's hut. Many minutes later the elder appeared and walked towards him. With no introduction Xapuri spoke. "Karaíva oikoi ñandéve mba'e vai eté." (Pale People have caused us great sadness.)

He told stories of violence when his villagers encountered the Pale People. Two flood cycles earlier they killed three of his people and forced the others to flee their village home. Ataqi remembered similar tales from his Igarapé People. Pale People carried magic fire sticks that could kill a monkey, tapir or man from many steps away in one loud flash. They invaded his people's land and forced them to flee further into the forest. Ataqi's knowledge of Pale People had changed when they saved his life at the FUNAI control post. He came to know many kind Pale People as he learned their ways. Ataqi had his own rifles now but would not tell Xapuri.

Ticata was smoking fish on bamboo racks over a nearby fire pit and Xapuri waved her over. He pointed to a hut across the village and she walked in that direction as Xapuri continued speaking of the Pale People. Ticata entered the hut and disappeared for a moment.

Ataqi was stunned as Ticata exited the hut accompanied by a tall blonde man with a scruffy stubble in tattered modern clothing. As they approached Ataqi looked directly into the Pale Person's eyes and saw fear.

Ticata and the blond-haired man sat on the log and tried to communicate. Knowing that Pale People spoke Portuguese or English, Ataqi asked him his name. Qual é o seu nome?

The man stared blankly.

"What is your name"?

"Michael Weston. You speak English?"

"Yes. I am Ataqi."

Mike Weston reached out and shook Ataqi's hand firmly. "I hope you can help me. I must go home."

"Where is home?"

"California."

"I know this California. My friend Professor Schmidt live there. She showed me with a map. Now she is near on Rio Sié."

"How did you get here?" asked Ataqi.

"Village men captured me and forced me to travel many days to reach this village. I have been here for nearly three weeks. I don't know why I'm here."

Ataqi turned to Xapuri with questioning eyes. They spoke their traditional language with voices rising and falling as Weston looked on. After a long discussion, Ataqi turned back with Xapuri's explanation.

"Xapuri say two years ago his people's village was on river you might know as Rio Celina. It was place of many animals and fish. His people were happy at their home. But then Pale People came in giant canoe. It had long arms and growled like howler monkey. I think it was gold mining dredge. Their river turned brown and fish died. Xapuri's people tried to fight Pale People with their arrows. But Pale People fought back with fire sticks...rifles. Three of Xapuri's people were dead in mud. His people left their village and mourned for many days as they searched for new home."

Ataqi continued. "Many days ago four men leave this village to find old village site on Rio Celina. They want to see if they can move back and build new village. The leader was Hatak. His father was killed by Pale People's rifle. When he saw you he think you with men who kill his father. They bring you back to this village. But Xapuri angry with Hatak. Does not want fight with Pale People. Anyway, Xapuri tell Hatak you do not look like Pale People who killed his people. You have yellow hair. You are taller and wear different clothes, shiny like water."

Weston nodded towards Xapuri. "Ataqi, can you take me to Professor Schmidt?"

"I tell you about her. I leave my village many years ago and cannot get home. Then I meet Professor Schmidt and she send me with other men to find my village, but we find Xapuri village instead. When I finished looking for my people we take you to Professor Schmidt and Orlando Rivas. Now I must take pictures for them."

Ataqi turned towards Xapuri and asked if he could demonstrate a miraculous tool of the Pale People. He unzipped the bag and removed his GoPro. "Ka'aguy rehegua." (Watch what happens.)

Ataq pointed his camera towards Xapuri and started the video recording. "Mborahe'i ko jape tekoánguéra." (Say welcome to my village.)

Ataqi ended his short recording and slid down the log next to Xapuri as he pointed to his camera and replayed the scene. Xapuri watched with wide eyes as Ataqi explained that the box did not hold his spirit, but instead a reflection like looking onto smooth water. Ataqi turned to Weston. "I'm not sure what he thinks of it."

"Nde ko'ãga rembiapó va'erã jape tekoánguéra?" asked Ataqi (Can I take more pictures of your village?)

Xapuri stood up and waved the men forward. Ataqi photographed and videoed scenes from around the village–thatched palm huts, women carrying babies in woven mat slings, clay pots alongside a gifted steel pot, manioc fields and children playing with a pet peccary.

"Where are the men?" asked Ataqi.

"Most are out hunting and fishing," replied Weston. "They will return this afternoon."

The three men walked towards the river and Ataqi continued his digital log. Three dugout canoes rested on the sandy beach. Mike spotted Ipixuna near the water wearing her plastic bead necklace and woven mat skirt. He called her name. "Can you take a photo of us Ataqi? They'll never believe this at home if I don't have proof."

Ataqi photographed the two of them on the riverbank and replayed it for the village princess. Ipixuna smiled with delight.

"Michael, please walk with me to my camp. Not far."

"Please ask Xapuri for his permission," replied Weston.

After a short conversation Ataqi turned back to Weston. "Xapuri say go talk to my men. Find way home."

"Michael, learn word 'aguéje'. Means 'thank you' in our language."

"Aguéje." Weston turned to Xapuri. "Aguéje."

Xapuri nodded in return.

"Ore nde'iy Mba'eapy," said Ataqi. (We will return tomorrow morning.)

An hour later Weston and Ataqi entered the expedition's jungle encampment. The four men in camp stared in shock at the tall blonde man in torn clothing. The first to approach was Urubu. "What the bloody hell do we have here?"

"My name is Weston. Mike Weston. I'm glad to hear you speak English."

"Urubu Pakha. Yeah I picked up a beet of yah language from me Aussie friend. What ya doing here?"

The three men sat around the smoldering fire pit where bugs were less vicious. Mike Weston shared his story as Urubu shook his head in disbelief.

"We need to report this. Yah family must think ya gone cactus fo good. We can send a message to our base and they can notify yah family."

"Thank you Urubu. That would be fantastic," said Weston.

"It's late in the aftanoon but if we hurry we kin get to the clearing and send out a message. Ataqi, set up a spare hammock fo our new friend. I think he'll be staying the night with us."

Urubu grabbed the operational **GPS messenger** and set out with Weston towards the clearing as a family of spider monkeys chirped and squealed above. Once they reached the canopy opening and Urubu locked in satellite signals, he pecked out a message to Andrea Schmidt. "Important message. We found a white man in the village who goes by the name Michael Weston. Hes American. Says he was misidentified and abducted from Rio Celina by the tribe here about three weeks ago. Please notify authorities."

Urubu handed the devise to Weston who typed in another message. "This is Michael Weston. Im alive and OK in a remote jungle village. Your expedition teams says they will lead me to your post. Please notify my parents Dan and Sue Weston in Klamath Falls Oregon and my company BetaCorp Technologies in Santa Clara California. I hope to meet you in person soon."

Urubu sent out one additional message to Doug on the Rio Sié as he turned away from Mike Weston. "Slight hiccup in our plan. Weve located a white man from California in the village. Says he was kidnapped by mistake. May need to change my plan a bit. Dont tell our contacts until Ive figured it out. Urubu out."

That night Ataqi shared his Secret Village videos with Urubu as Pelém took notes. "Show me the video of the rivah again. There it is. They build a bloody nice dugout canoe."

CHAPTER 17
Alive

Andrea Schmidt ran to the office of Orlando Rivas clutching her GPS messenger. "Did you know about the missing American? His name is Michael Weston."

"Sim, yes. He disappeared from the Rio Celina almost a month ago."

"It looks like our team found him alive in a native village. We'll need confirmation."

Professor Schmidt typed out a message to Urubu. "We know about the missing American Michael Weston. Confirm his description, home and physical condition. A. Schmidt out."

She did not receive a response until the following day. "Mike Weston is tall with blonde hair. He is thin and weak but happy we found him. He wants to get home to California as soon as possible. Urubu out."

Orlando Rivas contacted FUNAI headquarters in Brasília and the news spread quickly. First to be contacted were Mike Weston's parents who notified BetaCorp Technologies and Bill Greer. Ellie received the astonishing news within hours.

The story made worldwide headlines. "This is Suzanne Patel and you're watching BBC News. We have a breaking story. An American who vanished in the Amazon jungle a month ago has reportedly been found alive in an isolated native village in northwest Brazil. Michael Weston of Santa Clara, California has been located by a team of anthropologists in a region known as the Alto Rio Negro Indigenous Territory. The team will lead him out of the rainforest once their research is concluded."

Bill and Ellie had only met once but were soon on the phone. "I can't believe it Bill," Ellie sobbed. "I can't wait to see him. This will take a long time to process. I hope he's OK. I don't know what he's experienced but he must've gone through some serious trauma."

"I'm still in shock Ellie. I thought my friend was gone. Let's stay in contact. I'll be there whenever you think the time is right for a welcome home party. But I guess we don't want to get ahead of ourselves. He might need some quiet time to recover."

Professor Schmidt sent another message to Urubu. "Ask Mike Weston to begin documenting his experiences with the Secret Village People. Have Pelem set him up with paper, pencils and a plastic bag to keep his notes dry. Tell him it's important for our research project. A. Schmidt out."

Ataqi and Mike Weston walked back to the Secret Village the next morning. They arrived just as the men were leaving to hunt and fish. Jatabo waved to Weston but

Hatak looked away. Ticata came forward to welcome them followed closely behind by Ipixuna, her smooth brown skin glistening in the broken light. The four chatted as they waited for Xapuri. The elder woman spoke softly to Ataqi as Ipixuna stood by twisting her long hair in her fingers.

Ataqi passed her message on to Weston. "Ticata says Ipixuna is her daughter. Ticata's husband was killed by a snake while hunting many years ago. They believe the silver bird that flies overhead is his spirit looking down and protecting the village. We will not tell her about airplanes. As you can see, these people are like us–but different."

Ipixuna spoke to Ataqi and he turned to Mike Weston. "Ipixuna wants to know where you come from."

"Tell her I come from a place far away called California where people are the same but different. Tell Ipixuna she is beautiful."

Ipixuna looked towards the bare ground with a subtle smile as Ataqi relayed Mike Weston's words.

Ticata turned and spoke to Ataqi with a message for Weston. "Ticata says Ipixuna likes you Mike Weston. But she is wife with Hatak."

Weston, trying not to appear shocked, dipped his head towards Ipixuna. "Aguéje Ipixuna."

"Aguéje Michael."

The elder man Xapuri walked from the manioc field and signaled Ataqi and Weston to join him on the log bench. Once seated Xapuri spoke to Ataqi who then turned to pass the message to Mike Weston.

"Michael, Xapuri say you can leave with my men to find your home. But before we leave for FUNAI, Xapuri will lend his canoes and best men to help me find my Igarapé People."

Xapuri explained to Ataqi that his hunters had encountered other rainforest men far upriver in recent days. They had not communicated. The other jungle men carried blowguns not used by his Secret People who hunted with bows and arrows. Those men farther up the Rio Juri could be Igarapé People.

Ataqi turned to Weston. "Xapuri says bring my four best expedition men and bring supplies for two canoes and six men. Two men will come from Xapuri's village. We must pack tomorrow and depart upriver the next day. Rain is coming. When we look for my Igarapé People, you must stay here Michael and eat well and prepare for trip home."

Ataqi and Weston returned to the expedition camp to discuss the plan as afternoon rain began to fall. They would have only four days to paddle the Rio Juri upstream from the Secret Village to find Ataqi's people. Then they must turn back. The flood season would soon be upon the rivers. The first three selected to search for the Igarapé People would be Ataqi, Urubu and Pelém. The fourth was in question when Urubu spoke up. "Ishmi is me choice, the strongest paddlah."

Ataqi agreed. The other men would stay in the expedition camp and prepare for their team's return to the FUNAI control post escorting Mike Weston towards home.

Packing began early the next morning. Knowing they must paddle heavy dugout canoes up the Rio Juri, gear and food were minimized. Rifles, a curse of the isolated rainforest people, were left behind but bows and arrows were readied by the team. Steel machetes and axes would be crucial for clearing their campsites. Food and two pots were organized and placed in the dry bags and backpacks.

"Bring GPS messenger Urubu, but keep it hidden from Secret Village People," said Ataqi. "We already show them too much from outside world. I see they are confused by camera. I was same way when I saw first camera and video pictures at FUNAI. They are still magic to me today but I'm not shocked by pictures anymore. Magic things like computers is normal to me now. Like mystery of sunrise every day. We cannot show Secret Village People too much. Remember what Senhor Rivas said about his teacher Sydney Possuelo? He always tell Mr. Rivas once you make contact you begin to destroy their world. We cannot contact them without changing them."

The four men hiked to the Secret Village with their supplies that afternoon ignoring the orders of Orlando Rivas that only Ataqi could enter. Plans had changed with the discovery of Mike Weston and the Secret Village.

For Urubu, Pelém and Ishmi, it was their first encounter with Xapuri and his people. Mike Weston, carrying extra food from the expedition team to regain his strength, joined them. He would stay in the Secret Village to further document village life for Professor Schmidt until Ataqi and Urubu returned.

They met with Xapuri in the village center and Ataqi introduced the men. All six walked to the river where two village men, Hatak and Jatabo, were already loading dugouts. Ataqi and Xapuri introduced the team that would paddle up the Rio Juri in search of the Igarapé People-Urubu, Ishmi, Pelém, Hatak, Jatabo and Ataqi.

Ataqi spoke to the team in Nheengatu. "Ore kuarupu opu atarana." (We have a strong team.) Though Nheengatu varies from the Tupi-Guarani language of the Secret Village, Hatak and Jatabo nodded. When necessary, the forest men supplemented verbal communication with facial expressions and sign language.

The two long wooden canoes were loaded with an eight-day supply of food though the men knew they could be on the river longer. They would hunt and fish to supplement. Hatak and Jatabo who rarely wore body covering were curious about the other men's clothing and waterproof vinyl bags to store their food. They loaded their buriti palm-fiber hammocks while Ataqi's men's hammocks were colorful nylon. Ataqi loaded axes and machetes and promised to leave two of each for Hatak as reward for his support after their upstream journey. They loaded gifts into the canoes as well though most of the original expedition team's gifts had been handed out at the Secret Village. Two aluminum pots and four steel knives would have to suffice.

The men packed their canoes by late afternoon when the hunters returned with a giant tapir. Xapuri called for a feast to bless the team that would depart upriver in the morning. The entire tapir was butchered, enough meat for 100 meals. The hide was set aside to be tanned. Hooves, teeth and bones would make decorative and spiritual ornaments.

Urubu discretely carried the GPS messenger to the manioc clearing and activated the tracking function. He first messaged Professor Schmidt. "We have two dugout canoes and a strong team of six including Ataqi, me, Pelem and Ishmi plus two from Secret Village to paddle up Rio Juri in search of Igarape People. Must progress quickly. Heavy rain coming soon. Tracking seems to be working. Can you see my coordinates? Urubu out."

Urubu messaged Doug. "I leave tonight down Rio Juri. Where are my Colombian contacts?"

Ten minutes later Doug replied. "One day ahead of you. They will abandon their boat above Rio Sie rapids. Not passable. Meet there. If needed, help carry their bundles around rapids. Then take them to your hidden canoes. Good luck. Doug out."

In the excitement Urubu neglected to shut off the tracking function.

The villagers and their guests walked to the river and bathed. As they dried on the beach, women carried pots of red and black dye to the sand and the villagers decorated their bodies with intricate patterns. The women tied flowers into their hair and Mike Weston watched Ticata weave blue and yellow feathers into Ipixuna's long black mane.

With their fires stoked, bananas and yams baked while large slabs of tapir roasted. The entire meal was laid out on huge banana leaves and the village gathered round. The men ate first followed by the women and children using their hands and fingers as plates and utensils.

Xapuri stood and shared a story, often raising his hands to the sky and chanting.

"Ataqi, what is he saying?" asked Weston.

"Xapuri tell the story of their ancestors long ago. The people lived in rich land down where river is wide. Fish and rainforest animals fed their people well and village grew big. But then Pale People come looking for special trees and their sap. I think rubber. The Pale People carry fire sticks and deadly spells that kill most of village. Even shaman could not stop. Shaman call out to Great Jaguar Spirit who looked over their people. Villagers that still alive walk many days through jungle until river much smaller. Some die of hunger and fever on the way. But they find good new site and rebuild village far from Pale People. Great Jaguar Spirit watch over new Secret Village."

"Aguéje Ataqi," thanked Weston.

As Xapuri finished the legend of the Secret Village passed down by many generations, the wooden chicha bowl appeared. It contained the fermented manioc flour that village women chewed and spit back into the bowl days earlier. Everyone took a good swig except Mike Weston who held the bowl to his lips but did not drink. As alcohol took effect the people sang and danced. Weston joined in, this time unafraid of the spiritual celebration. An hour later it ended and the Secret Village slept, quiet except for the hum of jungle insects.

At first light Ataqi crawled out of his hammock excited to begin the paddle upriver towards his Igarapé People. He threw three small logs into the fire ring and went to wake his team. All were up and packing their gear– all except Urubu. "Urubu where are you?" called out Ataqi.

There was no response. Ataqi walked to the river expecting to see Urubu packing the canoes. He was not there and one of the dugouts was missing. Shocked, Ataqi looked up and down the river for the missing canoe. Nothing.

Ataqi ran back to the men gathering around the cooking fire. "Urubu E kïïpïï hee'pi!" (Urubu has taken a canoe!)

CHAPTER 18
The Chase

The Secret Village fell silent after the festal ceremony. Urubu, however, did not sleep. His mind raced with imminent tasks. He had helped Doug's contacts before and been well rewarded.

Urubu slipped out of his hammock, grabbed his pack and moved quietly towards the river. Stars in the clear sky illuminated the water's surface against the dark jungle. He walked carefully towards the light feeling the black ground with bare toes. Urubu reached the two loaded canoes and untied the smallest, still a beast for one man to paddle. Buzzing cicadas concealed his splashes as he crawled in and fashioned a comfortable paddling station.

In a brief moment he was off moving silently with the current. Urubu's paddle barely touched the water as he slipped past the sleeping Secret Village. Frogs croaked and fireflies lit up the shoreline as he drifted downstream.

Once he rounded the bend Urubu reached for the headlamp in his pack. The beam lit the path in front of him and he began to paddle with determination. Every stroke carried him farther from Ataqi, Hatak and the others who might pursue him in the morning. His contacts on the Rio Sié were likely past the mouth of the Juri and already near the head of the rapids. They would be waiting for him to locate the hidden canoes and guide them unseen far downriver towards São Gabriel da Nazaré.

Urubu paddled on in the darkness following the beam from his headlamp. At times where the Juri was gentle and wide, he turned it off. Once his vision adjusted to the darkness, starlight and glowing green eyes lit the dreamlike path. Adrenaline kept him moving knowing a pursuit party could soon be on the river.

By first morning light Urubu estimated he was two hours from the Juri's mouth at the Rio Sié. Downstream wind aided his progress.

* * *

The confused men gathered around the morning fire and discussed the disappearance of Urubu. The loaded canoe was too heavy for one man to paddle up the Rio Juri. He must have headed downriver towards the Sié. But why? That route led to the impassable rapids. They decided to follow.

Hatak readied an extra canoe and supplies from the loaded dugout were dispersed between the two. Each man packed his hammock while Ataqi made sure they had the most critical gear including pots, knives, bows and arrows. Hatak packed his club as well.

"Urubu ogueraha umi hakã guiguera ha machete kuéra!" cursed Hatak in Tupi-Guarani when he realized Urubu had the invaluable steel axes and machetes promised to his village.

Hatak recruited two more hunters to paddle the missing canoe back if they could find it. They joined the search party with Jatabo, Ataqi, Pelém and Ishmi. Within an hour the seven men were on the river paddling downstream away from Ataqi's Igarapé People.

Ataqi and Hatak guided the canoes side-by-side as they discussed their situation. They had no idea what they might find. Their efforts would be rewarded if they recovered their steel axes, machetes and canoe that required many weeks to shape from a single cedar tree with stone tools and fire. The men stopped late in the day to beach the canoes at a promising campsite. They saw no sign of Urubu or the canoe but fish were plentiful. Hatak estimated they could reach the Sié by midmorning if they broke camp at dawn.

As the other men cleared their campsite, Pelém and Jatabo stalked the riverbank with their bows and arrows ready. Pelém's bow was a modern fiberglass recurve while Jatabo's was a fire-treated rainforest jacaranda longbow. Jatabo took the first shot at an arowana fish suspended near a toppled tree branch.

Pelém shouted "îaîra apy!" (Good shot!) as the arrow's feather fletching twitched above the water's surface. Jatabo waded in, grabbed the arrow and dragged the fish to shore. One more and they would have enough to feed all seven men.

* * *

Urubu snacked on Brazil nuts and smoked boar but continued paddling taking short breaks in the strongest current to rest his arms. Clouds began to darken as he sighted the big river ahead. Moments later he turned onto the churning Rio Sié. He might make the head of the rapids by nightfall. His contacts should be waiting. Doug would know their status.

In a wide slow-moving reach of the river, Urubu removed the GPS messenger from his pack and immediately saw a message from Doug sent four hours earlier. "Your tracking function is on. Turn it off!"

In the excitement of the Secret Village, Urubu neglected to shut it off. "Sorry Doug. Tracking is off now. You know Ive reached the Sie. What is location of our contacts?"

Doug responded an hour later. "Bad move. Your professor friend will know the unit is back on the Sie. She will have questions. Your contacts set up camp at the head of rapids yesterday. Now packing bundles around towards your canoes. Move fast and stay hidden. Doug out."

Shaken by his mistake, Urubu paddled on.

* * *

At the Rio Sié control post a graduate student called out to Professor Schmidt through the wall of her tent. "Andrea, I have something strange to show you."

Andrea Schmidt threw open the fabric door while tucking her messy blond hair beneath her hat. "What is it?"

"Check out the GPS messenger app on my computer. It shows our team back on the Rio Sié above the rapids."

"Something's not right. I'll send a message to Urubu." Professor Schmidt tapped out her message. "Urubu weve tracked your GPS unit back on the Rio Sie. What's happening? Please advise."

She received a response three hours later. "Tracking must not be working. We are OK at Secret Village. Urubu out."

Andrea Schmidt suspected trouble.

* * *

Ataqi and Hatak readied their canoes to depart camp and continue downstream. The seven young rainforest men made two fine paddling teams. Jatabo and

Hatak were especially strong keeping their three-man dugout even with the four-man team. Perspiration glistened off their naked muscles as the brown men of the Secret Village dug into the river with long powerful strokes. Relief came as incoming storm clouds blocked the intense tropical sunlight.

CHAPTER 19
Confrontation

Urubu nodded off but snapped awake as his canoe struck a riverbank root. The dugout spun but sustained no damage. He paddled out to the main current that carried him swiftly towards his rendezvous. His first sign of the Colombians was a swirling ribbon of smoke rising through the rainforest canopy near the shoreline. Soon Urubu saw their boat in the distance, a 22-foot outboard skiff pulled onto the bank. Its useful life was over with no way to get down the treacherous rapids intact. He paddled on and heard cascading water downriver. Rain began to fall as Urubu approached the camp. He spotted a man washing in the shallows and called out, "Hola!"

The man did not hear him over the pounding water and Urubu called out louder as he drifted closer. The man turned and waved anticipating the rendezvous. Urubu beached the heavy dugout and the men introduced themselves.

"Urubu Pakha. ¿Cómo estás?"
"I've never heard anyone speak Spanish with an Aussie accent. But from Nick's accounts I expected something like that. Just call me Santiago."

"You speak English."

"Didn't Nick tell you? In our trade English is quite useful."

"Yea I guess it would be."

"Follow me to camp," said Santiago. "We've only hauled half our load around the rapids. I'd like to be in your canoes three days from now."

"Grab whatevah tools and food ya think we'll need from this canoe," said Urubu. "Crazy native dugout like me family made years ago. The owners upstream might be com'n to look fo it."

They walked the short distance to camp beneath the green canopy. Urubu's eyes widened upon seeing the remaining stash of cocaine bound in heavy plastic and organized in orderly rows.

"Twenty kilos each," said Santiago. "The street value of this run is in the millions. It's too dark to continue today but we'll get to work first thing in the morning."

"With a bit ah sleep I'll be ready to go hard at first light," responded Urubu. "I'll give you me canoe and hidden campsite co-ordinates. We kin paddle the Sié at night and hide under the trees in daylight if ya think they're on to us."

Urubu hung his hammock and rain cover as darkness fell upon the jungle. Before he slept he heard new voices in Spanish. The other men carrying loads around the rapids had returned to camp. Harder rain began to fall as two days with little sleep quickly rendered him unconscious.

"Grab a backpack and let's get to work," were the first words Urubu heard as early morning light trickled through the trees. He drank his coffee and snacked on plantain chips as he organized his gear. The Colombians wore wide-brimmed hats, stained white shirts and khaki pants while Urubu wore his jungle fatigue pants with no shirt or hat.

Urubu and the four Colombian men each loaded a twenty-kilo bundle into their backpacks and headed down the barely discernible trail. Two previous days of hacking, stomping and marking eased the task according to the men who rarely spoke. When they did it was in Spanish. Urubu knew there was no room for small talk or shallow friendship in their line of work. It could only get a man in trouble.

The trek around the rapids took nearly four hours. At times the men walked and climbed next to the thundering cascade before the path led them back into jungle thickets. Finally they reached the foot of the whitewater and Urubu saw other bundles stacked neatly in a palm grove.

Urubu pulled out his GPS messenger and divulged the locations of the hidden canoes and downstream camps to the Colombians. It was still nearly two kilometers downstream to the stashed canoes. The men decided to walk down immediately and paddle back upstream to their stockpile. Hiking on tangled game trails, they reached the concealed canoes in two hours. No one had touched them. In minutes they removed the brushy overburden and flipped the two aluminum canoes upright. The five men carried them down to the river and, an hour later, paddled up to their growing stash of contraband. Recent rains had raised the river level and Urubu was pleased his upstream paddling was complete. It would become increasingly more difficult as flood season commenced.

The men did not have time to pack a second load down from above the rapids so they dragged the canoes onto the bank and trekked back upriver to the main camp. They arrived four hours later in time for a big meal before dark.

* * *

Hatak, Ataqi and their team reached the Rio Sié with no sign of Urubu or their dugout. They continued downstream expecting to reach the head of the rapids before dark. Their search would end there. No canoe could survive the long stretch of crashing whitewater and massive boulders below. They paddled hard most of the day on the increasing flow they would soon need to ascend. Clouds once again darkened the late afternoon sky as they sensed the first rumblings of whitewater below.

Hatak saw it first, his dugout canoe lying on a clay bank. Just downstream a Pale Person's boat rested partially on shore. Smoke rose through the trees a short distance into the jungle. Hatak signaled his canoes to pull onto shore as the rainforest's evening light faded.

The dugout seized by Urubu was empty. He'd taken their priceless steel machetes and axes and the expedition team's only working GPS messenger device. They couldn't communicate with the FUNAI base without it. With quick eye contact, Ataqi and Hatak knew they must find Urubu.

The seven men walked towards the plume of smoke carrying their bows and clubs. In the distance fire flickered between the tree trunks. As they approached, silhouettes of five men contrasted against the fire's glow. Hatak called out, "Urubu, Urubu."

A loud voice echoed back in English. "Leave now whoever you are!" shouted Santiago. "Get out of here and don't come back. We have weapons."

Ataqi fully understood the warning and stopped, but Hatak and Jatabo continued their advance. "Urubu, Urubu."

"Leave now!"

"Urubu, Urubu."

Rifle fire rang out and the approaching men turned. Ducking branches and liana vines in near darkness they ran for their canoes. They stumbled and several fell, but fear lifted them immediately to their feet as they fled the gunshots. The men assembled on the shoreline and scrambled to pull the three dugouts into deeper water for the journey back to the Secret Village. But one man was missing–Hatak.

They heard a groan and turned to see Hatak emerging from the jungle gripping his abdomen. As he neared, Ataqi saw blood oozing from between his fingers. Ataqi and Jatabo grabbed their stumbling friend and helped him into the empty canoe. Ishmi handed them two paddles and they jumped in stroking before fully settled.

The men paddled with all their strength upstream and across to evade the fire sticks. As darkness enveloped the river, the three dugouts came ashore on a sand beach. The men rushed to Hatak. He was breathing but lying in a pool of water and blood. As rain continued to fall, three of the men removed their shirts and draped them over the badly injured warrior. One was packed around his wound.

Using sticks shoved into the sand, the men fashioned a shelter with Hatak's hammock cover. They lifted him from the canoe and placed him inside out of the rain. Ataqi offered him water from his bottle and Hatak took a sip. Occasional moans let the men know Hatak's heart still beat.

Hatak survived the night and was carried ten steps back to the canoe at dawn. He spoke a few words before falling into unconsciousness. "Akuã kuarahy paje'ỹ." (Take me to the shaman.)

The six paddlers manned their canoes and began the difficult journey upriver. The rainy season was upon them and the Sié continued to rise. All their paddling experience was needed to work against the current. They paddled close to shore and into the flooded forest where trees slowed the flow.

Hatak remained in the canoe laying between Jatabo and Ataqi. When he opened his eyes they offered him water. Sometimes he drank a sip or two. His bleeding had mostly stopped but Ataqi knew he was in grave condition. He flashed back to his caiman attack and knew Hatak's pain. This time though, there was no Ikanna or Dr. Sanchez and no Pale Person's medical tent.

The men had paddled from the mouth of the Rio Juri downstream to the head of the rapids in six hours. Paddling the same distance against the building current required two days. Beach camps were minimal to save the men's strength. They didn't bother hanging their hammocks. Some slept naked in the sand while others pulled the hammock covers over their shivering bodies. Rainfall rarely ceased. There was no time or dry wood for fires. The men grabbed a bite of molding dried fish or Brazil nuts whenever they could. Jatabo urged the men to rush Hatak to the village as quickly as possible. "Pajé tupãrã rẽ." (Our shaman can help him.) They turned up the mouth of the Juri and paddled on whenever light allowed.

Two days later the exhausted paddlers recognized the shoreline of their fishing and hunting grounds. They could reach the Secret Village by nightfall. "Hatak, oĩkoe okaa'ỹ ta'ỹna," said Jatabo. (Hatak, you will be home soon.)

Hatak did not respond and Ataqi watched his life force fade. Jatabo checked his pulse. There was none. Jatabo wailed and the other canoes came near.

CHAPTER 20
The Flood

Rain fell on the Secret Village as three dugouts approached. Villagers running to greet the tired men counted only six paddlers. As they waded in to pull the dugouts to shore, the people saw Hatak's lifeless body laying between Ataqi and Jatabo in a red puddle. A shout went out and a women rushed to the huts to tell Ipixuna. Villagers gasped and shrieked running to the water, their wet hair waving behind.

Mike Weston heard the commotion and moved quickly to the river. Among the many villagers maneuvering around the canoes, his eyes fixed on Ipixuna. As he neared he saw tears flowing down her delicate brown face. Mike waded in to help lift the dugout onto the flooding beach and saw the young warrior lying dead. He worked towards Ipixuna in knee-deep water but stopped himself. Instead he grabbed the canoe's bow and lifted it from the water. Weston and a dozen other men carried the heavy dugout forward.

News of Hatak's death spread through the huts in minutes. Villagers gathered behind the canoe carrying his body in a makeshift funeral procession. Ipixuna walked alongside her husband's dugout bier as the people chanted. Many raised their arms and faces to the grey sky. The canoe was placed near the palm thatched hut shared by Hatak and Ipixuna. Mike Weston stepped back to observe. With sharpened sticks village men began to dig in front of the hut's entrance. They continued under torchlight for hours as the entire Secret Village circled around singing. While they dug, Hatak's body and soul were prepared for burial. Images of jaguars and anacondas were painted in red urucum dye on his body as he lay at rest in the canoe.

Once completed, the pit was lined with fresh banana leaves and jungle fruits. In the dim morning light, village men lifted Hatak from the canoe and laid him in his grave. Gifts of manioc roots and caiman teeth were brought forward and placed near his body. His bow and arrows were set by his side. The shaman, with a headdress of vertical red and blue feathers, laid the wing of a harpy eagle over Hatak that stretched over much of his body. Ipixuna knelt sobbing as she placed a flower necklace over his head. Village women laid palm fronds over Hatak and his funerary effects.

Clouds wept as villagers tossed handfuls of dirt over the vanquished warrior. After it filled, all left except Ipixuna who remained throughout the day. Ticata brought food but she refused to eat. Finally, as darkness fell on the

Secret Village, Ipixuna walked the short distance to her mother's hut and slept for the night.

Mike Weston avoided Ipixuna not knowing the proper way to show his sympathy. While in Ataqi's expedition camp he documented his experiences and discussed their plight.

"Urubu must plan this long time ago," said Ataqi. "They have our canoes now going down Rio Sié I'm sure. Probably drug smugglers. Many people work with smugglers. You don't know. Now we need new way to get home."

"And now we have no way to communicate with Professor Schmidt. The **GPS messenger** is gone too," said Weston.

"We will find way home. But now rivers are flooding," responded Ataqi.

"How do you say, 'I'm sorry' in their language?" asked Weston.

"Say 'Añetavy'."

"Thank you Ataqi."

On the third day after Hatak's burial, Mike went to the Secret Village in search of Ipixuna. He wore a new pair of jungle fatigues offered by Ataqi that rose above his ankles. From across the village center Weston recognized Ipixuna's slender figure sitting on a mat weaving fiber cloth. Mike approached her as she stripped another palm leaf filament. Ipixuna stood as Mike called her name. As he neared she looked to the ground. Weston grabbed her hand lightly. "Añetavy," he said.

Ipixuna looked up, the green jungle reflecting in her amber eyes. "Aguéje Michael," she replied.

Then she surprised Mike by wrapping her arms around him and holding tight. Weston sensed the sweet fragrance of Yuripari flowers in her hair.

Ipixuna released her embrace on Weston and, seemingly embarrassed, reached down to show him her weaving. With intricately dyed fibers, her waist cover was nearly complete. Mike nodded his approval and touched his heart. Ipixuna smiled. He sat down next to her and she continued her project often stopping to show Mike the details. Clouds that covered the village for days grew thicker and rain once again began to fall. Ipixuna rolled her mat and weaving work, squeezed Mike's hand and walked back to Ticata's hut.

The tropical shower intensified until the beat of heavy raindrops echoed on thatched roofs throughout the village. Weston's bare feet made sucking sounds as he walked the mud slope to the river. The normally tranquil water ran fast and a heavy sediment load clouded the flow. The river's surface crept into the forest just a few feet below the huts.

Weston turned to head back and saw Xapuri, three other village elders and Ataqi examining the rising river. Ataqi waved for Weston to join them and the soaked men stepped and slid back to the communal hut. The fire inside warmed them as they sat on the log benches discussing their dilemma. Xapuri's stoic painted face and boar tusks drew the men's full attention as he spoke. Though Mike didn't understand their words, the elder's concern was obvious. Ataqi turned to him. "If rain does not stop we must move village to high ground of upper Rio Sié. Xapuri say no floods there. Many day walk, whole village. Everyone must prepare."

Weston nodded. "Do we walk towards the FUNAI outpost?"

"No. Rio Sié big flood. We walk other way," replied Ataqi.

CHAPTER 21
Forced Migration

As the Colombians finished loading the second aluminum canoe below the rapids, Urubu sent a final message to Andrea Schmidt. "All is well but problems with **GPS messenger**. See you soon. Urubu out."

A second message went out to Doug. "Plan working. Canoes loaded. River rising fast. Hidden campsites probably flooded. Tracking function off. Urubu out."

Doug responded, "Good. No worries about hidden campsites. With this stormy weather law enforcement should not be on the river or in the air."

* * *

At the FUNAI Rio Sié control post Professor Schmidt knocked on the office door. "Orlando it's Andrea."

"Entre Andrea."

"I received another message from Urubu. He says they're OK but didn't mention their journey to find the Igarapé People. Something's not right."

"We can only wait now," responded Rivas.

* * *

The rains did not cease and the people of the Secret Village prepared to move above the flood waters from their home on the Rio Juri to the upper Rio Sié. Objectives for Ataqi's expedition had changed. "Michael, it is time to help village move."

"Yes Ataqi. I understand," said Weston.

Ataqi's men, looking more like their rainforest ancestors as their bodies leaned and their hair grew, cleared the expedition camp and packed their gear. Ataqi asked his men to remove the stocks from their two .22 rifles. "Kúbehi musurá no umanyá." (Hide the rifles in your backpacks.)

The six remaining expedition team members plus Mike Weston slogged their muddy supplies to the Secret Village. The flooded Rio Juri lapped at the floors of the lowest lying huts as they entered. Four dugout canoes were already ferrying villagers to the far bank to begin their uphill migration. Ticata and Ipixuna came to greet Mike Weston and Ataqi. "Orembé peteĩ nhande kuéra", said Ataqi. (We are one people now.)

The women nodded. Ipixuna stared into Mike Weston's eyes. He pointed towards the hut she shared with her mother and Ipixuna understood, "I will help you move."

They sloshed through a thin layer of water as they entered. Black mold spread on the interior thatching. Ipixuna's belongings sat on the elevated bed platform–two waist coverings, feather jewelry, a palm fiber sitting mat, small clay pot, her plastic bead necklace and a short piece of bamboo filled with yellow jelly.

"Is that all you own?" asked Mike knowing she wouldn't understand.

Ipixuna squeezed his hand and smiled as warm rain droplets ran down her naked skin. Mike opened his blue waterproof river bag borrowed from the expedition gear. His own belongings inside amounted to little more than hers–nylon running shoes, his notepad and pencil sealed in a plastic bag, worn blue fishing hoodie, a hat and his spare tattered fishing pants replaced by new jungle fatigues. Mike pointed to her possessions and then to the river bag. Ipixuna placed the items inside and Weston sealed the top.

"Aguéje Michael."

Ticata entered the hut to pack her meager possessions including the new steel pot gifted from Ataqi. Weston's bag was full so he looked outside for assistance and called to Pelém, "Eipy Ticata." (Help Ticata.)

Ipixuna smiled at Weston, pleased with his new word in her language. From his backpack Pelém pulled an empty plastic trash bag and held it open. Ticata hesitated for a moment to inspect the strange black sack before packing her wooden spoon, feather necklace, tapir hide waist covering and bamboo container of medicinal dragon's blood sap in with her pot. Pelém lifted the bag and pointed towards the canoes. The four left the flooding hut for the final time.

By the time they reached the canoes most of the village had already shuttled across the angry Rio Juri. Each dugout with two paddlers could ferry four or five villagers and their possessions. Ataqi stood carrying a full backpack and Mike greeted him. "Jatabo and some hunters with our machetes already go across. They scout and make trail for others. Maybe get animal for people to eat. They make camp for the night for all village before we come," said Ataqi.

"That's smart," replied Weston.

Two young village men paddled a dugout into the flooded forest loading area. Weston led Ticata and Ipixuna forward. Soon they were on the raging river, the strong paddlers making less distance across than downstream. Brown waves rocked the canoe and broke over the carved wooden rail. With great effort they made the far bank and then paddled back upriver around flooded tree trunks where the current was weakest.

More village men waded out to steady the canoe and help the women disembark. Weston climbed out and slogged to the muddy bank carrying their bags. The elder Xapuri wearing his Swiss Army knife and jaguar claw necklace nodded to Weston as he gathered the villagers preparing to walk.

Most of the assembled women hauled woven fiber backpacks secured with forehead straps. Some carried babies while others held manioc, dried meat and fruit. Mothers held the hands of young children ready to walk. All were barefoot with scant clothing. Ataqi's men wore expedition boots and jungle fatigues except Pelém who refused the Pale People's shoes and clothing. He gave his boots to Weston who wore them without tightening the laces, his toes curled slightly.

Four packs containing assorted animal hides and fiber cordage sat against a tree unaccounted for. Ipixuna and Ticata each hoisted one and set the forehead bands. Once the entire village had crossed the Juri, eight paddlers pulled the heavy dugouts as high as they could above the flood. Their prized canoes were useless for the uphill migration.

When all were gathered, Xapuri gave a sharp call like the cry of a harpy eagle and the migration commenced. Two hunters led the women and children on the jungle trail blazed by the forerunners. Ipixuna and Ticata trekked behind the children with Weston following. Protecting the rear were Ataqi and his five remaining expedition team members carrying heavy backpacks. Two village men walked with them carrying caiman skull firebrands holding glowing hardwood embers to start the evening campfires. At Ataqi's request, his expedition team concealed many of their modern tools including their butane lighters.

The long line dipped and swerved through the tangled rainforest. Heavy water drops fell from the trees while monkeys warned each other of the villagers' advance. Where the canopy was thickest and light barely penetrated, they moved in straighter formation over the sparse forest floor. The nomads did not eat during the day stopping only for short breaks when they located clear rainwater creeks. Edible plants found along the way were collected and packed away for camp–Brazil nuts, palm fruits and camu camu.

The trek continued until late in the day when the villagers arrived at their makeshift camp under construction by the forward scouts. Simple lean-to shelters of bamboo poles and palm frond roofs sprang up as bustling rainforest men worked in teams. Some carried bundles of bamboo or palm fronds hacked from the jungle while others lashed the structures with fiber cordage. More palm fronds were laid in for beds.

As they arrived in camp, each villager went about specific tasks–firewood gathering, water collection, fire building, cooking and wound tending. Tired children rested but soon gathered with friends to play. Sticks and feathers made instant toys.

The villagers ate a full meal of dried fish, manioc flat bread and dried bananas to prepare for the next day's walk. They retired to their meager shelters to rest for the night. Weston and Ataqi left the expedition team's hammocks in their backpacks and shared a palm frond lean-to near Ticata and Ipixuna's shelter.

Ipixuna heard Weston swatting mosquitoes. She approached and tapped on his shoulder. Opening the blue river bag, she pulled out her bamboo container of yellow jelly. She rubbed it on his exposed skin and Mike realized it was a native insect repellent. Ipixuna handed the container to Weston and tapped on her own shoulder. "Ape terei." (Here please.)

Mike rubbed it gently on her naked back and shoulders enjoying the bittersweet fragrance. "Thank you," said Ipixuna to Weston's surprise.

"Ataqi?" he asked.

"Hee," giggled Ipixuna (Yes.)

The migration towards the upper Rio Sié continued the following day. Palm shelters collapsed as the women collected their valuable cordage. Lead scouts left early once again as villagers ate and prepared to walk. Other than minor scrapes and cuts they suffered no hardships. Weston followed the serpentine line through the forest marked by disturbed brush and snapped twigs at eye level left by the scouts. With no long sight lines through the tangled vegetation he wondered how they navigated.

As they walked Ataqi spoke to Mike Weston. "I think we are in Colombia now but it is hard to tell in jungle without GPS. Can't see anything. I will show you on map when we stop."

At the next water break while sitting on a fallen mahogany trunk, Ataqi pulled the topographic map from his backpack. As he leaned over to shield it from rainfall, Ataqi pointed out their location. "See Mike? I think we are here. We have been walking north. We pass from Brazil into Colombia. People of village do not know these borders or countries. Rivers are only borders."

As they entered the new temporary camp late that afternoon, Mike saw five fresh monkey carcasses hanging from a low branch. He turned away in disgust but did not feel the wave of nausea that typically came over him at such a sight. Rain continued to fall that night but the temporary palm shelters kept him remarkably dry. "It's amazing how well these instant huts keep the water out," said Weston.

"Yes. Jungle skills passed down many centuries," said Ataqi.

"What is the yellow jelly that repels mosquitoes?"

"Carap oil?" asked Ataqi. "From big seeds we find on ground. They are boiled and crushed to remove oil. Bugs don't like it."

Each night the elders met to discuss their progress. On the fifth night of the migration, Ataqi returned to the shelter he shared with Weston. "I talk to Xapuri. They hear strange bird calls all night. But not birds. They are calls of dangerous tribe Arabox. Xapuri say that many flood cycles ago they attack Secret Village at night. Kill four of his people with spears and take two young girls away. Very dangerous. We change direction tomorrow to get away from Arabox."

The next morning as their trek continued, Mike Weston deduced that their path veered sharply to the west. Diagonal shafts of light penetrating the dense foliage pointed the way.

That night Weston and Ataqi stayed awake longer than normal to listen for the bird calls of the Arabox. "They surround a village and talk like birds. Villagers don't know. Then they attack," whispered Ataqi. "But I think they gone away now."

Their migration route lead the people of the Secret Village to higher ground above the flooded headwaters of the Rio Sié. On the ninth day Xapuri proclaimed the end of their journey.

* * *

While the villagers prepared to build a temporary home above the floodwaters, Urubu, his Colombian associates, their multi-million-dollar stash and the expedition team's two aluminum canoes vanished under deep cloud cover.

CHAPTER 22
Hunger

Andrea Schmidt turned towards the deluged Rio Sié as she paced to the office of Orlando Rivas in relentless rain. The floating dock bucked at its tethers ten meters above its dry season elevation. Entire trees floated by in the chocolate soup, sometimes sucked under by massive whirlpools. *Tabatinga* had missed her last two scheduled stops, the captain hesitant about fighting the raging current and dodging hazardous debris.

Dr. Schmidt hadn't heard from the expedition team for over two weeks as she entered with barely a knock. Rainwater dripped off her messy blond hair onto his desk. "We need to get a search plane in there soon."

"I doubt they can fly in this weather but I'll make some calls," said Rivas. "Don't forget these jungle people have survived floods for thousands of years. They'll survive this one too."

"Poor Mike Weston. Just as he was headed back home bad fortune struck again," replied Professor Schmidt.

"He'll come out of the jungle alive. And when he does he'll have quite a story to tell. Just imagine the research paper you'll write, probably a book too," said Rivas.

"I hope so but my biggest concern now is getting everyone home safely."

As Professor Schmidt left the FUNAI office, Ikanna in her green scrubs walked out of the medical tents and called out, "Andrea, have you heard anything from Ataqi's crew?"

"Olá Ikanna. We're trying to get a search plane over the village site but the weather is not cooperating. I'm worried."

"Me too. I haven't seen a flood like this in years. But we both know how resourceful the rainforest people can be. They have the expedition team's gear now too. All those steel tools should help."

"Orlando won't be happy about that but I think he wants everyone back safely as much as we do," replied Professor Schmidt.

Two days later Orlando Rivas had Andrea Schmidt's answer. "The IBAMA flight to search for illegal gold mining and logging activity has been delayed three weeks. They've agreed to fly over the Secret Village site when the weather clears. I gave them the coordinates."

"Thank you Orlando. I'll be traveling back to California soon and I'd like to have some answers."

Clouds thinned enough the following week for the IBAMA environmental enforcement agency to search the upper Rio Sié. The flight out of São Gabriel da Nazaré on the Rio Negro stayed airborne for six hours at 3,000 ft. searching up and down the larger rivers and igarapés. At 1300 hours they radioed Orlando Rivas, "Estamos sobre o local da aldeia a 1.97 graus norte e 67.99 graus oeste. A área está completamente inundada." (We are over the village site at 1.97 degrees north and 67.99 degrees west. It is completely flooded.)

* * *

As the people of the Secret Village completed their migration above the vast flood plain of the upper Rio Sié, they built another temporary camp of palm frond shelters on the rainforest floor. This time, though, the lean-to huts were not abandoned the following day. The villagers planned to use them a short time, maybe ten days, until a new Secret Village could be raised.

Rainforest men who normally hunted and fished each day spent more time cutting palm and bamboo as food supplies dwindled. Fishing was unproductive when flood waters dispersed the fish populations many fold and the new village site was over an hour walk from the ever-moving shoreline of the Rio Sié. Like the villagers, animals were also on the move making them more difficult to find. Ataqi's men joined in the hunts determined to bring food back to the villagers.

"Michael, my men hunt for whole village. Pelém is good hunter. Bow and arrow or rifle," said Ataqi.

"I thought you wanted to keep the rifles hidden," said Weston as he pulled on the waistband of his expedition fatigues, growing baggier by the day.

"Yes for now. Village people are afraid of fire stick," replied Ataqi.

"They'll be more afraid of hunger," said Weston.

"All jungle people know hunger. But they do not worry. They continue to hunt and food will come."

"How can I help?" asked Mike Weston.

"Help build huts. You are tall. Can reach high. And don't forget to take notes for Professor Schmidt," said Ataqi.

"That's right. I might get out of this crazy jungle someday. Aguéje Ataqi."

The expedition team became one with the people of the Secret Village helping where they could. Palm and bamboo for construction was plentiful. Food was not. A few delicious peccaries were downed with well-placed arrows but they provided only a mouthful of protein for the 80 some villagers.

Large holes in the ground identified armadillo burrows. Village men excelled at coaxing the scaled mammals from their burrows with smoky embers and Mike Weston sampled bites of another strange rainforest fare. But armadillos were also scarce. Ataqi's team had exhausted their expedition food supplies weeks earlier and refused to eat the villagers' meager sustenance. But Xapuri insisted all would share in both famine and abundance.

Ipixuna and Ticata spent much of their time foraging the forest for food whenever the rain abated. They found palm fruits, Brazil nuts and leafy chaya but in small quantities. They tore decomposing logs apart to find protein-rich insect grubs. Three nearby dragon's blood trees refilled the women's pots with the red wound-healing sap.

In an old kapok tree, Ticata spotted a bee hive but it was too high to reach. That evening Ipixuna asked Ataqi to pass a message on to Mike Weston. "Hello Michael. Ipixuna ask if you can follow her into forest tomorrow."

"Why?" asked Weston.

"She need help to collect food."

The next morning Ipixuna met Mike as he cut bamboo. She pointed towards the rising sun. Ipixuna carried Ticata's steel pot containing glowing coals from the village fire. Weston nodded and followed her for nearly an hour. They reached the old kapok and Ipixuna pointed out the swarming bees. Weston nodded not knowing her plan. She sat the pot down and commenced collecting sticks from brush and trees off the moist ground. Ipixuna stacked them under the bee hive and dumped the coals among the fuel, blowing on them until the thinner twigs ignited. Soon the pile of sticks smoldered and burned. As the fire increased Ipixuna cleansed the pot with wet leaves from the ground and created more smoke by sprinkling them on the fire.

A thick cloud rose to the hive and the buzzing bees settled back into their nest. When their activity ceased, Ipixuna swept the fire from the tree trunk's base with branches, Weston assisting wherever he could. When the hot coals were moved away from the trunk, Ipixuna grabbed Weston's wrist and guided him beneath the hive. She grabbed the pot and gestured for Mike to crouch low. Finally, he understood her plan and he stooped down holding Ipixuna's hand. She climbed on his back and stood on his shoulders. Mike stood upright and Ipixuna balanced with one hand on the huge tree trunk as Weston grabbed her ankles. "Porã," she said. (Good.)

Gently, Ipixuna plunged her hand into the hive up to her elbow and pulled it out covered in thick honey and wax. With the pot wedged between her stomach and the tree, she wiped the dripping goo off before repeating the process four more times. The pot filled as the bees revived and several stung her hand. Quickly she handed the pot down to Weston and jumped to the forest floor.

They sat on a nearby log and Ipixuna held her sticky arm in front of Weston's face. He smiled not understanding until she licked a bit of honey off. Mike nodded and grabbed her hand licking the sweet delicacy off her forearm. Other than a few larval fragments, it was perfect. They laughed enjoying their delectable meal as Ipixuna passed her honey-covered arm between them. Weston finished nibbling the last sticky remnants from her fingers as she giggled. A flock of parakeets chirped from high in the canopy.

The new Secret Village grew gradually during the following days as hungry men cut, lashed and thatched. Gaunt Mike Weston joined in and learned new words in their Tupi-Guarani language. "Ikytá taquára." (Cut the bamboo.) But hand signals and facial expressions accounted for most of his communication with the villagers. Usually hungry, Weston took strength from Jatabo, Ataqi and other rainforest men who continued with their duties uncomplaining.

With instructions from Ataqi and help from other villagers, Mike constructed a sturdy rainproof hut for Ticata and Ipixuna. Its straight walls and pitched roof like the Igarapé People's huts formed a unique design for the Secret Village. A small stone fire ring was laid beneath the highest portion of the roof pitch and raised bed platforms were built on either side with bamboo stakes driven into the dirt floor. Layers of palm fronds made hard mattresses. The small door of thatched palm could be partially closed to trap heat from the fire and keep some insects out.

Like most of the single young village men, Weston constructed his own small hut. Ipixuna helped him weave palm frond leaflets as the thatching was tied in place. Ataqi's expedition team of six erected three huts for themselves. They also built raised bed platforms choosing to save their hammocks for the trek back to civilization whenever it might come.

A nearby stream emerged from a rocky bluff far in the distance. It was too small to be named but ran through a shallow canyon that did not flood. A pool beneath the overhanging rainforest canopy was large enough for communal bathing. Pelém and other villagers fished there but shot only small wolffish with their arrows. Pelém hiked further downstream and caught more with a baited hook and line, tools most villagers had never seen.

Damp firewood was difficult to burn and the villagers sometimes slept through cool rainy nights with no source of heat. With little to cover them but giant palm fronds, many of the famished people shivered as they slept. In pitch dark one cold night, Mike Weston woke to stirring in his hut. He wondered if a jungle animal had entered. Something moved closer to his bed and his eyes opened wide though he couldn't see. He twitched as he felt a cool touch on his chest. A lean body nestled in next to him. He recognized the fair scent of jungle flowers and pulled himself tight to Ipixuna.

CHAPTER 23
Children of the Village

Children ran and played with jungle bugs on the edges of the new Secret Village. "When I can't see their naked bodies through the trees, the laughter reminds me of kids at my local park in Santa Clara," wrote Mike Weston on his note pad. "Every parent seems to be the parent of every child in the village. But they don't parent much. I don't see them discipline the children even when they play in dangerous snake habitat or accidentally singe a hut's wall playing with burning sticks. I guess the children learn by example."

As final layers of woven palm sealed their new huts, the people stayed drier and the village men had more time for hunting. The fortunes of their excursions improved as the men learned the ways of the new forest environment. Wild boar and tapir sometimes came to a creek meadow downstream. They disappeared into the jungle at dawn so hunting parties began departing their huts in the dark. Two months into the rainy season, Jatabo and three other bowmen carried two huge tapirs into the village hanging hooves-up from stout poles.

Villagers feasted all night around three outdoor fire pits under palm frond awnings. Hefty chunks of fresh tapir baked on rocks and sizzled on bamboo skewers. Singing and laughter echoed through the jungle until early morning light seeped through the foliage. As a chorus of birds awakened, the villagers retired to their huts and slept. Barely a human stirred until late afternoon when the rainforest people emerged preparing for their evening baths. Many were naked though Mike Weston, the only Pale Person among them, preferred the modesty of his black polyester briefs. Ipixuna wore her intricately woven fiber waist covering, a short skirt open on the sides. They walked to the communal pond together but not within touching distance. Weston didn't know how the villagers would react to their relationship. He wasn't sure either.

Ipixuna's best friend Curiari joined them as they walked the slippery trail to the creek. The two young women spoke excitedly though Mike Weston did not understand a word. He turned to Ipixuna and grinned. She laughed softly and resumed her conversation with Curiari.

The midstream pool was barely large enough for half the villagers to bath at one time. Mike Weston stood out in the throng of shorter black-haired rainforest people, yet most of the villagers no longer seemed to notice. Many rubbed their bodies down with shoreline mud before they entered. Ipixuna and Curiari carried jasmine-scented leaves to wash themselves. Ipixuna offered some to

Weston as they entered the pool and he scrubbed his arms and chest. The leaves secreted a soapy foam as he ran them over his body.

In a smaller pool a short distance downstream children splashed and giggled, playing more than bathing. A sudden scream silenced their laughter and adult heads snapped around. Children ran from the water as village men waded quickly towards them. A disturbance caught their attention. Within the churning water a serpent's tail the thickness of a man's leg swirled. "Sucuri!" (Anaconda!)

In the thrashing emerged a horrific sight. The feet of a young child protruded from the giant snake's head as it swung above the raging surface. The men dove in and swam with all their strength. But as they reached the horror's exact location, the water fell silent. The snake and child were gone. The villagers rushed towards the children gathered on the shoreline counting their faces. A mother howled and the people encircled her as she cried. Somber wailing filled the evening air. The child's mother removed her colorful bead necklace and tossed it into the water where it sank out of sight.

The villagers shuffled solemnly back to their huts in a tight pack, the mother sobbing as she looked towards the sky. Mike walked to the rear, shocked by the sudden death. That night he wrote in his journal, "Nature surrounds us here, both the magnificently beautiful and the magnificently tragic. It's no surprise that humans have sought to isolate themselves from the uncaring whims of nature since we first appeared on earth."

Cries, bumps and shrieks of disembodied spirits haunted the Secret Village for many days. Mike Weston was awakened by the wind one night shortly after the child was lost. Within the swirling jungle breeze the faint wailing of a child called to him. He shook his head in disbelief and the cries were silenced. But after a moment the wailing resumed.

Eleven days later a new baby was born into the village with Ticata assisting the birth. Mike Weston sensed that the pall hanging over the people was gone. Voices around the village seemed uplifted, especially those of the women. Ataqi and Mike Weston visited Ticata and Ipixuna's hut the next morning to ask them. After some discussion in Tupi-Guarani, Ataqi turned to Weston. "The people believe new baby shares spirit with dead girl. They are same. Mother of dead child is second mother for new baby. She is happy now."

Mike took notes in his journal while Ipixuna observed closely. "Michael, your writings are new to them," said Ataqi. They draw characters from nature with plant dyes and fire ash. Sometimes carve in wood. But they have no letters like Pale People. They do not write words, just speak them. People like Professor Schmidt make villagers' speak words into written words."

Mike wrote Ipixuna's name in large letters on his paper "Ip-EESH-oo-nah". He pointed to her and then back at his letters. "Ip-EESH-oo-nah," he said and she smiled. Mike handed her the pencil and she copied the letters crudely. He smiled. "Yes. Ip-EESH-oo-nah."

Ipixuna reached out and grabbed Weston's scraggly blond hair. She pointed to the pocketknife in Ataqi's pocket. "Eíporā?" (Please?)

With the sharp edge she trimmed the ends of Mike's hair until it hung in waves neatly above his shoulders. Ataqi was next and Ipixuna cut the stringy black mane that had grown far below his shoulders since his departure from the FUNAI control post three months earlier. The women continued to talk as Ticata collected the long useable strands off the earthen floor, compacted by hundreds of footsteps. Before they departed, Ticata and Ipixuna turned the men around to face them. They smiled, apparently pleased with Ipixuna's work.

Thin rays of sunlight danced on the forest floor early the following morning. The rainy season was nearing its end. Manioc roots planted by the villagers had not grown to maturity but small amounts were harvested to produce their cassava flour. The Rio Sié flood plain began to recede, the shoreline now a two-hour walk from the village.

Xapuri gathered the elders and Ataqi to plan for drier days. A priority was finding trees to build new canoes. Many of the largest trees were flooded in the river but would soon emerge onto dry land. Those felled near the shoreline were favored. Carrying a heavy dugout through the rainforest to the river could be as laborious as building it.

Canoes allowed hunters and fishermen to travel further from the village and transport their heavy kills along the slick waterway. Canoes could carry the people back to the mouth of the Rio Juri and upriver to find a better village site near their old village. Dugouts could take Ataqi's men to the head of the Rio Sié rapids within reach of the FUNAI control post.

Ataqi and Pelém made the long hike to the retreating Rio Sié shoreline hunting for both game and suitable canoe trees. Pelém carried his steel machete and bow while Ataqi held a tall wooden pole with a knife blade lashed to the end.

As they approached the water through the jungle thicket, two prime cedar trees with thick trunks protruded above the surface, out of reach for now. Further down the muddy shoreline, Ataqi froze and stretched his arm in front of Pelém to halt his progress. He pointed and Pelém nodded. A caiman as heavy as the two men combined rested in the shallows with half its armored body out of the water.

Ataqi raised his spear slowly and crept forward on bare feet. The caiman did not stir, its eyes open but blank. When he came within range Ataqi did not hesitate. He thrust the spear forward letting out a grunt as it left his hand. The caiman reacted instantly spinning away from the bank as the sharp tip penetrated its scaled hide. Ataqi's strike missed the vertebra but slowed the giant reptile. Sharp teeth flashed as the primitive beast hissed. Pelém reacted as quickly as the caiman lunging forward with his machete held high. His powerful blow landed just behind its eyes and penetrated halfway through the caiman's neck. It thrashed mightily once more but then lay motionless. The men shouted warriors' victory calls.

The caiman was too heavy for the men to carry whole so they cut it into manageable pieces. The massive head and claws were left behind, perhaps to be collected in upcoming days. A long tree branch as thick as the men's arm was cut and trimmed. The tail, body and meaty legs were lashed on tightly and the men began the long walk back.

Villagers greeted the hunters later that afternoon excited by their great kill. Ataqi knew caiman were a favorite food of the people for both their bodies and souls.

CHAPTER 24
Feast and Plunder

Mike congratulated Ataqi on his hunt as village women prepared the caiman meat, enough to feed all the people. "It must feel good to kill the animal that almost killed you."

"Michael, our jungle home always provides in both life and in death."

The villagers enjoyed any reason to celebrate and a caiman feast was more than enough. Women decorated their hair and bodies in colorful feathers and flowers while the men painted themselves in red urucum and black genipapo dyes. Ipixuna beamed in elegance that evening with long scarlet feathers tied into her streaming hair. She wore two as earrings that glimmered like fire embers when she turned. Delicate patterns in red and black adorned her face telling a story Mike Weston did not understand.

Xapuri spoke before the feast standing between Ataqi and Pelém with the prized Swiss Army knife hanging from his neck between six jaguar claws. The villagers stood quiet and Mike Weston thought he picked out some of the elder's words–"brothers", "great hunters", "thank you"–as he recorded with Ataqi's GoPro. Xapuri finished by raising his arms to the spirits of their ancestors watching over the Secret Village.

Villagers laid their mats on bare ground around the fires and came forward. Most used their fingers to pull pieces of the delicious white meat directly off the cooling fire pit. Others like Ipixuna used sticks to place the meat onto woven palm trays. Warm acai berries sweetened the meal. When everyone was satiated, enough caiman meat remained to place on the smoker. Mike recognized the singing that broke out after the feast. "Michael, this is to thank animal spirits for feeding us," said Ataqi. "We are happy now. We drink chicha."

Mike watched as the wooden bowls passed from person to person. He had avoided the ceremonial drink before after seeing its unique production process–boiled and cooled manioc root chewed by village women and then spit into wooden bowls where it was left to ferment. Mike had held the bowl to his lips but never sipped. This time he convinced himself the alcohol had sterilized the foamy liquid and he drank. The buttery taste warmed his throat and he drank again. Another bowl of chicha was passed and he drank a third time.

Soon the singing led to dancing and Weston joined in for the first time. He watched Ipixuna move gracefully, even erotically, from a distance not wanting the villagers to know of their relationship. He suspected many already did. Their eyes met.

A young village man maneuvered close to Ipixuna and they danced to the rhythm in unison. Surprised by his jealousy, Weston moved towards the dancing couple but stopped short. Ipixuna looked into his eyes once more.

The Secret Village fell silent many hours later when only the fireflies continued to dance. Once again Ipixuna visited Mike Weston's hut and then departed before the daybreak calls of howler monkeys echoed through the jungle.

The village men did not hunt the next day. They played with the children–lessons disguised as games. The children shot arrows and threw spears at a monkey pelt target. They built swings with vines and fiber cordage. The rainforest men and Mike Weston cheered them on. Village women left their tasks to join in and laughter filled the sultry air.

As the children shot their arrows, kind Jatabo approached Mike Weston and handed him his bow and four arrows. Jatabo pointed to the monkey pelt target. Weston remembered summer days in Oregon when he joined his brother to shoot straight aluminum arrows from his father's recurved fiberglass bow. Jatabo's bow was shaped from a long, strait limb of jungle hardwood, his arrows of bamboo fletched with blue and red macaw feathers lashed with animal sinew.

Nervous in front of the villagers, Mike took the bow and nodded. The pelt hung at eye level on a palm trunk and Weston counted out twelve paces towards the crowd from there. He turned and drew. His hand quivered and the first arrow flew just right of the target. The villagers sighed. The second arrow came close grazing the brown fur. Determined to hit the target, Mike Weston drew and held the third arrow longer before he let it fly. Bullseye! The rainforest people cheered and Weston pumped his fist in the air. The fourth arrow struck the pelt again and the people celebrated Mike Weston like an honorary hunter of the Secret Village.

Longer periods of morning sunshine announced the gradual return of the drier season. Hunters alerted by the musky odor of rooting peccary and boar brought home greater bounties. Older boys joined the men on their excursions, eager to take their first shots that mattered. Mike joined Ataqi and Pelém on a long hunting day along the river and they saw that the Rio Sié shoreline had retreated beyond the trunks of the canoe trees. "Canoes can be made soon. They carry us down Rio Sié to rapids. We must find way to get home from there," said Ataqi.

The men carried bows and spears ready for encounters at both short and long range. They could not get a clear arrow shot on a boar or peccary. But just as they prepared to depart the shoreline for the village, Pelém spotted long writhing bodies in the shallow mouth of a

seasonal   creek.   "Electric   eels,"   cautioned   Ataqi.
"Dangerous. Watch way we hunt."

Ataqi and Pelém did not stand in the water but
were able to stalk the prized fish with their long spears. The
eels did not swim off as the men approached cautiously,
their weapons held high. When the moment was right they
struck with strong thrusts that pinned two thick eels to the
bottom. The men held firm knowing the powerful shock of
the delicious fish faded with their heartbeats. Weston
followed the example of his jungle friends and speared a
third. Static tingling moved up the wet pole to his hands
but he held tight. The eels squirmed and splashed but the
three men in close proximity gripped their spears tightly
encouraging each other with hoots and shouts. The
thrashing finally ceased and the men dragged the heavy
eels onto the bank.

"Ataqi, I will show you what we do in California to
celebrate a good shot. Hold your hand like this," said Mike
as he raised his clenched fist to shoulder level.

Ataqi imitated Weston and Mike gave him a fist
bump. "Great hunting my friend."

Mike turned towards Pelém, his fist held high.
Pelém understood the universal gesture and connected his
fist with Weston's. "Great hunting my friend."

They returned to the village that evening with eels
around their necks, both heads and tails hanging to their
waists.

As the rainy season waned, villagers spoke of moving back to the lush forests of the Rio Juri. The flood had likely devastated the old Secret Village site but they might be able to rescue the canoes abandoned before their long migration. The elders discussed building a new village lower on the Juri where hunters rarely ventured. Once the new dugouts were built, the people could travel by canoe down the Sié and up the Juri. Even if it required multiple round trips, the river route was easier than hiking many days through dense jungle.

Plans were made to begin cutting trees for the new dugouts as their rainforest world began to dry. Monkeys and parrots grew more numerous in the canopy and the hum of the tropical forest grew louder each night. But one bird call concerned the hunters. "Michael, the Arabox may be near," said Atari early one morning. "I hear their calls last night. They are not birds. They are savage tribe that raid villages in middle of night."

The proximity of the hostile tribe hastened the villagers' plans to move to the shoreline of the shrinking Rio Sié. Xapuri announced they would make the short migration in three days. Guards would be posted at night to warn the people of nearby Arabox savages.

Two nights later as all but four village lookouts slept, calls of human birds echoed through the Secret Village over the shrill buzz of jungle insects. The calls came closer and the guards prepared to warn the sleeping people. But before they could wake the villagers, Arabox raiders struck swiftly and silently. Screams filled the darkness as villagers snapped awake. The last flames of the central fire pit illuminated silhouettes of thin, long-haired jungle men and their spears moving cat-like from hut to hut.

Pelém, knowing the Arabox were near, had assembled his expedition rifle two days earlier and hid it loaded under his raised bed. He grabbed it and stepped outside the hut he shared with Ataqi. His first shot into the air silenced the forest. The second shot was followed by more human bird calls as the Arabox fled the fire stick. The screaming of young girls faded into the jungle with their captors.

Villagers awakened by the attack searched the huts with torches, cautious of any remaining savages. All remained awake until morning when the tragedy was fully assessed. The daughter of Ipixuna's friend Curiari and another village girl had been kidnapped. Curiari and her husband Umarik lay blood-soaked and dead outside their hut, victims of the invaders' spears. The people wept.

Preparations for moving the village ceased as the village mourned for Curiari, Umarik and the kidnapped girls. The young couple was placed together in a grave lined with palm fronds and bright feathers. Umarik's bow and arrows were placed on his chest and Curiari wore a headdress of jungle flowers. Chants rose to the spirits above as villagers poured handfuls of soil over their lost family.

Ipixuna cried softly most of the day and Mike Weston accompanied her on a long walk into the rainforest. Without speaking, their deep eye contact expressed Ipixuna's despair and Mike's empathy. They held each other often, Weston running his fingers through Ipixuna's smooth hair. Ipixuna pointed to a blue bird with a large rainbow-colored beak in the tree above. "Tukã. Ikatu xe irû Curiari." (Toucan. Maybe my friend Curiari.)

Rumors circulated through the village that a counterattack by the Secret Village People could be in the making. The elders, though, agreed on a more cautious plan. "Michael I talk to Xapuri," said Ataqi. "He say small groups of two or three men can hunt near Arabox territory but always hidden. If they find our girls they try to bring them back at night. Xapuri say big attack no good. Not enough men in this village."

Weston was surprised when the villagers returned to their tasks the next day as if the Arabox attack never happened. "Michael, the people have much work to do but still mourn. They help each other like big family. Hard to understood but I think death makes village stronger."

Their move downhill to the Rio Sié was planned for the next day and villagers packed their minimal possessions. Against the advice of Orlando Rivas, most of

Ataqi's remaining expedition team had used their modern equipment in the presence of Secret Village People, especially during the peak of the rainy season when food and comfort were scarce. The brightly colored nylon, steel, aluminum, polyester and flashing picture box no longer elicited the surprised reactions of a few months earlier.

Once again the expedition team filled their backpacks preparing for the uncertain journey home. As they prepared to leave, Ataqi could not find the GoPro camera. He asked his men and several villagers but no one claimed to have seen it. "Michael, have you seen the camera?" asked Ataqi. "We had two but Urubu take one. Now both are gone."

"I haven't seen your GoPro since I used it to video the caiman feast," said Weston. "I put it back in your hut inside the backpack."

"Michael, some villagers fear camera will take their soul and lock it inside. Maybe they take camera away."

"Maybe, but I think I understand," said a frustrated Weston. "Our worlds are so different. This must be why Dr. Schmidt studies people with few possessions and no modern technology. Everything is stripped away but their humanity."

Morning broke and the people of the Secret Village made final preparations for their trek to the Rio Sié. Immature manioc roots dug from the village field the day before protruded from palm fiber packs along with pots, stone knives, digging sticks, bamboo containers, body coverings and adornments. Every able villager loaded their arms with poles, cordage and mats. Hunters carried their bows, arrows, spears, prized steel knives and machetes. Elders carried less except Xapuri who insisted on hauling Ticata's load with his. With hand gestures Mike Weston offered to carry Ipixuna's possessions, but she refused. "Thank you Michael."

"Aguéje Ipixuna," replied Weston.

They did not walk together.

Many hunting parties had walked to the Sié so the pathway through the jungle was obvious with broken twigs and compacted soil marking the way. The tribe walked two or three abreast not forced into the serpentine line of their previous migration through the untrodden rainforest. By late afternoon, after stepping through concentric lines of drying mud in their bare feet, the villagers reached the shore of the Sié.

Giant water lilies the diameter of a tree trunk spread out along the shallows providing cover for fish, caiman and anacondas. The village women collected *tracajá* buried on the sandy beaches. The turtle eggs provide a seasonal bounty. A temporary village of simple palm frond shelters went up in two days. The more challenging task of building five large dugout canoes began on day three.

CHAPTER 25
Dugouts

Six thick-trunked cedar trees submerged in the flooded Rio Sié two weeks earlier now stood on dry ground rising high into the canopy. Master canoe shapers of the Secret Village selected five to begin their laborious process. Mike Weston pitched in swinging a steel axe like he did as a teenager in Oregon. "This cedar wood is strong Ataqi. Almost as hard as oak. It should make a great canoe," said Mike as perspiration dripped down his shirtless chest.

"Think how long it can take to cut with stone tools. That's what they use over there," said Ataqi as he pointed to four men cutting another cedar. "Maybe two days to chop down. We help them with our steel tools."

Once the trees were down the men swarmed over the trunks like ants chopping limbs and bark. Treetops were cut off where the diameter was best which customized the length of each canoe. The men cleared tangled brush on the river side of each trunk to bare earth for an unobstructed work area, sometimes singing while they worked.

Continuing with axes and machetes, each log was chopped, carved and shaped for many days until a smooth upside-down hull emerged from the cedar wood. Tapering the ends to the proper form required the most experienced shapers who often stepped back and inspected their work from a distance.

When the hulls were formed and smoothed, hordes of grunting rainforest men strained to roll them over onto soft beds of wood chips accumulated over days of chopping. Small logs wedged beneath kept them stable for the work to follow. By the fifteenth day all five hulls rested upright spread along the river that continued to recede.

The village celebrated while bathing in the Sié splashing and chatting. Yet Mike Weston saw apprehension on the faces of many villagers. Xapuri sent two small hunting parties out each day but there was no sign of the barbaric Arabox or the two abducted girls. The blasts of Pelém's fire stick could have sent them deeper into the jungle, but they might still be near.

After washing, the Secret Village People dined on piles of baked turtle eggs. The easy harvest of tracajá buried along the Rio Sié beaches allowed many hunters to focus on canoe building. Ipixuna wore a beautiful necklace of multi-colored macaw feathers and delicate red body paint that Mike Weston had never seen before. With the first step of his journey home taking shape along the shoreline, he considered her motivation.

Burning of the canoes commenced the next morning. Remnant wood chips and sticks from the hull-shaping process were stacked in small piles atop the partially finished dugouts and lit with embers from the village fire pit. Experienced artisans supervised the many small flames as they gradually burned out the hulls' interiors. With long sticks, they pushed the smoldering cinders into position avoiding the dugouts' sides. Men chiseled out each charred section with stone adzes and then pushed more glowing coals over the area to continue the process. Cedar smoke swirled through the forest.

While waiting for dozens of small fires to hollow out each canoe, the men shaped paddles from the largest limbs using the same tools. Each canoe required at least four paddles with one or two spares.

Working with the fires day and night, the village men roughed out the canoes' interiors in four days. To widen the narrow hulls while the wood was warm, thick limbs removed earlier in the process served as levers. Each was cut to the desired interior width of the hull and wedged inside at a diagonal. The men hammered the limbs with wood and stone mallets forcing the canoe sides outward until each limb lined up perpendicular to the length of its canoe. Additional scrapping smoothed the dugouts' interiors and removed the last of the embers.

With the fires extinguished, final shaping began. Holes drilled in key locations with stone augers revealed the hull thickness. Wooden plugs sealed them later in the process. Half the length of an index finger plunged into each hole indicated the proper finished thickness. Smaller stone adzes chopped and smoothed the interiors until each wooden sculpture was complete.

The men rolled the canoes over again. Rubber trees located along the migration route from the upper village supplied the final ingredient–latex sap to seal the hulls. The milky secretion dripped from V-shaped slashes in the bark into bamboo containers lashed to the trees. Clay pots of raw sap heated over fires boiling off water and thinning the liquid. Allowed to cool slightly, the men dipped flattened sticks into the rubber and spread it onto the exterior hulls. Others smoothed it into a thin layer until the five hulls were complete.

The entire Secret Village walked in a ceremonial procession the next day as each canoe was blessed with caiman blood and carried to the river on the shoulders of twelve heaving village men. Mike Weston sensed he was living in the pages of *National Geographic* as he watched the black-haired brown men in scant body coverings move their new craft proudly towards the water. Mike joined them as they waded into shallow water and assisted in turning the dugouts over to set them in the river. He clapped and fist bumped several of his to new friends to congratulate them on their extraordinary craftsmanship.

Amid the excitement, Mike did not see the fresh gash on his lower leg. The cool sensation of blood trickling down his calf finally caught his attention on the walk back to the huts. "Michael your leg bleeding," said Ataqi.

Ipixuna heard the concern in Ataqi's voice and came over to investigate. The cut was clean but deep, perhaps caused by a thorny palm along the shoreline. Ipixuna washed it with dragon's blood sap and then motioned Mike and Ataqi to follow her into the forest. "What are we doing Ataqi?"

"Michael I think I know. I will bring my bow and arrows in case we see peccary or capybara."

The three walked the jungle for several minutes before Ipixuna stopped near a thick tree trunk crawling with ants.

"Michael this work good but sting a little bit," said Ataqi. "Sit down here."

Ipixuna kneeled next to Mike while Ataqi plucked the first ant off the tree, its large mandibles snapping open and closed. He handed it carefully to Ipixuna.

"Ouch!" grimaced Weston as Ipixuna skillfully held the wound closed with one hand and touched the mandibles across the cut with the other. The powerful ant pinched down on the wound as its sharp mandibles dug deep. The ant refused to release its grip and Ipixuna twisted its body off leaving the head clamped to Mike's skin.

"Michael, these army ants good for fixing cuts," said Ataqi.

Ipixuna applied six more, Weston wincing in pain each time. When she was done Mike looked into her amber eyes. "Aguéje Ipixuna."

Ipixuna nodded as she held Mike's head in her hands.

After a moment's rest Weston asked Ataqi if he could practice with his bow. "Yes my friend."

A scar on a thick mahogany trunk made a good target. From fifteen paces Mike put two of three arrows on the mark. Both Ipixuna and Ataqi called out with encouragement. Weston gathered the arrows and walked to Ipixuna. "You try," said Mike as he handed her the bow.

"Village women do not shoot arrows," said Ataqi.

"Maybe they should," replied Weston.

He held her hand and led Ipixuna towards the mahogany tree target. Standing behind her, Mike put one arm around Ipixuna's waist and pulled her gently backwards a few steps. "Right here."

Mike placed the bow in her left hand and reached around her with an arrow. Ipixuna placed it in the fiber bowstring. With both arms wrapped around Ipixuna, Weston aided her draw while enjoying the flowered aroma in her hair. When the arrow reached its proper position, Mike released the grip on her wrists and said "now."

The arrow flew far left of the tree and Ipixuna growled softly. Determined, she walked forward to find the arrow in the thicket. A red, yellow and black-banded coral snake slithered into the brush as she searched, barely slowing her hunt. Soon she located the bright fletching feathers and pulled the stray arrow free from the underbrush. Ipixuna strode back and spoke to Ataqi. "Mike, she want to try it alone."

Weston nodded, proud of her resolve.

Lean but strong, Ipixuna focused on the target and drew her arrow intently. For several seconds she adjusted her aim and then released. The arrow traveled true and struck the mahogany trunk. Mike let out a hoot and grabbed Ipixuna's shoulders with excitement as she beamed. Ipixuna shot a dozen more as Ataqi and Mike Weston applauded her skill.

CHAPTER 26
Xapuri's Spirit

Wild boar returned to the upper Rio Sié as flood waters receded. The Secret Village might remain there if the savage Arabox tribe did not hunt nearby. "Michael, elders say we all must leave," said Ataqi. "Canoes are ready."

Hunters preparing for the villagers' departure located bountiful game. Weston, Ataqi and Pelém hunted together with bows and arrows preparing for the exodus. As they entered camp after a successful day Pelém shouted out, "Michael opu'a ko porã!" (Michael shot this boar!)

Many villagers abandoned their tasks for a moment to congratulate Weston. Within an hour the butchered meat smoked on wood racks alongside the previous day's game. A sumptuous aroma filled the air. After a day enveloped in warm dry smoke, the preserved meat was wrapped in broad leaves and stored in palm fiber bags for travel.

The next day Ataqi joined Xapuri and the elders to finalize plans for moving the people of the Secret Village back to the Rio Juri and returning the expedition team with Mike Weston to the FUNAI control post. After a long conversation standing among their new dugouts, Xapuri announced that the first trip with all five canoes would depart the following morning.

Ataqi searched for Weston and found him trimming more boar's meat for the fire, his hands covered in blood. "Michael we have plan," said Ataqi. "Xapuri think canoes going down river Sié get to mouth of Rio Juri in one day plus one-half day. Then maybe three days to paddle back upriver and return here. You go in canoes with my team and other village men to find mouth of Juri. We make camp there until whole village comes. Then we split up. Villagers go up Rio Juri to find new village site and we go to rapids, try to find a way down Rio Sié to FUNAI. Then you go home."

"That sounds good Ataqi. But what about you? Are you going to look for your Igarapé People?" asked Weston.

"They probably move because of flood. Maybe we find them when we going back. Maybe Orlando Rivas let us come back to look again next year," responded Ataqi.

Each cedar dugout had a capacity of six or seven villagers and their meager possessions. With two paddlers needed for the return trip, the five canoes could move the entire village in three or four round trips. Ataqi's original expedition team of eight, minus Urubu and Nauta, plus Mike Weston prepared to depart down the Sié the following morning. They loaded their backpacks with clothing, tools, the two disassembled rifles, pots and the colorful nylon hammocks that saw little use around the villagers. Smoked boar meat, Brazil nuts and dried acai berries were packed in every dry space.

Knowing she would not see Mike Weston for many days and then maybe never again, Ipixuna entered his hut and presented Mike with a woven leather necklace adorned with wooden beads and boar's tusks. "Aguéje Ipixuna," said Weston as she slipped it over his neck.

The two walked to the river that evening to bathe but the sight of glowing yellow caiman eyes kept them from the water.

The village fell silent earlier than usual that night in anticipation of the canoe migration beginning in the morning. Croaking of frogs drowned out the insect's buzz and lulled most into deep sleep. The two guard's eyelids grew heavy with the mesmerizing drone.

Two hours later Ataqi sprang from a deep sleep and listened intently through the darkness of his hut. The frogs' chorus had faded enough that other jungle sounds broke through. There it was–an unmistakable chirp. Ataqi exited his hut. The full moon cast faint shadows through the forest and village. He woke Pelém who grabbed his rifle from the backpack and snapped on the stock. They moved silently towards Jatabo's hut. Another chirp spoke from nearby and then another from the opposite side of the village. Before they could reach Jatabo the village erupted in chaos.

Shouts and screams filled the heavy air and Pelém drew his rifle. He shot into the air but the assault continued. A second shot did not deter the Arabox raiders. "Usá kusé!" yelled Ataqi. (Shoot them!)

As Pelém squinted to pick out a fast-moving savage in the dim light, the unmistakable face of Xapuri flashed by him running towards the Arabox. The elder carried his long hunting spear ready to defend his people. Two Arabox ran near and Xapuri thrust his spear bringing one down. The second turned towards Xapuri and reached him just as Pelém pulled his trigger. Stunned by the blast the warriors froze in place for an instant. Pelém fired a second shot at the attacking Arabox. As Pelém and Ataqi approached, both men collapsed to the ground. The jungle fell quiet.

Villagers holding torches came forward to access the scene. Two Arabox lay dead, one by Xapuri's spear and one by Pelém's rifle. A third man lay next to them gasping for breath as blood pumped from his chest wound. An Arabox stone spearpoint protruded through his back. The helpless onlookers watched as his life force faded, his painted face transforming from agony to peace–Xapuri. The villagers stared in stunned silence as more approached. Their supreme elder for over twenty flood cycles was gone.

Immediately four village men grabbed the two dead Arabox savages by the ankles and dragged them into the river, casting their bodies into the current. Sobbing women rolled Xapuri to his back as the spear was removed. They rearranged their leader's arms and legs into comfortable positions.

The shaman rushed to his hut and returned with the Secret Village's most sacred mask to begin his rituals. He kneeled beside Xapuri chanting and raising his arms to the dark sky. Torches lit up the mask–the spotted face of the great jaguar. The shaman's incantations mimicked calls of rainforest animals, including the unmistakable snarl of the jungle king.

The masked shaman continued his mantra and the people joined in while others washed Xapuri's prone body, first with dragon's blood sap and then with clean river water. Artists decorated him with red and black dye in the form of monkeys, snakes and caiman. The largest paintings over his heart depicted a fierce jaguar and the face of his deceased wife Pucapena. The artists moved his jaguar claw and Swiss Army knife necklace until their images dried.

As morning broke over the somber scene, men constructed a bamboo and palm frond bier to carry Xapuri's body. The entire village continued their solemn chants and songs as they set him onto his eternal bed.

The shaman led the villagers on a procession up a hill overlooking the upper Rio Sié. Six men carried their great leader. For three hours the Secret Village People followed the bier carrying Xapuri, their songs never diminishing. Many carried food, gifts, adornments and tools to serve Xapuri in his afterlife. Mike Weston took up the rear carrying a smoked slab of his boar to feed the bravest elder on his journey through the threshold.

On the peak of a rock outcropping at the crest of the hill, Xapuri's body was laid to rest. Manioc, fish and Mike's boar meat were left to sustain him, flowers to adorn him, and spears to protect him. As a final offering to carry his spirit to the body of the jungle lord, the shaman set his jaguar mask alongside Xapuri's painted face, still strong with its bold stripes and boar tusks.

Villagers placed layer after layer of palm fronds and stones over Xapuri to protect him from the bright sun and dark spirits. They walked silently back to their temporary village arriving just before dark. Three days of fasting and grieving commenced.

The morning after Xapuri's long vigil, Ataqi's men and Mike Weston departed towards the Rio Juri with Jatabo, sixteen other village men and eight women. Paddling down the soft currents, the five canoes moved easily and the Rio Sié grew as small igarapés entered along the route. The shade of tall trees extended onto the river through much of the day offering relief from the sweltering heat.

The first night's camp was hastily set on a sandbar with no shelter and only small fires to deter the insects. At one point while sleeping in the faint glow of dying embers, Weston opened his eyes to see Jatabo staring back. Mike flashed back months earlier to a similar nighttime scene on the beach during his capture. On this night he knew Jatabo's name and considered him a friend.

Late on the second day of river travel, the canoes reached the mouth of the Juri. They crossed and landed on the southside sandbar. Most agreed the junction of the forest and sandy beach would make a good temporary camp site while waiting for the entire village to arrive. Pelém was the first to walk into the forest. On his fifth step he jumped and raised his machete as a startled fer-de-lance fled deep into the jungle. Jatabo and his Secret Village crew prepared to paddle the five dugouts back up the Sié to ferry more villagers.

Days passed slowly for anxious Mike Weston as he waited for villagers at the mouth of the Juri. "How do we get home from here, Ataqi?" asked Weston.

"We need canoes to get down river Sié to rapids. Then we walk around rapids through jungle. Then we must find way to get back to FUNAI. Maybe need another canoe," replied Ataqi. "We had good canoes there but they are probably gone."

Weston passed time building palm frond shelters for the villagers arriving later. He stalked the banks of the Sié and Juri with Ataqi and Pelém hunting peccary, boar and tapir with their bows and arrows. Peacock bass and arowana fish resting in the shallows were sometimes too easy to pass up. While in camp, Weston wrote observations and thoughts about the people of the Secret Village. Since Ataqi's cameras had disappeared he sketched scenes of the jungle and village, pencil on line paper. His teenage artistic skills returned.

When the canoes returned five days later with more villagers, Ipixuna and Ticata were not among them. A rough count indicated two more round trips were needed to bring everyone down to the Juri camp.

The next canoe shuttle arrived late in the afternoon surprising the naked villagers bathing in a shallow eddy. This time Ticata and Ipixuna were aboard and Mike Weston embraced them both as they stepped onto the dry sand. He led them to their new shelter he had built with Ataqi. The elevated bed platforms were already covered in thick stacks of palm.

After the women unpacked their small bags and settled in, Weston brought a gift to Ipixuna. As they sat on the bed she opened the clear plastic bag and removed a sheet of paper. On it was a pencil drawing of her and Mike sitting together near the river. She removed another sketch, a delicate portrait with her face adorned in dye art and long feathers tied into her hair. Ipixuna had never seen herself except in the river's reflections. She beamed gracefully and leaned over wrapping her arms around him.

Ipixuna turned to her mother sitting on the other bed platform and asked her a question. Weston observed their thoughtful discussion with no idea of its meaning. When they were finished Ticata stood up and called out to Ataqi in his neighboring hut. He came over and spoke with Ticata before turning to Weston.

"Michael. Ticata and Ipixuna have important question for you. They ask if you can stay in village and live with Ipixuna forever."

Weston fought back his surprise, showing the thoughtful poker face he used for important client meetings.

"Tell Ipixuna I am honored that such a brave, kind and beautiful woman would want to spend her life with me," said Mike staring into her eyes. "Tell Ticata that I have great respect for her and her people. They have treated me well. But I come from a different world. A much different world, though I will not say it is better. I must go home to be with my family and friends. You will live in my heart forever but I cannot stay." Mike was not sure how his words would translate.

As Ataqi spoke for Mike, a tear ran down Ipixuna's smooth brown face. He wrapped his arms around her and kissed Ipixuna on the forehead.

CHAPTER 27
The Gauntlet

When all the Secret Village People plus Mike Weston and Ataqi's remaining expedition team had assembled at the mouth of the Rio Juri, the village elders called a meeting. Without the leadership of Xapuri they asked Ticata to join them. Weston could not remember a more contentious conversation in the village as their heated exchanges resonated through camp. When the tone and volume settled, Weston knew a strategy was taking shape.

Ataqi assembled his team and explained the plan before turning to Weston. "Michael, here is what we do. Tomorrow elders send out all five canoes. Three go up Rio Juri to find good new place for Secret Village. Two canoes take us down Rio Sié to top of rapids with thirteen men, six from village and our seven men. We make camp there and try to find way around rapids and back to FUNAI base. Village men stay to help us. After we find a way to FUNAI the dugouts go back up to Rio Juri to help move their village."

That night around the fire Mike Weston spoke to the people of the Secret Village. He stood barefoot wearing his expedition team pants, remnants of his blue fishing hoodie and the boar tusk necklace from Ipixuna. His scraggly blonde hair rested on his shoulders. "Ataqi, please give the people this message."

The villagers stood silent as Ataqi translated Mike's words. "We started as enemies but are now friends. Our worlds are much different but we have found respect for each other. We all do what we must to sustain our families and friends–this is what all people share in common. I have learned much from you that I will take back to my people. Thank you for your kindness."

Many villagers bowed and some spoke softly. Weston stood face to face with the elders and extended his arms. He searched for Xapuri before realizing he was gone. He turned towards Ticata to thank her for her care. "Aguéje Ticata," he said, knowing she understood his sincerity.

The village sang as darkness enveloped the jungle and nocturnal creatures awoke. Ipixuna sang as well but did not make eye contact with Mike Weston.

Sunrise illuminated the green cathedral as it had each new Amazon day for millions of years. The expedition team, Weston and six village men including Jatabo prepared their canoes for the short run down to the Rio Sié rapids. They planned to arrive in time to set up camp before dark.

Mike Weston approached Ipixuna's hut and pointed towards the river as she stood and came forward. Could they walk together one more time? Ipixuna would not go, lowering her head and staring towards the earth. Weston hugged her and kissed her on the forehead before turning and walking away.

He loaded his backpack and walked with Jatabo to the waiting canoes. Ataqi's map lay unfolded on the dry sand. "Look Michael. Only about 25 kilometers to rapids. Maybe four or five hours in canoes."

With their gear packed tight in the two dugouts, the thirteen men expected an easy day paddling downstream in fine weather. Many villagers came to the loaded canoes to wish their new friends well as they traveled back to their mysterious world. Many touched and embraced knowing they might never see each other again. Several rainforest men approached Mike Weston with clenched fingers held high and he fist bumped them all.

The crews stepped into their canoes as villagers surrounded them and cast the dugouts into the current. The strong flow carried them swiftly downstream. As they came to the first bend, Mike turned back upstream to watch his strange home of eight months vanish behind the forest. The distant silhouette of a tall woman stood waving. Then she was gone.

The canoes stopped only once on an exposed sand bar. The men paddled just enough to stay in the shoreline shade letting the powerful Rio Sié carry them forward. The jungle pulsed with life. Monkeys chatted high in the canopy while green parrots swooped in. Iridescent blue morpho butterflies the size of a man's hand fluttered between the tree trunks while green vine snakes curled through the branches. A family of giant river otters rested on the shoreline barely disturbed as the men passed.

By late afternoon the distant din of the rapids reached the men upstream. The approaching rumble of heavy whitewater reminded Mike of the locomotives passing through Klamath Falls at midnight. He doubted the other men had ever heard a train. Within an hour the din grew to a roar and the men knew their day's journey was done.

Ataqi, Jatabo and Pelém searched for the campsite where Urubu and the Colombians carried their bundles around the raging water, where Hatak was shot. They found it within minutes.

The canoes landed near the clearing and the men jumped out to inspect. Little trace of the drug runners remained after the flood, just a few sawed tree trunks and displaced fire ring stones. As they walked back to the canoes to gather their gear, Mike spotted something unusual in the jungle foliage near the shoreline, a heavy rope. "Look over there Ataqi."

"Michael, the drug men have big boat they bring from Colombia upstream," said Ataqi. "Cannot go down through rapids so they tie it here. We see the big boat right here but flood must have broke this rope and carry it away."

Weston untied the rope from a thick tree trunk and coiled it near the canoes. The frayed end told the story of wild flood water and straining line holding a bucking boat until it finally gave way. "Ataqi maybe we can use this for something. It's in good shape and we have at least sixty or seventy feet here," said Weston.

The thirteen men set up camp knowing they would be there until they devised a plan to get Ataqi's team and Mike Weston safely back to the FUNAI control post a hundred kilometers downstream. Ataqi and Pelém led the men on an inspection around the rapids by foot the next day. The narco-trafficker's path worn through the jungle was still evident though flood debris had lodged in the branches above their heads. Whitewater along the route crashed over boulders and churned through rocky chutes, impassable to any watercraft. The crashing water continued for hours until the men eventually reached gentler flows below.

Before they headed back to camp, Jatabo and the five other Secret Village jungle men waited at the foot of the rapids while Mike Weston, Ataqi and his expedition team walked downstream through the shoreline brush. "Michael we leave big canoes down here before hiking into jungle. I think Urubu and Colombians take them or floods carry them away. But we must check," said Ataqi.

As they expected, no trace of the aluminum expedition canoes remained and Ataqi lead his men back to the bottom of the treacherous rapids. When they reached the Secret Village men, Jatabo signaled Ataqi over. He had an idea. Mike Weston sat by unable to understand their discussion. "Michael, we think maybe we can tie rope to one canoe and lower it down rapids," said Ataqi. "We have many strong men to hold rope. Then we have canoe to take us downstream to FUNAI and Jatabo men have one more canoe to go back to Secret Village."

"That sounds very difficult but I guess we don't have many options," responded Weston. "It would take many days to build a new canoe. Can we build a log raft?"

"Too hard to control in the big rocks and current," said Ataqi.

Thirteen men hiked back along the cascading whitewater arriving at camp after dark.

Work began the next morning preparing the smallest of the two dugouts. Two holes were needed high on one end to pass the thick rope through. Pelém dug with his steel knife blade from one side while Jatabo used the tip of a borrowed machete on the other. The process was slow but within a few hours, two coin-sized holes were bored through the tough cedar wood.

Ataqi passed one end of the nylon rope through both and formed a bowline knot. Jatabo stretched the frayed end of the rope to its full length backing into the forest.

"Great," nodded Weston. "It's about 60-feet long."

Jatabo called the men over to test the process of lining the canoe downstream. They assembled at the head of the whitewater that crashed downstream as far as they could see.

Their first river obstacle was a drop the height of a man and a thousand times more powerful. As the water churned, nine of the men grabbed the rope and secured their feet above the falls while the others worked the shoreline clearing brush downstream. Slowly the men fed their line out straining against the surging canoe.

Near the brink of the falls the unmanned canoe hung on a submerged boulder. Ataqi ran back to camp and returned with two canoe paddles. Two men leaned over the raging water pushing the side of the dugout further into the flow with the paddles. The constant boom of crashing water drowned out their shouts of instruction and encouragement.

As the men forced the dugout away from the boulder it slid downstream until the end extended partially over the drop. The men on the line upstream gripped with all their strength and prepared for the drop. But the power of the rushing river was too great and the canoe pulled them forward as it spilled over the falls. Four men still gripping the rope were pulled to the brink. On the edge of the whitewater with their toes digging for grip on the wet rock, they were forced to let their prized canoe go free.

The empty canoe landed upside down beneath the drop and spun wildly dragging the long bow line in spirals. In a stroke of good fortune, the line tangled in boulders near the shoreline and the obedient canoe swung down towards the riverbank. With a long branch they snagged the gunwale and pulled the dugout back within reach.

The men regrouped and emptied the swamped canoe before lowering it through two easier whitewater chutes. As the Amazon sun dropped towards the western canopy, it was time to quit for the day. They hauled the dugout partially onto shore and secured it firmly to a tree trunk before hiking back to camp. Fish were abundant above the rapids near camp and the thirteen men ate well that night in preparation for the difficult work ahead.

While sitting around the fire the men decided they should attach a second line to the opposite end of the canoe. Two men on the shoreline downstream could help pull the dugout over stubborn rocks with the second rope and it could be a safety line to retrieve the boat if it went free again. The next morning they searched the narco men's old camp but found no rope adequate for the job.

Mike Weston had another idea. "Ataqi, tell the men I will sit in the canoe with a long pole to help control it. I can push off boulders so it won't get stuck."

"This is very dangerous Michael," said Ataqi.

"I'll be OK. I'm a good swimmer if I go in the water. I want to help."

In the morning the men searched the forest floor and Jatabo returned to camp with a long section of dry liana vine. They trimmed it to the length of the canoe. Mike Weston hoisted the pole and swung it through the air. "Yes I think this will work."

An hour later all thirteen men reached the canoe partially beached alongside the crashing current. Before they cast off a team worked down the bank chopping brush with their machetes. Once an adequate path was cleared, eight men grabbed the bow line and the others pushed the canoe into the river. With his long pole in hand, Mike Weston jumped aboard.

Progress improved as the line of rainforest men, like a naked tug-of-war team, gradually lowered the heavy dugout down the whitewater. Kneeling in the center for balance, Weston fended off large boulders with his pole and pushed off the bottom to align the canoe down the chutes. When the swirling currents pulled him too far from shore he extended the long stick out to the path clearers to pull him closer. By late afternoon they had worked their way halfway down the rapids.

As the thirteen men hiked back to camp Ataqi congratulated Weston. "Good Michael. Maybe one more day to get through rapids."

The dangerous task continued the next morning as the dugout made tedious progress downriver lowered through a maze of cascades and boulders. At midday the men saw smooth water in the distance. Two hours later they reached the last major obstacle, a fast chute dropping between a jutting shoreline outcropping and bus-sized boulder. The men pulled the canoe into a calm pocket and regrouped.

They gathered on the rocky point downstream of the canoe holding the rope while searching for footing. When they were ready the men waved to Weston who stepped into the canoe and pushed it outward into fast water. At first the heavy dugout moved uncontrolled towards the rope men. Seconds later, as they planned, it passed them and swung in an arc as the line tightened. Mike steadied himself holding the pole in the middle like a tightrope walker, ready to push off either side of the chute. The rope men curled their bare feet into the rock ready to bear the full force of the canoe as it neared the precipice.

But the line was too short and the canoe slammed into the outcropping below the men as Weston attempted to fend off with his pole. The accelerating current proved too powerful and the rope men could hold no longer. Two held on past their limit and were pulled into the raging flow. The dugout flipped as it fell over the drop tossing Mike Weston into the seething whitewater.

In a swirling chaos of bubbles, he fought for the surface. As he gasped for breath the current pulled him back under. Mike swan upward with all his strength and his head thumped against a hard object–the spinning canoe. The rope swung around his leg and he reached down to grab it. Hand over hand he worked his way to the overturned dugout.

As the turbulence released its grip Weston pulled his chin above the surface and filled his lungs with fresh air. Still grasping the rope he looked around. A head popped up nearby–Jatabo. He swam to the canoe and held on. As the two men clung to their life buoy the dugout drifted into a back eddy. Mike watched as men ran down the bank towards them.

Weston's feet touched sand and he began to walk submerged above the waist. As the water shallowed Jatabo stood up pulling the rope and half-sunken dugout. More jungle men splashed in tugging on the rope until the canoe bumped the bottom. The exhausted men fell to the beach catching their breath. The canoe was finally below the treacherous rapids but one man was missing. "Aracu!" called out Jatabo.

No one responded. Nervous chatter mixed with the water's rumble. They had watched their brother plunge over the drop alongside Jatabo. The twelve remaining men spread out along the shoreline and searched the water and rugged riverbank for two hours. But Aracu was gone. Gradually they returned to the dugout resting on its side in the shallows. The solemn men hauled it up the sandy bank for inspection.

The sturdy cedar canoe had sustained gouges and cracks as it hurtled over the drop and slammed into solid river rock. A crack extended two meters midway along one side.

The hike back to camp could not be completed until after dark so the men decided to sleep in the sand. Pelém carried a butane lighter in his minimal gear and collected dry flood wood suspended in the branches of riverbank trees. They had no food but Jatabo and his Secret Village men found enough palm fruit for the twelve men to snack around the campfire as they discussed their next plan.

"Ataqi, why do the men do not mourn for Aracu?' asked Weston.

Ataqi translated the rainforest men's conversations.

"Michael, Jatabo say men are sad to lose brother Aracu. There is nothing more they can do but plan to meet him in next life. Now they must fix canoe. They can fix it with tree sap. But we need pot to boil it. Tomorrow we hike up rapids to camp and prepare."

After an uncomfortable night in the sand swatting pium flies, the men reached their camp at the head of the rapids by late morning. Half went to fish and half readied supplies for return to the damaged canoe. "Michael, we bring everything with us. Maybe you go home this time," said Ataqi.

Ataqi's expedition team loaded all their gear into backpacks for their long-awaited return. Jatabo's men carried the canoe paddles, knives, hunting bows and spears. The next day the twelve men hiked back down alongside the rapids to the damaged canoe.

The beach next to the overturned dugout was large enough for a temporary camp to prepare Ataqi's men and Mike Weston for their journey down the Sié. Ataqi's team hung their covered hammocks around the wooded edges of the camp while Jatabo and his four Secret Village men built lean-to shelters and hunted. Pelém stalked the shoreline, bow in hand, searching for fish.

Once their new camp was established, Jatabo set out into the rainforest with several of his men carrying knives and Ataqi's aluminum pots. Soon they found a suitable grove of trees and began the task of extracting sap. V-notches were slashed deep into the bark with the pots lashed below. They returned to camp collecting nuts and palm fruit along the way.

That evening while the men ate around the fire, they honored their lost brother Aracu with songs and stories of his life. A marker of egret and macaw feathers tied into a fan and topped with three harpy eagle feathers was tied from a branch in his memory.

Jatabo inspected the sap pots in the morning and determined an additional day was needed to collect a sufficient supply. The men spent the time hunting and resting while Weston sat by the riverside sketching and penciling notes.

"I'm beginning to feel that I'll make it out of here. I don't understand many of their ways but the rainforest people have worked hard to get me home, even with the tragic loss of their brother Aracu who drowned in the river. I am grateful for their friendship. We are different in many ways but come together when we share a common goal. In the jungle our goal is survival."

Mike looked up to see three pink river dolphins playing and fishing near the foot of the rapids, a sign of good luck he hoped.

Jatabo returned to camp the next morning with pots full of sticky sap. The men stoked the campfire and set the pots near the flames. They stirred the thinning sap with sticks and removed bugs and other debris. The men propped the canoe on its side in the sand with the long gash facing upward. A pile of broad leaves was collected and set inside the dry hull.

Once the sap was well mixed and cleaned, the pots were removed from the fire. As the pitch cooled, six jungle men stood shoulder to shoulder facing the canoe's interior.

Others placed stacks of the large leaves on the palms of their open hands for protection. They six pressed the leaves up against the inside of the open crack to seal it as the thickening sap was poured into the crack's upward-facing exterior. With their knives, both stone and steel, they smoothed the pitch from the outside. Within minutes it cooled and thickened enough for the men to remove the temporary leaf barrier. Once they were satisfied with the hull's exterior the men rolled the dugout on its other side. They poured more hot pitch into the interior of the crack and spread it with their knives.

"The rainforest men seem quite proud of their ingenious repair work," wrote Weston after they rolled the dugout upright and pushed it into the water.

Ataqi looked towards Mike Weston, "Are you ready to go home?"

CHAPTER 28
Rendezvous

"Oiké amuixi para yamõ," directed Ataqi to his team in Nheengatu. (Leave gifts for our friends.) His five remaining men and Mike Weston packed their gear into the patched cedar canoe preparing to head down the Rio Sié. "Michael, we say goodbye now."

Ataqi's team pulled offerings from their packs to leave for Jatabo and his Secret Village men before they departed upriver. The knives, hats, machetes, nylon bags, twine and axes would be cherished in the jungle. Pelém selected four of his best steel-tipped fiberglass arrows to leave with Jatabo. He kept the disassembled rifles buried in their backpacks. The drug runners' rope was cut to share, one-third to Ataqi's canoe and two-thirds to Jatabo's men.

The twelve gathered on the riverbank one last time as slivers of sunrise penetrated the rainforest and reflected off the river. Ataqi's men presented their gifts and Jatabo's team packed cooked meat, nuts and berries into the patched-up canoe.

Mike Weston handed a sealed plastic bag to Jatabo. He showed his Indigenous friend how to slide the lock and then removed a pencil drawing–a sketch of the two returning from a hunt together, each holding a peccary by the hind legs. Jatabo grabbed Mike's shoulders and smiled.

Weston pointed upriver as he handed Jatabo a second bag, this one of red nylon. "Ipixuna," he said. Jatabo's eyes showed he understood. Inside was a blue skirt Mike had fashioned from his polyester hoodie. Extra loops cut from the sleeves could be used as decorative arm bands or a jungle tiara with the addition of a few bright feathers. "Aguéje Jatabo," said Weston as he grabbed the young jungle man's shoulders and looked him straight in the eyes.

Ataqi's men and Mike Weston walked the canoe into calf-deep water and boarded as Jatabo's men cast them off. Though packed tightly, the four paddlers and strong current moved the seven men swiftly downstream. The hum of the devil rapids faded behind as the rising Amazon sun lit their wide pathway.

With less than 100 kilometers to the FUNAI control post, Ataqi figured they could make it in three or four days. Their food supply looked adequate to focus on downriver progress instead of hunting. The sun glared intensely but they moved downstream with little effort often choosing the faster mid-river flow over the shaded shoreline. The men paddled until dusk and camped at the mouth of the Rio Celina where the trees met an exposed sand bar. Mike Weston recalled how his ordeal started in a similar place.

Light rain fell but many of the tired men slept on the open sand using their hammock covers as blankets. They didn't bother to light a fire the first night.

* * *

At the FUNAI control post, Orlando Rivas typed an email to Professor Schmidt.

Hello Andrea,

I hope all is well in Berkeley. We're looking forward to your return next month. I just received the recent overflight report from IBAMA. The Rio Sié drainage is finally back in its banks after the big flood. Last year's village sites were inundated. Some new clearings are emerging. We can't tell if these are new village sites or if they identify illegal logging or mining activities. We've received no sign of the expedition team. Not a peep from their GPS messenger unit. I know you fear the worst but don't give up on them.

Your new students are doing well. With our medical clinic shut down for so long during the flood, we have a surge of patients coming in. Tabatinga is back on her regular schedule. The students have plenty of Indigenous people to interview and assist.

See you soon,
Orlando

* * *

Higher upriver on the Sié seven men continued paddling. The bare-chested crew in their cedar dugout would not be distinguishable from a canoe of Secret Village People except for the lone white man in the center wearing his borrowed expedition shirt. During midday at the apex of the tropical sun, all the men but Pelém donned their shirts.

The team pulled into camp early on the third day to fish and forage, their food supplies from Jatabo's men dwindling. "Michael I know this camp. We stay here on first night of our trip. We are close to FUNAI."

The excitement around the campfire that night was more than Mike had seen from the expedition crew for many months. The men laughed and chatted well after dark. "Ataqi I wish we had chicha for our celebration tonight," said Mike.

"Yes."

After a quick bath in the river, the men were off early the next morning before heat enveloped the valley. The songs of Amazon birds seemed brighter than Weston could recall. By midday the men saw a familiar structure on the riverbank, the large sign at the entrance to the Alto Rio Negro Indigenous Territory. Minutes later Ataqi pointed out stained white tents on a river bluff in the distance. "Michael we make it back."

Ataqi heard barking and watched in the distance as an excited dog ran down the grassy riverbank. "Carlos!"

As they approached, the crew saw men replacing missing planks on the weathered pier. Ataqi did not recognize them but called out, "Olá. Ikanna está aqui?"

A head popped out of the medical tent and a short dark woman in green scrubs walked slowly down the hill staring intently. Ataqi waved and shouted. "Sou eu, Ataqi!"

Ikanna ran for the canoe and met the men as they touched the dock.

As he stepped out of the dugout Ikanna hugged her old friend and sobbed. She pushed off his shoulders to confirm her amazement and held him again. Ikanna turned and ran uphill towards the office of Orlando Rivas as the expedition team and Mike Weston unloaded their gear.

Students and FUNAI staff heard the commotion and spotted the big cedar canoe. They raced towards the pier. A crowd soon gathered as the haggard expedition men looked for friends. Ataqi spotted Orlando Rivas walking with Ikanna and grabbed Weston's hand. "Come Michael."

They met just before Rivas stepped into the throng. "Michael Weston meet Orlando Rivas." The men grabbed each other's hands firmly and shook.

"Welcome to FUNAI Mr. Weston. I've been waiting for your arrival. Many others have as well."

"Thank you Mr. Rivas. There were many days out there when I didn't think I'd make it."

"Mike Weston, this is my good friend Ikanna Baré," said Ataqi through a smile. "Ikanna, this is my good friend Michael. Ikanna speaks English and every other language here."

"I'm very pleased to meet you Ikanna. Ataqi speaks of you often."

"Ikanna, take Mr. Weston up to Andrea's tent," said Orlando Rivas. "She won't be here for a few weeks and I'm sure she won't mind. Do we have any clothes that might fit him? Ataqi, some beds are open in your old tent. Get your men cleaned up. We'll all meet in an hour at the dining tent."

"Can I communicate with home from here?" asked Mike.

"After our meal you can come to my office and use my email and sat phone. Do you remember the phone numbers and email addresses?"

"I wrote them down when Ataqi's men gave me a pencil and paper–miraculous tools in the jungle when you add a plastic bag to keep them dry."

"Go get cleaned up. Ikanna will drop off some clothes. I'll see you in an hour."

Orlando Rivas walked to the kitchen just as fresh arapaima was delivered from a local fisherman. He pointed to the giant fish and grinned. "Temos convidados especiais esta noite." Rivas hurried to his office and grabbed the satellite phone tapping rapidly.

"This is Andrea Schmidt. I'm not available now. Please leave a message."

"Andrea it's Orlando. Big news. A dugout arrived from upriver a few minutes ago. Ataqi and most of his men and the missing American are here. That's all I know for now. We will meet in a few minutes to get some answers. I'll talk to you soon."

Mike Weston stared at the shower head and knew he would never take the basic implements of his regular world for granted. Yet he felt a twinge of longing for his village friends he would never see again. The soap was luxurious but no better than Ipixuna's aromatic bathing leaves.

Ikanna dropped off several clothing items in tall sizes. Mike chuckled as he slipped on the slightly used t-shirt with a red, white and blue New York City logo. He headed for the dinning tent.

Everyone at the control post gathered to hear the men's stories. The tables filled quickly with Ataqi and his expedition team, Mike Weston, four of Professor Schmidt's grad students and Ikanna. FUNAI staff members filled the remaining benches and four stood outside looking in through the rolled up wall flaps. Orlando Rivas presided. Dinner plates of steaming arapaima fish, fresh farina bread and fruit were placed in front of the hungry men.

"May we video this?" asked a grad student.

"Take photos now but let's wait until tomorrow for videos. Then you can video anyone who's willing," responded Rivas.

Two of the students secretly recorded the audio with their smartphones knowing their professor would ask for every scrap of information from the remarkable journey.

"OK let's get started. Feel free to eat while others are speaking. You all look hungry. I'll speak in English in honor of our special guest Mike Weston. We'll take some short breaks for translation. Ikanna and Ataqi can you handle that?"

"It's fantastic to see you all gathered here. We've been concerned with your fate for many months. I'm sure each of you have great stories to tell. Mike Weston let's start with you."

"Thank you Mr. Rivas. It's amazing to be here, almost surreal. I feel like I'm standing on the boundary of two completely different worlds. First of all, thank you to Ataqi, Pelém and all of your team. I owe my life to you.

Last November I was on my last day of a fishing trip on the Rio Celina, not too far from here. During lunch I walked into the rainforest to take some photos. Out of nowhere I was attacked by a group of young native men. They tied my hands and forced me to walk through the jungle for many days. We could not communicate so I had no idea why they captured me. Eventually we came to a wooden canoe like the one down there," said Mike as he pointed to the shoreline."

"They paddled for another day until we got to their village. As you can imagine I was terrified. I thought they would kill me. But it turns out I was abducted by mistake."

Mike Weston continued his harrowing story for two hours often pausing for Ataqi and his team to fill in details. Ikanna and Ataqi translated between English and Nheengatu as fascinated students and FUNAI staff listened intently. During his speaking breaks Mike took bites off his dinner plate getting reacquainted with utensils.

The graduate students had many questions. "How did you communicate?"

"Initially with facial expressions, hand waving and pointing. It was frustrating until Ataqi came along to translate. That's when I began to understand the Secret People's ways. Eventually we learned some of each other's words."

"Where did you sleep?"

"How do the people stay clean?"

"What did you wear?"

"What do the Secret Village People do for fun?"

"Do they use medicinal plants?"

Mike Weston, Ataqi and his team answered questions until their tired eyes began to droop.

"All right let's wrap this up for tonight. These men need some sleep," said Orlando Rivas. "Thank you very much Michael. Your story is incredible. We can meet again tomorrow after you're rested. I'll need to file an official report with FUNAI. Michael, I know you're tired but come to my office to make your calls and send emails."

CHAPTER 29
Message from the Jungle

Immediately after finishing their meal, Orlando Rivas led Mike Weston into his office. "Use my satellite phone to make some calls. Dial zero zero one, the area code and then the phone number. I'll be back in a few minutes."

Mike pulled a folded sheet of paper from his pocket and dialed the first number.

"Hello."

"Mom is that you?"

"Michael?"

"Yes it's me. I'm OK."

"Oh my God I can't believe it's you."

"I'm at a government outpost on the River Sié in Brazil. I spent months in a jungle village trying to get home. It's a long story but I'm safe. Is dad there?"

"No he's at Fred's but he should be back soon."

"Tomorrow I'll start making plans to get back home. I have so much to tell you but it will have to wait. We can email each other now. I love you mom. I'll see you soon."

Mike dialed Ellie. "Hi. You've reached the voice mail of Ellie McIntosh. Please leave a message and have a great day."

"Ellie it's Mike. I made it out of the jungle. Well, almost. It will take days to tell you all I've experienced. Your wish that I'd have an enlightening adventure came true ten times over. I hope I'll be back home in the next week or two but I'm not sure yet. I'll call you again soon but let's email in the meantime. I miss you."

Mike sent emails to Bill and BetaCorp Technologies, thanked Orlando Rivas and slept thirteen hours straight.

Just before noon Mike exited Professor Schmidt's tent into the sunlight.

"Hello my friend. How are you today?" called Ataqi from across the lawn. "Let's get some lunch."

Ikanna in her medical scrubs joined them at the table next to the four graduate students who could not contain their excitement. "Mr. Weston we've told our anthropology professor Andrea Schmidt that you're here. She can't wait to meet you but she's in Berkeley now."

"I live in Santa Clara if the bank hasn't taken my home. You know where it is, a short drive across the bay from Berkeley when the traffic isn't bumper to bumper. Can you believe I haven't seen a car in eight months? I'm sure I'll meet Professor Schmidt soon."

"She planned to get back here in a few weeks but now she's trying to get here sooner."

Ikanna invited the grad students to their table and they talked for two hours. Mike walked back to his tent and retrieved his sketches of village life. The students laid them out on the tables and took photos.

"Thank you so much Mr. Weston. It's hard for us to study Indigenous people in the rainforest that we can't meet face-to-face. You've not only met them, you've lived with them."

"Call me Mike."

"Thanks Mike."

"Mr. Weston, we're running routine medical exams on the men today. When are you available?" asked Ikanna.

"In an hour?"

"Yes, thank you. I'll see you in that tent over there," said Ikanna as she pointed across the lawn.

"This is a nice little facility you have here in the middle of nowhere," said Weston as he entered the medical tent.

"It is when we're not low on supplies," replied Ikanna. "Dr. Sanchez, the director here, is in São Gabriel da Nazaré downriver on the Rio Negro right now buying more. We get long lines of river people here when diseases spread. Malaria is pretty common. How have you been feeling?"

"I hardly know. It seems like I always have some level of nausea and headaches. But I guess I've gotten used to that."

"Can I take a blood sample?"

"Of course."

Ikanna examined the blood smear under her microscope. "Michael you do have signs of malaria. I see this all the time." Ikanna stepped to a shelf half full of medicine jars. "We're out of prescription containers so I'm going to put these pills in a plastic bag. Keep them dry and take two each day. You should feel better soon. We'll follow up with you and your doctor when you get home."

"**Aguéje** Ikanna."

"Very good Michael. You're welcome."

Later that afternoon Orlando Rivas summoned Mike Weston to his office. "Mike we have the government wheels rolling. The American embassy has agreed to charter a float plane to pick you up here. Expect a big gathering at the Manaus Airport with reporters and dignitaries. From there you can fly to San Francisco. Don't worry about a passport or airline tickets. All of that will be arranged in the next few days."

Rivas dialed his satellite phone. "Michael I have someone here who would like to speak with you."

"Mike Weston this is Andrea Schmidt from the anthropology department at U.C. Berkeley. I'm thrilled that you made it out of the Alto Rio Negro."

"Thank you Andrea. I've heard so much about you."

"I hear you've met my students."

"I have. I love their energy. Reminds me of my college days."

"You must feel relieved but a little overwhelmed right now. I hope you can rest the next few days while the preparations for your flight home are finalized. I'm going to try to meet you on the tarmac in Manaus if I can squeeze through all the reporters they expect. Your story, what is known of it, is already on the news here."

"It sounds like there's a lot of interest."

"Yes there definitely is. The modern world is fascinated by isolated human cultures that haven't changed much in hundreds of years. That's why I became an anthropologist."

"It's going to take some time to process all of this."

"It may take years Mike. I don't want to push you but feel free to email me with any questions or anything you experienced at the Secret Village. My students have already sent your pencil sketches. Nice work. How is Ataqi doing?"

"He saved my life and we've become good friends. Only a few of us have lived in two different worlds. We'll always have that in common. I'm already planning on seeing him again in the future. If the culture shock won't be too great I'd even like to bring him to California someday."

"He's a little shy but he could be a great ambassador for the plight of uncontacted people. He would have the attention of many ears here on the Berkeley campus," replied Professor Schmidt.

"OK thanks Andrea. I'll be in contact again soon."

CHAPTER 30
Weston's Notes

"Is the internet back up? I'm sending an email to Professor Schmidt," said Mike Weston as he typed on a student's laptop in the dining tent. A flock of Amazon green parrots sped over the Rio Sié headed upriver towards Ipixuna and his rainforest friends.

"Hello Professor Schmidt,

It was great speaking with you yesterday. Excuse my rambling notes here. Consider these disorganized thoughts a rough outline of my experiences for our future conversations. Your students are kind and have peppered me with questions. They've told me my experiences as an outsider living in an isolated native village are unprecedented in recent years.

As I'm sure you can imagine, being abducted was the most terrifying experience of my life. I was in a state of shock and physical pain as the men marched through the jungle. My mind raced with thoughts of escaping their leader Hatak and the other three tribesmen. They tied my hands and legs making my capture even more painful. The jungle men were salvages in my mind but that began to fade when I realized one of them was concerned for my safety. I learned his name was Jatabo days later when we reached the village.

I became friends with Jatabo even though we could not speak each other's language. When Ataqi wasn't around to translate we communicated with hand signals, facial expressions and laughter. We learned a few of each other's words. Jatabo even allowed me to hunt with him and his brother, an honor I humbly accepted. Ataqi joined our hunting party. We used bows and arrows and returned to the village with many peccaries, my favorite jungle meat. It felt like an initiation and many villagers came out to greet us as we returned from our hunt.

Hunting is a man's main task in the village. The meat of peccary, boar, tapir, capybara and monkey are most popular. I never got used to monkey meat. They seem too human to me. Game hides are used for many purposes and the claws and teeth for necklaces and facial adornments. The village men hunt nearly every day. The only exceptions are during heavy storms, burial ceremonies and sometimes the day after a good hunt when the entire village eats until they are stuffed and everyone rests the next day.

The women spend most of their time preparing food or making fiber mats and cordage from palm fronds. They weave thinner cloth for bags and some of the minimal clothing they wear. At the main village, before the flood forced a migration, the women spent hours each day harvesting manioc root. They process the roots by grinding, boiling, washing and drying until they have a delicious flour. They make flat bread and porridge with the flour that is served almost every day. The Secret People might be clearing a new manioc field on the Rio Juri right now. Peccary is one of the villager's favorite foods but they invade the manioc fields at night digging up the roots. The men try to shoot them with their arrows but it's difficult in the dark.

While the women work, the youngest children stay with them during the day. It's not unusual to see a young woman digging manioc root while carrying her baby in a sling. The older children are not closely supervised. They play most of the time and sound like children everywhere. They run, jump, throw sticks and make up games. I saw them play with tarantulas and with peccaries that came into the village looking for food. The children are rarely reprimanded. If they wander from the central village there are many hazards, especially snakes. One child was killed by an anaconda while we were at the upper camp, a horrible tragedy. The people mourned but believe the child's spirit was passed on to a baby born soon afterwards.

The villagers use medicines from rainforest plants. My female friends Ticata and Ipixuna used the red dragon's blood tree sap to treat my infected leg wounds. They have other medicinal elixirs, brews and ointments to relive pain, reduce inflammation and repel mosquitoes. Your students and Ikanna told me that many of our modern pharmaceutical drugs today come from the rainforest and were first discovered by Indigenous people. It's interesting to me that organic remedies and supplements have become more popular in America in recent years while the rainforest people have been using them all along.

We've had some good discussions regarding Indigenous languages and spelling. Ikanna is especially helpful translating local names into written language. I spelled the name of my Secret Village friend phonetically as Ip-EESH-oo-nah. Ikanna suggested it could be spelled "Ipixuna". I learned that "X" is pronounced "SH" in translations of native languages in the region. The elder Shah-POO-ree can be written as "Xapuri". Your students tell me the old Tupi Indigenous languages of this region were unwritten until early European missionaries translated them to written words in the late 1500's. Fascinating.

The kindness shown to me by Jatabo is not uncommon in the village. Some of the women were very helpful to me once they got over the initial shock of seeing a white person in their village. The men tended to be more reserved but many became friendlier when I worked alongside them building shelters, hunting and chopping dugout canoes.

The 80 or so people in the village function like a large family. It's probably an important key to survival in their dangerous jungle environment. Everyone contributes to their wellbeing though some make a greater effort than others. The villagers argue like all families. I saw young men fighting over women a few times. Ataqi can give you more details since he understood what they were saying.

Village elders Xapuri and Ticata, and Ticata's daughter Ipixuna were especially kind to me. Xapuri frightened me at first. His face painted red with black stripes and boar tusks protruding through his septum was intimidating. But soon after meeting him I realized he was wise and deliberate, a man of prominence respected by the villagers. I considered him Chief of the Secret Village.

Other than my shoes and torn clothing, the only personal item that accompanied me on my forced march was a red Swiss Army knife. I gave it to Xapuri and he wore it on his leather necklace with jaguar claws. He enjoyed using the sharp steel blade and other tools. I think he considered the knife a symbol of pride and friendship, perhaps a bridge between our worlds.

Xapuri was killed fighting a barbaric tribe called the Arabox that raided the Secret Village twice while I was there. During the first midnight raid they kidnapped two children and killed their parents. Xapuri bravely defended his people during the second attack and was struck by an Arabox spear. His death stunned the Secret Village. The shaman and every villager performed a mystic wake and burial ceremony that lasted for three days. There was spiritual chanting and singing and his painted body was carried up to a rocky crest overlooking the Rio Sié. He was buried there under palm fronds with many artifacts. The shaman left his spotted jaguar mask in Xapuri's grave. Ataqi says it will transport Xapuri's spirit to the body of a jaguar so he can live forever as master of the jungle.

Ataqi and Pelém kept the expedition team's rifles hidden except during the Arabox attacks. All the rainforest people seem to fear fire sticks. Pelém's rifle shots forced the savages to flee. The raids on the village might have been much worse without the rifles. So the villagers knew Ataqi's men had rifles. But as far as I know they never asked about them again, perhaps because they are believed to be evil.

The Secret Village People might have stayed in the upper Sié drainage if the Arabox did not live there. When the flood waters receded the village men cut five large cedar trees and build dugout canoes, a long process with hand tools and fire. The steel tools we gifted the people definitely helped. Once the canoes were completed, the entire village was ferried downstream to the mouth of the Rio Juri to look for a new village site.

Hopefully my rainforest friends are completing a new village on the Rio Juri right now. That's where I left most of the villagers before we set off down the Sié in an attempt to get a dugout through the rapids. We got it down the hazardous whitewater but a village man Aracu drowned in the process. It was tragic but the men were quite stoic. The rainforest that gives the people everything is also deadly. Death often felt too close for me. The villagers believe their departed reside in an alternate world, always near the living. Their spirits may come back as animals–strong, beautiful, patient and wise or vicious, dark and deadly. Often they return as birds flying high above the forest. That's how they describe aircraft passing overhead.

Day-to-day survival is the villager's main task but they love to celebrate and praise the spirits of the forest. Any time the hunters have a good day the entire village joins in a feast. There is singing, laughter and dancing and sometimes a second feast a few hours later. During their celebrations the people drink alcoholic chicha made from chewed manioc root that ferments in a wooden bowl. It's not bad once you put the idea of fermented saliva out of your mind. When hunting is slow the village may go two or three days without eating much so they stuff themselves when they can. No one is overweight.

People of the Secret Village have little concept of wealth or property like we do. Materialism is almost nonexistent. Once they have adequate food and shelter, they seem content to rest and socialize. Their families and the rainforest are their wealth. I'm concerned our introduction of steel knives and other tools could change their way of thinking. The sharp tools make common tasks like skinning game and building dugouts much easier. We left some tools behind as gifts but there weren't enough to go around. I hope we didn't cause any jealousy. Since they have so few possessions, there is little or no theft in the village. As you already know our cameras disappeared but we think that was more for spiritual reasons. It's not surprising. If I had never seen a digital image of myself I might also think it was black magic.

We have many ways to record our histories—writings, visual and preforming arts, photographs, videos and verbal descriptions passed down through the ages. The Secret Village People have only unwritten recollections passed from generation to generation as stories. Memories of their history are often acted out in dances with chanting and signing. Some of their oldest history seems elevated to legend.

As I spent more time with the villagers, I became less judgmental of their ways. They know there's another world downriver but choose the life their ancestors have lived for centuries. The outside world is frightening to them since most of their limited exposure has been violent. Their lives move slower in the jungle than anything I'm accustomed to. Perhaps the greatest difference in our societies is the constant stream of news and digital information that inundates us in the modern world. For months I caught myself reaching for my iPhone or computer. I was uncomfortable living without video screens, text messages and mechanical noise. Ataqi's GPS messenger unit felt like a small piece of home until Urubu stole it. There was a spare that we couldn't get to work, probably Urubu's dirty work as well.

Life in the rainforest is physically uncomfortable. The tradeoff is that villagers seem to suffer less from stress. I'm no psychologist but I see stress every day in my line of work in Silicon Valley. It seems to be a requirement for success. The Secret Village People seem more accepting of good and bad in their lives, not striving like we do to alter fate. They are not aware of the world's many problems and conflicts except through stories of "Pale People" that occasionally infiltrate their rainforest home.

Once we moved with the rainforest people to higher ground I became more adapted to village life. There wasn't much choice. With the incessant rain, food was scarce and we were all hungry. I helped as much as I could and gained more respect for the villagers' way of life. With everything they need provided by the rivers and jungle, change comes slowly. Yet they are highly adaptable to fluctuating food supplies, weather conditions and outside threats often choosing to migrate to greener pastures. Their nomadic lifestyle seems infinitely sustainable when commercial-scale resource extraction by outsiders is not destroying their rainforest home.

I wonder if the Indigenous people see beauty in nature like we do. The rainforest that sustains them and provides their colorful feather and flower jewelry can also kill them in an instant. We might describe the Amazon rainforest we see on television as beautiful while their relationship with the jungle is deeper, more complex and spiritual.

Most of the villagers seem content with lives we consider primal. Their daily tasks center around survival. Life in Silicon Valley couldn't be further from the lives of the Secret Village People but we do have things in common: family, friends, music, identity, games and recreation, problem solving, emotion, pride, curiosity, fear, spirituality, hope and love. Now that I've written it down for the first time, I can see this list describes all humans. It's possible these people we call primitive are no less fulfilled than we are. I suppose the measure of human wealth is not always obvious. I want to read more about early societies when I get back. I'm sure you can point me in the right direction.

I hope we can meet in person soon.

Sincerely,
Michael Weston

"Hello Michael. How do you feel?"

"Hey Ataqi. I'm doing better. The malaria pills and a soft mattress seem to be working. I guess adrenaline has been masking my physical issues. If you don't know, ask Ikanna about adrenaline."

"That is good. Mr. Rivas ask to meet in his office now."

"Alright. Let me get this email on its way to Professor Schmidt and I'll be right with you."

Mike and Ataqi walked together across the lawn as the golden sunset's glow lit up the Rio Sié.

"Hello Mr. Rivas. We are here."

"Come in Ataqi. Come in Michael. I have good news. The U.S. embassy and FUNAI have been working hard to get you home Michael and they have a plan. Three days from now they'll send a chartered floatplane here to pick you up. I will join you. Ataqi, I would like you to come with us."

"We are going to Manaus? I never see a big city."

"Yes we will all fly to Manaus. Expect a crowd of reporters and government officials. We will stay in the city for two days while both of you are interviewed. Reporters will have many questions and so will the government. Professor Schmidt is trying to get there in time to meet you. After our two days in the city the embassy will fly you to San Francisco Michael. Ataqi and I will return here."

"Fantastic!" responded Weston. "Thank you."

CHAPTER 31
Manaus

Mike Weston woke before the monkeys, anxious to continue his long journey home. A dim electric light illuminated his meager clothing options–faded, tattered or too small. He chuckled at the attire, appropriate for a man of good taste emerging from eight months in the jungle.

His memories of the Secret Village just weeks earlier seemed more surreal each day. Excited to return to a life of physical comfort, he missed his village friends. Ticata, Jatabo and Ipixuna were gone forever. He caught himself subconsciously turning towards the jungle, hoping to see Ipixuna emerge from the trees.

Ataqi sat in the dining tent as Mike entered in the first dawn light. "Are you ready to see the big city?"

"Yes but maybe nervous," replied Ataqi.

"It will feel strange to you, but I know you'll like the good food and soft beds–and no bugs. You guided me in the jungle and I will help you in the city."

"Aguéje Michael."

"Thank you Ataqi."

"Bom dia, homen," called Orlando Rivas. "The plane refueled in São Gabriel da Nazaré and will be here in an hour. Let's eat some breakfast and be ready to go. The kitchen staff is busy."

Soon the dining tent filled with students and staff there to wish Mike Weston good luck on his travels home. One by one they stopped by his table. Ikanna handed him a tiny plastic bag. "Don't forget to take your malaria medicine. Check in with a doctor when you get home. The infection should be gone from your body soon. Remember to email me."

"Thank you Ikanna. You've been so helpful. I hope you make it to California someday. I'll talk to Professor Schmidt about it."

"Thank you Mike. That would be amazing."

"Ataqi I have an idea for you," said Ikanna. "In Manaus, they will ask you for your full name. Tell them you are Ataqi Igarapé, a nice name I think."

"I like that Ikanna. I wish you could go to Manaus with us," responded Ataqi.

"I have too much work to do right here."

Orlando Rivas supplied compact travel bags for Ataqi and Weston and they carried them half empty to the dock. Blazing sunlight emerged above the rainforest canopy as a plane engine droned in the distance. Moments later the Cessna Caravan amphibious plane swooped low over the Sié and touched down with a soft thud. The rooster tail of spray diminished as the plane came to rest and began its taxi towards the dock.

Mike recognized the plane from the same charter company that commenced his odyssey eight months earlier. The co-pilot waved as he stepped out and tied a pontoon to the cleats. "Bom dia."

"Good morning. It's a beautiful day to fly."

Minutes later Orlando Rivas, Mike Weston and Ataqi, with Mike's assistance, secured their seat belts and waved to the students and staff outside the windows. Ataqi's expedition team had received their cash and departed the FUNAI control post–all except Pelém who stood on the grass wearing only ragged shorts and his necklace of armadillo claws. "He wants to hear stories from the big city when I return," said Ataqi.

The Cessna taxied from the dock and turned downriver to gain a speed advantage. The propeller surged and the plane accelerated forward. White spray rose to the passenger windows for a moment before the floats lifted off the Sié. The plane climbed rapidly above the canopy and made a U-turn upriver–the wrong way.

"I have a surprise for you," said Orlando Rivas loudly as the plane leveled off at 3,000 feet. "We will retrace your journey."

They followed the winding Sié for an hour. Wrapped in towering green and flowing gently, no sign of human activity showed on the river or in the jungle. A major tributary entered ahead from the west. "There's the Rio Celina. The *Wild Amazon* is up there fishing. They've added a line to their contract for visiting anglers," yelled Rivas over the engine's roar. "No guests are allowed to walk into the forest beyond sight of their fishing guides."

"I looked hard at maps," said Ataqi. "My village when I was boy must have been on Rio Celina. I walk from my village to FUNAI nine years ago."

"A long walk for a sixteen-year-old by himself," said Rivas.

A large white ribbon appeared ahead and soon they were above the thunderous rapids. "I can't believe we lowered a canoe through that," said Weston.

"I am sad for my brother Aracu," said Ataqi.

"Yes, all of Jatabo's men are very brave. I am sad that Aracu gave his life to help us get home," replied Weston.

"OK that's the mouth of the Rio Juri up ahead," said Rivas.

"See that disturbed area down there? I think you can see some huts. That was our temporary village while they shuttled their people down from the upper Sié. That's where we said goodbye to most of our Secret Village friends," yelled Mike.

The plane continued up the Juri. "There it is," said Rivas. "That's probably the new Secret Village."

Mike pressed his face against the window. A large round structure sat in the middle of the clearing, not yet fully thatched. "That's probably the new communal maloca."

Tiny dots appeared to be huts and a clearing was likely the new manioc field. Canoes were visible along the riverbank and Mike felt pride in his contribution to their construction. He squinted attempting to see any movement between the huts and imagined Ipixuna moving gracefully and singing to the birds. He lifted his hand slightly and waved.

Thirty minutes further up the Juri another clearing appeared. "Ataqi this might be your village," said Rivas.

"See they have a different maloca hut, like a big FUNAI tent. I still want to find my people someday," replied Ataqi.

The Cessna turned north towards Brazil's border with Colombia and the upper Rio Sié. "Urubu's drug trafficker friends came from somewhere up there," said Rivas. "Look up ahead. There's always trouble up here. That looks like an illegal gold dredge down there. If they're on Brazil's side of the border then they're in the Alto Rio Negro. I'll send an IBAMA flight in to check when they can get it on their schedule."

The Cessna banked sharply and headed downriver for several hours flying directly over the FUNAI control post and on to the Sié's junction with the great Rio Negro.

Small developments carved from the jungle became more numeruos as the float plane traced the route of the riverboat *Tabatinga*.

"We're going to take a quick break while we refuel in São Gabriel da Nazaré," said Rivas. "Then we're three hours to Manaus."

The amphibious plane with wheels on its pontoons touched down and taxied to the terminal. While the passengers ate lunch the crew refueled. An hour later they continued on their last leg towards Mike's flight home and Ataqi's immersion in the modern world. As they flew down the Rio Negro river traffic increased below–fishing boats, tankers and riverboats. Finally they began their descent as the world's greatest river confluence loomed ahead, the Rio Negro and mighty Amazon.

"It's a giant river," said Ataqi, his voice barely discernable over the engine's hum.

"In some places it's too wide to see from one bank to the other," shouted Orlando Rivas.

Soon tall buildings lined the horizon. The plane began its descent and a huge runway came into view. As they approached Mike Weston and Ataqi Igarapé glued their faces to the passenger windows. Just off the runway behind a temporary white fence, hundreds of greeters waited to meet them–reporters, dignitaries, military, friends and well-wishers. Bright flags and banners waved in the breeze. "Bem-vindo de volta, Michael Weston!"

Author's Postscript

Inspiration for this story began in November 2022 while flying low over the Rio Negro in Brazil. I expected barren swaths where logging, gold mining and farming scarred the rainforest 3,000 feet below. I soon learned the major clearcutting is further south. Dense jungle spread to the horizon in every direction. Tall palms poked their fronds through the towering cover of leaves and bright yellow flowers. The impenetrable canopy divulged no sign of human activity below.

Scattered clouds floated above the treetops as we flew four hours deeper into the Amazon. Occasional serpentine headwater tributaries carved the only breaks in the vast sea of green. Cutaways along the riverbanks provided our only view of the rainforest's full height. While the canopy's intertwined leaves reach high competing for sunlight, shadows beneath inhibit growth allowing larger creatures to prowl the forest floor. I imagined pig-like peccaries, tapirs, giant rodent capybaras, jaguars and armadillos roaming the moldy soil while spider monkeys and scarlet macaws looked down from their perches high above.

The previous day our small group of adventure anglers signed contracts with FUNAI allowing us access to the Médio Rio Negro I Indigenous Territory, property of the Baré, Baniwa and Tucano Peoples. We paid our entry fees and pledged to take nothing except photos and leave nothing but goodwill. We agreed to measure and release our fish as part of a scientific survey of the river's health.

That day we toured the enormous Manaus fish market, a bustling emporium of multi-colored Amazon fish of every size and shape. Pirarucu, arowana, redtail catfish, matrincha, peacock bass, **pacu and bizarre armored catfish** cooled on trays of ice while lively merchants negotiated their sales. A spirited vendor of rainforest medicines preached the benefits of his potions and elixirs in English and we bought small plastic bottles of boiled anaconda fat guaranteed to reduce inflammation and heal wounds.

We visited the waterfront where dozens of flat-bottomed riverboats in every vintage, color and size from skiff to ship rested on their docks and moorings. A few were freshly painted and well maintained but most were rust stained and deteriorating. Trucks pulled up to the largest riverboats as pallets of supplies were offloaded. Passengers boarded for journeys to unknown destinations that could be over a thousand river miles in either direction. They strung their colorful hammocks on the covered upper decks.

Our tour guide flagged a powerboat and we sped towards the far side of the river, barely visible from the opposite bank. At an anchored offshore dock away from the current, a man threw baitfish into the water and huge pink river dolphins known as botas rose from the murky depths. We crawled nervously into the water and the powerful botas bumped our legs beneath our depth of vision. My heart raced as the enormous dolphins surfaced next to us, their long toothy jaws snapping for more fish.

We climbed in our motorboat and headed back towards Manaus stopping at another floating dock. This one was open in the center and held a net pen full of giant arapaima fish, known locally as pirarucu. We dangled dead baitfish tied to stiff lines and stout bamboo poles over the water. Three-hundred-pound fish crashed the surface to grab the hookless baits. These arapaima were raised in lagoons along the Rio Negro that are netted once every three years. The attendant explained the environmental benefits of aquaculture to farm the over-fished delicacy compared to slash-and-burn cattle ranching. We dined on delicious arapaima at a local Manaus restaurant that night as we chatted enthusiastically about our morning flight deeper into the Amazon.

Back on the Cessna 280 float plane the following day gazing down on the canopy, my mind flashed to dramatic photos from a *National Geographic* article years earlier. From the vantage of a low-flying plane, thatched huts stood in a rainforest clearing. Standing outside glaring upwards at the photographer were four black-haired men, their naked bodies stained in red dye. Expressions on their painted faces were a mixture of surprise and anger. The rainforest men held spears and bows overhead threatening their skyward intruders. During pre-trip research I learned that our destination, the upper drainages of the Médio Rio Negro, are also believed to be the home of several isolated and uncontacted Amazon tribes.

An hour later we landed on the river's surface and motored to the houseboat we shared for the week. Local Indigenous people made up much of the hospitality and guide staff. Each day two anglers with two guides boarded fast outboard skiffs and searched the river's inlets and lagoons for giant *Temensis* peacock bass.

Our fishing guides discouraged walks into the jungle when they beached their boats along the river. Dangerous animals hid in the dense rainforest and FUNAI did not want outside contact with isolated peoples. Despite their warnings, I could not resist a solitary inspection of the jungle on our final day.

Ten steps in the foliage obscured me from the others near our boat. My perception sharpened immediately–perhaps the ingrained survival instincts of our ancestors that we all retain. Shadowed colors intensified and faint sounds resonated. Scanning the jungle floor two steps ahead occupied most of my short tour but I stopped briefly to photograph bizarre and beautiful plants. I imagined an uncontacted tribesman moving silently through the thicket, his bow ready to draw.

During our week on the remote Amazon tributaries we saw no sign of humans besides those on our team. One area cut out of the rainforest may have been a seasonal fishing camp. I asked our guides if they ever saw boat traffic on these igarapés that flowed from across the border in Colombia. On rare occasions in the dark of night they heard boats headed downstream and suspected nefarious activities.

A month after returning home from Brazil, I spoke over the telephone with a service rep for a fishing tackle company. "The Amazon was amazing. I want to get back there soon."

"Oh, I'll never go there. About ten years ago one of our customers was captured by a native Amazon tribe. They held him for nearly a month before he was rescued."

"Really?" I asked.

"Yes, it really happened. It made the evening news."

I spent hours scanning Indigenous Protected Territories of the Rio Negro drainage on Google Earth–a desktop expedition. In regions with the highest resolution, clearings could sometimes be found. Occasionally I located huts and canoes on the riverbanks.

Drawn back by the mysteries of the rainforest, I returned to the Amazon in Yasuni National Park, Ecuador with my wife Mary the following year. Towering Andes peaks capped with equatorial snow formed the western skyline as we boated down the Napo River, a major Amazon tributary. Our Indigenous Kichwa Añangu hosts guided us proudly through their jungle lands and waterways. Massive Yasuni Park is also home to the uncontacted Tagaeri and Taromenane People who have chosen to remain isolated. Rare encounters with outsiders have resulted in deadly confrontations.

Spirit of the Jaguar

In the late 1990s the Kichwa Añangu Community along the Napo River faced a difficult decision. Since the mid 1960's oil companies have explored, drilled and extracted petroleum from the rich deposits beneath the Napo River Basin. In Yasuni National Park, the protected park status has not entirely prevented oil production within its borders. Roads, pipelines and drilling platforms have been constructed within the 10,000-km² national park.

Petroleum production is Ecuador's largest industry and often conflicts with environmental protections. Other Napo Basin Indigenous communities have exchanged oil rights on their rainforest lands for quick profits. Some have come to regret their decisions as they witnessed degradation of the land and water that have sustained their people as far back as their legends tell.

The Kichwa Añangu elders studied their options thoroughly and ultimately turned down oil profits to create a sustainable ecotourism economy for their lands and community. They constructed and operate the Napo Ecolodge and Wildlife Center, visited by guests from around the world. The native guides now lead tours into their unspoiled rainforest where biodiversity is among the highest on earth. Quietly stalking the jungle and paddling the waterways, we encountered twenty-foot-long anacondas, alligator-like caimans, piranhas, macaws, sloths, parrots, myriad species of lizards, bizarre insects, huge arapaima and giant river otters. Each morning we woke to haunting calls of howler monkeys, no less magnificent than the roars of African lions. On this journey the great jaguars eluded us though their snarls sometimes echoed through the jungle. They knew our whereabouts, no doubt.

REFERENCES

Everett, Daniel L. *Don't Sleep, There Are Snakes: Life and Language in the Amazonian Jungle*. New York: Pantheon Books, 2008.

Hemming, John. *People of the Rainforest: The Villas Boas Brothers, Explorers and Humanitarians of the Amazon*. London: Thames & Hudson, 2018.

Millard, Candice. *The River of Doubt: Theodore Roosevelt's Darkest Journey*. New York: Doubleday, 2005.

Wallace, Scott. *The Unconquered: In Search of the Amazon's Last Uncontacted Tribes*. New York: Crown Publishers, 2011.

Nheengatu and Tupi-Guarani languages translated from English by ChatGPT

Amazon Journeys of Author David M. Schultz:

November-December 2022. Journey to Manaus, Brazil and the Médio Rio Negro I Indigenous Territory with authorization of FUNAI–home to the Indigenous Amazon Baré, Baniwa and Tucano People.

November 2023. Journey to the Napo River Basin and Yasuni National Park, Ecuador–home to the Indigenous Amazon Kichwa Añangu, Tagaeri and Taromenane Peoples.

ACKNOWLEDGEMENTS

All my gratitude goes to a fine group of editors for your expertise and insight: Gary Ruppert, Kailie Anderson, Adam Schultz and Karen Ruppert. Special thanks to Mary for her patience as I focused on my keyboard for days on end.

PHOTOGRAPHS

Title page:	Indigenous Amazon man in Brazil by David M. Schultz
Interior photos:	Capuchin monkeys by Sean Sharpe All others by David M. Schultz
Back cover:	Aerial view of Rio Negro tributaries in Brazil by David M. Schultz
Author page:	Author in the Ecuadorian Amazon by Frank Ghamari
Back pages:	Amazon Rainforest in Ecuador by David M. Schultz

AUTHOR

David M. Schultz is an author, biologist, adventure traveler and civil engineer with degrees from the University of California, Berkeley in Engineering Science (M.S.) and Biology (B.S.). His previous books include *International Misadventures with the aid of a Fly Rod* (2020) and *Peril in the Deep-Adventures of the WWII Submarine USS Burrfish* (2022).

Thank you for reading *Spirit of the Jaguar, Abducted by an Uncontacted Amazon Tribe.*

Please consider rating this book and writing a review at Amazon.com/*SpiritoftheJaguar* or goodreads.com

Contact the author at freewaterpress@gmail.com

David M. Schultz

Made in United States
Troutdale, OR
06/01/2025

31810702R00186